# *Almost Heaven*

## Country Roads Series: Book Two

Grea Warner

Almost Heaven
Copyright © 2018 Grea Warner
All rights reserved.

ISBN: (ebook): 978-1-945910-65-4
(print): 978-1-945910-80-7

Inkspell Publishing
5764 Woodbine Ave.
Pinckney, MI 48169

Edited By Vicky Burkholder
Cover art By Najla Qamber

## OTHER BOOKS BY GREA WARNER

# DEDICATION

Singing every word on top of our lungs, buying only the best seats, tailgating ... to my country music concert friends. Such great memories. Here's to many more! Rock and read on!

And, as always, with love to my parents.

# CHAPTER ONE

It was weird thinking that we were leaving him there. Sure, the beach was picturesque and serene with its rippling water and stretching coastline. It was a place where any young boy would love to spend hours on end running, swimming, and making creative structures along the bank. But knowing that the sandy shore was, in part, his final home instead of a bedroom full of books, stuffed animals, and model airplanes, still seemed so wrong. And hearing his sweet, three-year-old sister ask when he was coming back broke our hearts. No matter how much we tried to keep a positive spin on the evening by eating Wyatt's favorite mint chocolate chip ice cream and splashing in the water, the fact that we were scattering some of his seven-year-old ashes could not be eclipsed.

It had been one day less than a week since the accident and, consequently, Wyatt's passing. It was only three days since the funeral parlor. Three days since I found out the real truth about Finn's erratic behavior. Three days since I had been able to understand. Three days since I had held Finn's hand as we listened to the preacher say a few words of supposed closure.

Finn offered to drive me home from his nephew's

beach memorial. His parents, who were staying with his only sibling, Nola, had driven me there, which, I am sure, was an obvious set-up to have Finn make the return offer. He didn't need the push, though, which made me feel a little more secure about our questionable relationship status. That drive would be the first time we would truly be alone together since the gut-wrenching day, over a month before, when I had told him I didn't want to see him anymore. I hadn't understood back then. He hadn't told me why he had acted the way he had. But after the tragedy, I had learned that Finn suffered from a form of PTSD and had gone off his meds. Now back on, I hoped we were too.

We rode in silence for the first part of the ride, both of us overwhelmed by where we had just been and the finality of the situation. It was almost painfully obvious how tentative we were with one another—not knowing exactly how to start being ourselves, being a couple, being together after our separation. But the love could not be denied. We just needed the time together to express that— in person and not via a text, which was the only way we had spoken with each other during those three days prior.

Finn was the one to break the stillness in the car, thanks to a minor miracle in the sky. "Look, Lara."

I lifted my head from the side window where I had been watching a few straggling raindrops trickle from an earlier quick shower. It was if they were our tears racing down the pane to see which could reach the deep, dark crevice first. Through the front windshield, though, was something much more uplifting. There was not only one rainbow but a double rainbow, creating an almost protective, secure, safe, dome-like picture.

"Oh, my God. It's almost like touching heaven," I acknowledged in awe.

"Yeah," Finn agreed softly. When I started to sing the "Rainbow Connection" and got to the lovers and dreamers part, he glanced in my direction before staring back at the road and saying, "I'm the lyric king, show-off."

It was the first semi-relaxed statement I had heard him say in such a long time that I almost cried. "I'm glad you sang at the beach." I recalled Finn's voice, although broken at times, at the memorial.

This man, who had first been a good friend in college and then seven years later became my soulmate, took a moment before responding to my comment. He grasped my hand in his and placed both on his thigh. "I've had so many number one hits." His eyes, grayish not only in color but in mood, remained focused on the road. "But that song was Wyatt's favorite. It never even became a single."

I liked the touch of his skin entwined with mine. I liked that he wanted our bodies touching. "It was beautiful, Baby." I let the term of endearment fall from my mouth before I had a chance to filter. I wasn't sure we were back to that stage yet. I wanted to be, but did he?

The squeeze of his hand in response didn't help define his feelings. It only sent me another mixed message. Was he squeezing in encouragement or thanks? Or was he squeezing because the statement made him tense?

I didn't have much time to ponder the conundrum because Finn was already pulling his steely blue roadster into my apartment parking lot. He had to remove his hand from mine in order to put the car in park. Once he did, though, he looked at me with a sad smile and allowed his hand to once again find mine and cover it. I turned my body and placed my remaining hand on top of his, reminding me of the hand sandwich game my brother Lane and I used to play as kids. Now facing Finn, I hoped he would take the opportunity to kiss me. I missed that. I missed him so much.

But instead, what I got was, "Well, you're back."

My shoulders sagged, defeated. I pulled my hands away and reached for my passenger car door. I was debating if I should invite him in as I walked around the front of the car to his open window.

"Do you want me to walk you up?" Finn asked in reference to my second-floor apartment.

"You don't have to." I tried to sound casual but was thinking that I really did want him to, if just for the fact that I wasn't ready for the night to end.

I felt like we hadn't said anything or progressed in any manner. Though, of course, I knew the night was not about us. It was about that precious little boy and the loss we all felt.

"I'll call you tomorrow, then," was his response.

I should have known to just say what I wanted instead of being so passive, especially when emotions were so high, and we weren't as in sync as we had been. I didn't need him to walk me up, but I did want him to know how I felt. So I took the opportunity, leaned down, and kissed him. It was the first time since our break-up, and it was a fast peck on the lips, but I felt like I needed to make that statement of love. Unfortunately, I didn't feel much reciprocation from his side.

Because of that, I turned, and then, just as quickly, walked into my apartment building. I only made it around the corner of the hallway and, fortunately, out of sight, before collapsing to the ground. Sliding my body down the hallway wall, I felt so worn and so confused. The day and days preceding had been extremely emotional, but I thought the silver lining was the fact that Finn and I had found our way back to one another. But his distance confused me, especially when we needed each other the most.

With sudden determination not to give in, I boosted my body up from the floor and decided to try again, if only to get a more definitive response. I walked back out to the parking lot just as Finn was putting down his phone and starting to pull out. Spotting me, he put the car back in park and leaned out his window.

"Do you have plans for tonight?" I asked.

"No." Simple answer.

"Oh, all right." I didn't know where I expected to go with the question. It was already past eight p.m., and I had to be up for work in the morning. I just knew I wanted to hear his voice or see his face for a little longer for my sake, as well as making sure he was all right.

But he had given me nothing. I stood awkwardly for another moment and then, once again, turned to head back into the apartment building. It was then that I heard the window go up and the car door shut. I turned around to see Finn standing next to his car looking around as if scanning the parking lot. I knew why. Immediately following Wyatt's death, Finn, Nola, and her husband, Will, had been dealing with media interference. But, thankfully, there wasn't any at my apartment building.

Seeing that, Finn asked, "Lara, do you want me to come up so we can talk?"

"Is that what...?" I trailed off, thinking he hadn't seemed to want to talk the entire car ride over.

"I want to hold you." It was raw. It was emotional. It was real.

"I'd like that," I admitted.

I wanted to talk. We needed to talk. We had yet to talk about the elephant in the room—his diagnosis—since I had learned about it. But, more than that, I agreed.... I needed to be held.

Finn hit the alarm on his car without taking his eyes off mine. He closed the space between us by taking a few steps to meet me. Putting his hand on the small of my back, he guided us to and through the front door of the complex. Still, we were silent as we climbed the steps to the second floor.

When we entered my apartment, I could feel the energy change. It was as if a re-wound movie was appearing in front of us in that living room. I flashed back to the last time both of us were in my place. We were screaming at one another, blaming one another, hurting one another, leaving one another...not knowing the truth or the pain that was yet to come. I wondered if Finn could "see" it too. I turned to face him, and he caught me with his eyes. Yep. He felt it.

Without a word, I sat down on the sofa. Finn sat down too. There was a gap, and it wasn't just physical.

"I know I screwed up…before," Finn started, obviously referencing his choice to go off his meds months before. He looked at me, waiting for a response. When I didn't give one, he took a breath and said, "Ask me. I want you to ask me whatever you need to."

So, we *were* going to talk, I thought. "Why couldn't you tell me about it in the first place?"

That was the thing that hurt the most. He never told me that he suffered from a disorder due to being abandoned as a child—a form of PTSD with a twinge of depression. I had trusted him with my deepest, darkest secrets, including giving up a child right after high school, and he never told me what he considered to be his. I only found out because his behavior had changed after going off the meds.

"It wasn't you."

"I know that, Finn." I admit it, I was a touch angry.

With a sigh, "I didn't know what I wanted to tell you. I wasn't ready, because I was afraid I would lose you. And I did anyway."

I could see how genuine and sad his statement was. So I moved on. "It's like an oxymoron. You are the easiest going…one of the happiest people I know."

"You can see more than that, though, can't you? You can see *me*, right?" He was looking at me so intently, like his heart was going to be torn in two if I didn't understand what he was talking about.

His question made me think though. I reflected on all our moments together—from undergrads in college to friends and, years later, much more. I knew him. I knew the important stuff…not what he put out for others. There was just one thing he neglected to let me see.

In the brief moment that I took to reflect, Finn grew weary and decided to let me off the hook. He got up to leave, not trusting my answer. "Okay. It's all right."

"Don't." I touched his forearm in an effort to get him to stop. "I know you...the real you. And nothing has changed. It just maybe makes more sense."

As he slowly sat back down, he asked, "What do you mean?"

"Well, for one thing, how you don't let many people in on a personal level. Instead, you work on being there for others...making other people happy. When you're performing, I see you feed off of how you make the audience feel. I know you don't want me to say this, but I'm sorry that your performer persona is a mask for what you are keeping inside."

"It's not. No, not a mask," he denied. "I understand now that I've always been a little—I don't know—sad or numb or something. Music from when I was real young brought me to life. It's a healer...not a mask. There's a difference. But when all that crap happened all at once all those years ago—Audrey leaving"—he spoke of his fiancée straight out of college—"and my career taking off, it suddenly wasn't enough, and I turned to drugs. It wasn't until I rehabbed that I truly realized what was going on in my body...in my mind—what happened when my grandmother left me alone. Performing? Music? It's not a mask. It's not covering anything. But without it, I would need so much more than a pill and a therapy session. Playing music allows me to feel...to feel free and loved and wanted."

That last statement broke my heart and urged me to contradict it immediately. "You don't think you are loved and wanted? God, Finn, you grew up with one of the most loving families I could ever imagine. You always had friends in college. You are a natural magnet to people, even if they don't know 'who' you are."

"I know." He avoided my eyes as if he was being

chastised. "It makes me sound selfish. I don't know if I'm explaining this right."

But I understood enough about mental illness, having been around the education field. I just needed him to know the positive effect he had on people. I needed him to understand how important he was to so many of us who knew the "real" him. "You don't have to. You just can't see all that is wonderful in your world—not without help...meds, whatever. It's not you being selfish. It's deep-seated, and it's an imbalance."

"I know."

"Do you?" I forced him to look at me by not allowing my eyes to move in the slightest. "Because I know it, and it still breaks my heart that you would ever feel so alone...unloved."

"You want to know why I went off the meds? Because I had you. You completed the picture. You were my personal music muse. I felt the same way when I was with you as when I was playing." He exhaled and spoke slowly, like he had been since the funeral—all the energy taken away from this once amazingly lively man. "I thought I didn't need them anymore. We were so happy. We could live a normal life. Why would I need medication? But,"— he paused still embarrassed by the disorder—"it doesn't work that way."

"No."

"I eventually realized if I wanted any true normalcy back, I needed to take those meds." He nodded slightly at me, wanting me to agree or accept his explanation. "What else do you want to know?"

"Who all knows about—?"

"My family," he answered succinctly.

When he didn't offer more, I prompted him. "Your family...?"

"Yeah. Just Mom and Pop and Nola and Will." He paused. "And now...you." He said it in such a final way, but I knew there had to be more.

"No one else?" I paused wanting him to insert other names. But when he didn't, I trudged on with the obvious people that were on the list. "But who in your crew? Your band and agent, right? And—"

"No, Lara," he interrupted with a hint of agitation. "It has nothing to do with them. It has nothing to do with how I sing, how I perform…nothing. Nothing. I don't want their pity, and I don't want yours."

"I already told you," I replied just as adamantly, "I won't do that. But worry about you? Yeah. Just like I'm worried about your sister, and I'm worried about Will, and I'm worried about little Kelsea. It has nothing to do with…I care about you. Even if you told me not to,"— I emphasized dramatically, knowing that he had tried to push me away at the funeral parlor, but I wouldn't let him — "I would still care. I just need to trust you again. And I will."

"I didn't mean to lie to you, Lara."

"But you did. You lied when you didn't tell me. And you knew you were doing it. There were so many times you could have said something. I asked what was wrong."

"But the thing is, I didn't want there to be anything wrong. My mind was telling me it was going to be okay. And if it wasn't, I certainly didn't want you to see that there could be something wrong."

"Exactly. I need to be able to rely on you to tell me everything. If things aren't the greatest, fine. Just tell me the truth. No omission clauses."

"All right." Finn paused before taking the opportunity to try to change the tone. "I wasn't being deceitful earlier when I said I wanted to hold you."

I smiled. Who wouldn't when hearing their guy say that? I scooted toward Finn who opened his arm for my impact. I leaned my head on his upper chest but just for a minute, because I realized I needed to be even closer. Re-adjusting, I moved so that I was sitting on his lap facing him. I pushed my body as close as I could. We sat there

9

for countless minutes arms wrapped around each other's backs and ear to ear. It was the most comforting, secure warmth I could imagine.

I felt Finn's lips on my neck—soft, gentle, gliding. When he moved to the other side, I backed up slightly so we could see one another. I bracketed my hands on his face and then slowly went in to kiss him. This time, it was reciprocated. I held back tears, feeling the butterfly touch of his lips, as well as, the ones in my stomach.

Knowing where this was going, Finn stopped and asked, "Is this wrong? I mean, should we...today?"

I grasped his hands in mine. My eyes dipped down. I was feeling what he was feeling. I wanted—no, I needed Finn. I needed our connection back because I missed him and because of the pain of losing Wyatt. It had been months since we had made love. But was I sure it was appropriate? A tear started to slide down my face. When I went to move my hand up to brush it away, Finn's went with me.

"God help me. I need you so much." The tears may have been coming from my eyes, but they were ever so prominent in his voice.

"I...me too," I admitted. When Finn hesitated, I encouraged him. "Finn, it's okay."

His eyes searched mine darting back and forth, looking for confirmation, looking for permission. Not to make love with me, necessarily, but to allow himself to feel again. I nodded ever so slightly.

He kissed me suddenly with greed...with passion. His tongue parted my lips, savoring every inch. Then I felt his hands—those large worn hands—in my long hair. He was tugging and pulling. It was as if he was trying to claw out of himself and into me.

I must have moaned because he pulled away, saying, "I'm sorry."

"No. It's all right." I needed to feel the pain, knowing that it was nothing compared to the ache and loss that had been ravaging my soul.

And it wasn't as if he was actually hurting me. I liked the pressure. I liked feeling. I liked knowing how much he needed me. It was how much I needed him.

I could see he was leery though. And I didn't want him to second guess himself or us. So I dug my fingers into his bare biceps urging him toward me. When I removed his black polo shirt and began kissing his pectorals, I heard Finn groan and felt his reaction—my lap snuggly on top of his. He lifted me up so we were standing and we both fumbled around, frantically unzipping each other's pants— mine shorts, his casual khaki slacks. I don't remember my top being removed or much of anything else for that matter. I just sought that feeling of temporarily losing myself with the one person who I knew echoed my sentiment. And I hoped the piece of the puzzle that had been missing over the past month plus was finally found.

\*\*\*

Afterward, we laid there in a disheveled mess on my living room sofa. I had drawn the white-and-blue throw blanket on top of us. Finn was twirling my slightly sweaty hair, but his eyes were focused elsewhere—a faraway place I couldn't recognize or was too scared to. I put my finger to his lips, tracing their beautiful shape. Returning from wherever his mind had taken him, he slowly eased his body around mine to a sitting position at the end of the sofa. I scooted up slightly, allowing him room.

I wasn't too concerned when he put his boxer briefs on, but when he reached for his shirt, I questioned, "Where are you going?"

He turned, leaned over, and kissed me on top of my head. "I'm going home."

"What's this—wham, bam, thank you, ma'am?" I teased to keep things light but also because I was guarded. Sarcasm had always been my shield.

"Don't," he said adamantly while piercing his eyes at me, obviously not appreciative of my comment. His shirt was already over his head, and he was working on his pants. He relaxed slightly, though, with his next statement. "I'll call you...tomorrow."

"You're being serious?" What?

"Yeah, Lara." He was matter-of-fact—back to that place of the unknown.

"What? Why?" My mind was racing. Had I pushed him too far? "Was it something I...wasn't it—?" I was near tears from the emotional roller coaster called today, the week...life.

"Don't. You're perfect. Try to understand. I just don't have anything more to give right now. It's a lot."

I knew that. That was why we needed each other. That was why he needed to stay. Hadn't we broken through?

"Finn—"

He stopped me with not only his words but his pleading eyes. "Please, Lara."

"Okay," I consented, knowing that he was just as fragile as I was...even more. I didn't need to add to his stress. I didn't want to be another pressure point for him. For those reasons, I agreed to not only stop questioning him but gave into his desire to leave. I agreed verbally, but internally those pistons were re-igniting with concerns about him, us...everything. "Be careful."

Finn took a second look at me with the slightest curve of his lips that was more like a twitch, and he left. I brought my knees to my chest, wrapping my arms around them. I felt naked and exposed in more ways than one.

# CHAPTER TWO

The following day, the final Friday of the school year, was Field Day. Half the classes went out on the field in the morning and the other half went out in the afternoon. It was a nice release for the kids and staff who had been dealing with counselors, the press, grief therapy dogs, and memorial plans along with final grade testing during the week. Wyatt seemed to have touched so many people in our community—his immediate classmates and those in his grade level, his homeroom teacher, his specials teachers, the administration, other kids who knew him from his baseball team, and those who just knew him because of his infectious smile in the halls...so much like his uncle's used to be.

As the technology coordinator for his private school in upstate New York, it was pretty much a fun, free day for me too. I walked around, monitoring and taking pictures of the bouncy houses, Olympic style races, face painting, hula hoops, snow cones, popcorn, carnival games, etc. I hoped to get some good shots to use on the district website and calendar. I was not at my computer or checking my messages, which was probably a good thing, because I would have dwelled on Finn and how we had left things the night before. I knew we had broken through major barriers. Yet, somehow, things were still unsettled. The logical part of me realized that healing from grief took time. But the insecure, needy part of me wanted a magic re-start wand.

I stayed late, downloading the Field Day pictures and making sure the electronic report cards were set up and working correctly. I wanted to get as much done as I could so I didn't have to take too much home over the weekend, but it was inevitable with only two more student days left of the academic year. I would still have to file the report cards, as well as compile the special technology summer packets.

I was double checking the report cards when I came across Wyatt's. He was the last one in his particular first grade class because they were in alphabetical order by first name. Seeing his name hit me like a sledge hammer to my chest. How did it manage to shock and strike me down every time I saw it? And how long would it be until I didn't get that reaction? He wasn't just Finn's nephew, but he had been a student where I worked… and a great, amazing, kind one at that. Without him, Finn and I would have never reconnected. I owed him so much. And he was gone. I wondered if his uncle was too, since he hadn't called or texted me at all. As I contemplated whether to contact him, the night custodian walked into my room. I glanced at the clock. It was just a couple minutes before six p.m.

"You're still here? It's Friday!" His act never got old.

"Yeah, beginning of the year and the end of the year— killers! But you haven't seen me stay this late in a while, though, have you?"

"No. And you shouldn't be now."

"You know, with everything that's happened, I'm just a little behind."

Thane leaned his mop against my desk. He pulled up a chair and sat across from me. "All of it," he said. "It's such a sad, sad story."

He knew everything from the elderly driver having a fatal stroke and hitting Wyatt to Finn and me breaking up prior to that. Everyone on staff was being overly cautious around me, not knowing what to say or do. They had brought a meal over to the Jamison's along with gift cards for restaurants so that Wyatt's parents wouldn't have to worry about food while they were grieving. Of course they understood the family wasn't in need of food or money, but they didn't know what else to do. There was talk about establishing a memorial plaque for Wyatt on the playground near the tree that bloomed every spring, and they approached me on the matter. But they also knew that things with Finn and I were tenuous and, as much as any group likes to gossip, nobody ever truly wants to listen to other people's woes, especially when they don't know what to say in response.

"I still can't believe it, Thane. I mean, God, it's been a week. Wow," I added because it just hit me. "It was a week ago today."

"Yep. Seems like yesterday yet so long ago, right?"

"Yeah, it does. It all just messes with your mind and what you believe in, you know?"

"Keep on keepin' on, girl. That's all you can do—for you, for that little boy, and for those who loved him." I used his wink as encouragement not to give into my sad thoughts and think instead of helping Finn and his family.

"I know. Thanks, though. I needed that."

"You got it. You know that. It will be all right. I promise." Somehow, coming from Thane, a grandfather-like figure, I believed it. "Hey, I gotta get a move on. The fifth graders are about to start pouring in."

"Oh, crud," I immediately started gathering up my papers and binders. "I forgot. Today is the dance, huh?"

"Yep. The gym is all decked out. Just so they can stand against the walls and stare at one another."

"Really? Kids still do that?" I asked.

"Yep. Good old-fashioned ro-mance."

"Those were the days, huh? They have no idea how easy they have it."

"Look at you—young twenty-something girl—acting like you're ancient like me."

"First of all, I just turned thirty."

"Really? Well, thirty is the new twenty."

"Ah, to do that all over again," I said, thinking of when I originally met Finn in college.

We had been no more than friends back then and had drifted apart after graduation. It was only in September when we had re-connected on a whole new level. What time we had wasted.

"Girl, you have an old soul. Get out of here now, before those hormonal pre-adolescents invade us. I'll lock up for you."

"Thanks. You're the best," I praised honestly and scooted myself and my homework out the door.

I did not hear from Finn that night, and I decided not to call or text him either. I wanted to give him whatever space he needed, particularly on that day. I hoped he was with his family—with his sister, brother-in-law, and niece, but also with his parents, who were staying in town a few days longer for support. Support I knew was not only for their daughter but also for their son. I prayed that Finn knew I was there for him—for all of them. He was in my heart. He knew that, didn't he?

*** 

Over the weekend we spoke just once, and it was me who called him. But it was mostly about seemingly random things that didn't matter, like the rain that didn't seem to be ending, the updates he wanted to make to his house in Nashville, and the energy water he loves. When I questioned him about his parents, his tone changed. Not that it had been particularly jovial, but it became even less so. He said he loved them, but they were either going to drive him or his sister, Nola, crazy with their hovering. Their family was the definition of all-American nuclear. So I expected nothing but. When I asked about his niece, he paused and said that Kelsea's had to understand way too much for a three-year-old. And then his voice caught, and he quickly found a way to end our phone conversation.

\*\*\*

I felt like, even though Finn was responding to me, he was still, somehow, slipping away. I didn't know why and I, for sure, didn't like it. I tried really hard to put myself in his shoes, but I was only human and took things personally. I needed that reassurance.

So, with the encouraging sound of birds chirping outside my work window that Monday, I texted Finn, telling him I wanted to see him. His response back said he was in a meeting, but he was just thinking the same thing and had been planning on texting me when he was done. I smiled, happy that he had been thinking of me. Just as instantly, though, I wondered if he had just said that. But, like Finn had said, he wasn't a liar.

Before I could overanalyze further, another text from Finn came in. He said that his parents were flying back home the next day. After seeing them off, he wondered if he could come to my place. We could watch the CMT awards that were being broadcast that night. It was another thing, along with some of the tour dates, which he had to cancel out of.

Of course I was thrilled, relieved…almost giddy. Maybe things were all right. He sounded, albeit the written word, all right. And once we saw one another again and held each other again, the awkwardness from the other night, from the past few days, could dissipate. We just needed the moment to happen.

\*\*\*

That next day was the last day of school for the students. It was technically a half day. They were dismissed, in the midst of balloons and photographs and thank-yous, before lunch. It left those of us on the staff the uncommonly rare opportunity to go out to lunch before spending the afternoon listening to a speaker for in-service.

It was a bittersweet morning for me. I liked my job. I liked the students and the faculty I worked with, and I liked being able to use both my creative mind and my analytical mind. In one sense, I hated to see the year end. But, exhausted by the daily grind and all that life had thrown at me, particularly in the past couple of months, I was also more than happy for summer to begin and have a couple months off.

I thought of calling Finn during lunch to confirm our evening plans. But there was a bunch of us at the restaurant chatting away. We barely got our lunches in and paid for before scurrying off to the auditorium to find a seat.

My phone vibrated a missed call about ten minutes into the in-service. It was Finn's number, but he didn't leave a message. So I texted him: *Saw U called. Listening to a speaker. Thinking of U. Still on for tonight? My place? When?*

Despite my constant checking, I did not hear back from him for over an hour. And when I did, the uncertainty came racing back. It came back big time.

Finn's text read, *Bad feeling about tonight.*

I responded with, *Me???*

His response took a moment. *No, not U. No. Just can't be there.*

I hated texting. And the ironic thing was, for the most part, Finn always had too. Nothing ever seemed clearly defined in texts. But it couldn't be helped. I could not get out of the mandatory in-service, but I needed answers for his reversal. Sitting next to me, Wyatt's first grade teacher, Gwen, gave an eyebrow raise probably wondering what the sudden texting was about.

I simply shook my head and tried to stay positive as I typed back, *Tell me. I'm here for U.*

*I know. Meet up another time?*

Sarcastic and scared, I poured out, *Bad feeling about THAT.*

I did have a bad feeling. He was backing out and not giving me a reason. Even though he said it wasn't me, I was most definitely an element. I had to be. If I agreed to another time, would he put that off too? And if so, why?

*I'm sorry. I just don't think I can.*

I was so frustrated, I couldn't even type back. I didn't want to be mad. I wanted to talk to him. I wanted to see him. I dropped the phone in my purse, pushing it away from my brain. I closed my eyes and tried any type of breathing routine I had learned from yoga. It didn't help.

At the conclusion of the in-service, I decided to walk the track that encircled the football field next to the building. The monotony of the cushioned ground and the cooler than normal beginning of June temperature helped clear my mind of angst. Well, some of it.

I decided to try texting Finn again before I started for home. Yes, texting. I was afraid of what I might say verbally. My mind wasn't that clear, yet.

I kept it simple. *Finally done. Starting for home. How R U?*

In a few moments, he was even more matter-of-fact. *Heading to airport to see folks off.*

Thanks for your itinerary! That was not what I asked! Sighing, I gave in and texted, *Hope they have a safe flight.*

I made my way home, willing myself not to cry. I was stronger than this…this whatever was going on. And I was not about to give up. I just needed to sit back and carefully think about how best to proceed.

Luckily, I didn't have to stress too long. I had gotten home, showered, and started a load of laundry. I was thinking of having just ice cream for dinner when I heard my phone announce a text from Finn. I don't know what made him text again, but I thank God he did.

*U still up for tonight?*

I tried to sound casual. *Yeah. @ home checking messages. When?*

*U tell me.*

Feeling a little more positive, I texted back, *an hour ago, now, or ASAP*

*LOL—I'll be there in a half hour or so!*

\*\*\*

In typical Finn fashion, he actually arrived close to an hour later, but he arrived. I was just finishing creating a creamy linguini with bacon and shrimp for us to eat for dinner. I figured it would give us a home base for starting the evening.

"Love the ball cap," I said as a greeting to him and his Mets baseball cap. "But, you know, a gentleman takes his hat off indoors."

He obeyed and then rustled his hands through his longer than usual brown hair. "I didn't think you liked baseball caps."

"What? Oh yeah, especially down low like that. It accents your eyes." I knew Finn was wearing it as a pseudo disguise for taking his parents to the airport—he would blend in quite naturally with the other baseball fans in the area.

Finn's gray eyes that I liked—not the fake green contacts he wore to perform in—glistened. "So I don't look like a cancer patient?"

"What?" I asked not knowing where his comment came from, and then a flashback hit me square on. It was something that I had told him the first time we had met years ago. I hadn't meant it seriously, but he obviously remembered it. "Geez, Finn. How do you remember so much?"

"Probably having to memorize so many lyrics. But the important things…I think everyone holds onto, right?"

I could have cried at that moment. He was more himself than I had seen him since before we broke up. Looking him in the eyes, I nodded and quickly stroked his not norm, beyond five o'clock shadow. I wanted to say, "I love you," because God knows, I never stopped, but I didn't want to scare him. And being a girl, a stubborn one at that, I wanted him to be the first to say it, Part Two.

"You haven't eaten, have you?" I said instead.

"A snack bar. I could eat." He made his way toward the dining area.

While I served the linguini, Finn poured a glass of bourbon from the bottle he'd left at my place prior to our split. He then devoured the pasta like he hadn't eaten in days. And from the look of him, I knew the past month or so had taken its toll. It was obvious he had lost some weight. So I was glad to see that he was eating. Although I knew his mind still wandered and drifted during our conversation. I decided not to question his indecisiveness on whether to come over in the first place and was just happy that he was there.

I asked him about the concerts being rescheduled. He said his first one back was now going to be in just over a week, and he would have to perform into October to do the rescheduled events. I cringed, thinking that he was going to be leaving so soon. I wanted more time. We needed more time.

When the CMT awards were set to begin, Finn and I were on the same sofa where we had made love less than a week before. I commented on a champagne colored dress of one of the female singers. It was beautiful, but so thin and sheer. Finn was about to say something back when his phone buzzed just like it had been all evening. While he chose to ignore some of the messages, there were others, like this one from his agent, that he had to field. He left the sofa and started walking around the apartment discussing the predictions, including his possible win for Video of the Year. During another conversation, I saw him in the kitchen pouring a drink. In addition, his social media sites were constantly updating on his phone with condolence notices and best wishes on the awards.

I had just settled back down with a bowl of caramel popcorn when Finn told whoever he was on the phone with that he needed to go. He put his glass down on the coaster and sat on the sofa's edge with his elbows resting on his knees. I wished he would have warned me that it would be hard. I was so thankful then that, in the end, Finn had chosen to come and watch the awards with me. I couldn't have handled it on my own. And I was scared to know what would have happened if *he* had.

I scooted up to meet him, looking from him to the television screen—both of us silent. Feeling the special stillness in the air, I slowly rubbed his knee. Finn had been scheduled to be one of the presenters. Of course, he bowed out of the event due to Wyatt's passing. It was now the time where he should have been up on stage presenting. Instead, one of his counterparts, Danny Roth, did the duty for him.

"I am honored to present Female Video of the Year. I'm here on behalf of Finn Murphy who, unfortunately, as many of you may know, recently lost his young nephew. All of us here are thinking of you. We love you, man."

I leaned into his shoulder afraid to do much more. I was afraid of my emotions as much as I was afraid of his. He tilted his head onto mine and rubbed my leg. Slowly, we both leaned back into the sofa. I hadn't heard a thing on the television after that announcement. I'm pretty sure Finn hadn't either.

"So sweet," I finally offered.

"Yeah." God, he was near tears.

His phone started to ring with a distinct retro tone. I looked down to see Nola's name appear on the screen.

Finn pressed ignore. I twisted my eyebrows at him. Why wouldn't he pick up for his sister, especially knowing she probably just saw the same nationwide comment about her son?

"Finn?"

"I can't."

Then Nola's text came into his phone. *We all love U too, and R so lucky to have U in our lives.*

I read it across Finn's lap before he put it on mute and slid the phone onto the side table, obviously wanting to ignore anything else that would come through. I admired Nola for putting her brother in front of herself during such a difficult time. I wished that he would reciprocate, but I guess she knew his emotional condition. Hence why she sent the text in the first place. I decided to let it be between them.

Finn stretched his arm wide so that I could curl into his body. We watched a couple more performances before my phone alerted me of a text. Since it was sitting on the kitchen counter, I got up and went to look.

The text was from Nola. *Where R U? Is he w/ U?*

She was worried. I had to put this poor woman's mind at ease, at least about her brother's sanity, for the night. She was dealing with too much as it was. I texted her back, giving Finn an out by saying he was with me and his phone was off.

Before Finn could question who I was texting, I said, "I'm glad you decided to come over." I sat back down next to him, noticing that the show was nearing its final half hour.

"Me too."

"No more 'bad feeling' then?" I referred to his earlier text.

Finn altered his body so that he could see me. "I was just sitting at my place watching the rain. I didn't want to go out—do anything. Then I had to see my folks off." He paused. "You know, if you wanted your own fan club, they would be the first members."

I smiled. I was glad Finn had seen his parents and that they were such supporters of both of us. "And what about you?" I teased, anticipating his response and hoping that it could redeem his hesitation from earlier.

"Beauty," He used one of his terms of endearment for me. "I would be president."

Yep. "Right answer, Cowboy." I took the initiative and kissed him—something we had yet to do that evening.

His answer back to me was seductive. His kissing was long with his tongue searching as if he was just waiting for me. "You wanta?"

I did but asked instead, "Don't you want to see if you win?"

"Lara, what difference does it make? Those trophies don't mean a thing. The more I think about it, I don't want to hear the statement I made in case I won."

I gathered from his comment that his acceptance speech had something to do with Wyatt. I understood. Just listening to the comment that Danny had made nearly shredded him.

I found the remote and turned off the television. The silence that filled the room was both stark and calming. I kissed him and spoke one word, "Bed." I wanted a secure, more "us" place than the last time on the sofa. I took his hand and led him down the hallway into my bedroom.

I opened my heart and my body up to him completely, letting Finn take charge of our lovemaking. His pain was still evident by the way his body met mine. But it felt good. He felt good—fuller and lasting longer than the other night. I wrapped my legs around him wanting him to know that I was there for him. Finn and our connection were what I needed to heal too.

# CHAPTER THREE

Exhausted from grief, worry, and my job, I took refuge in Finn's strong arms as we lay in bed after making love that awards show night. With his lips resting on top of my head, I felt secure. I loved that feeling after days of uncertainty. I let my mind drift and my eyelids shut, but I wasn't quite asleep when I felt Finn adjust his body.

"Hey, Sleepy, I'm going." His voice was soft.

"No, stay," I murmured back, thinking he just needed a reassuring invitation, although he never needed one before.

But Finn sat up on the edge of the bed. "Gotta go."

Whatever peace my body had been in was snatched away. Covered with the sheet, I scooted up toward the head of the bed. "Why? I don't get it. You know I want you to stay."

"I know. I just…I don't know…I can't…just not now. Go to sleep. The band came in. So we're practicing a little tomorrow, anyway." He glanced at the bedside clock. "And you have to be up in less than five hours."

I should have been impressed that he remembered what time I got up, but that didn't matter at all. The fact that he was both figuratively and literally pulling away, as his previously glorious naked body was now being clothed, disheartened me tremendously. I pulled at his arm, wanting to draw him back to bed…back to me.

"Please." I didn't want to beg. I wouldn't. But I was close.

He obliged as far as leaning toward me and giving me a swift, yet tender, kiss. "Bye, Lar."

I suspect my mouth probably hung open long after I heard the front door to my apartment close. I was in shock. Maybe I shouldn't have been. I knew things still weren't quite right. I knew there were things Finn had to work through, and we, as a couple, did too. It wasn't just Wyatt. It was all of it wrapped up in one emotional ball. But I just didn't think he would go home. Not again. He had always stayed before. And now? Why did he keep leaving? What was different?

I was trying hard not to resent his actions, but it wasn't easy. Hurt and fear and disillusionment weren't just creeping in, they were crashing in. The more confused I got, the angrier I got. Did Finn not see us the same way as he had before? Was I now just a proverbial bootie call?

I forced myself to wait. I knew being impulsive was never a good idea, especially when high emotions were at play. But I also knew I had things that needed to be said or at least questioned. There was too much at stake to hold back.

I waited a while, worked out my thoughts, and then texted Finn. *Maybe I will need that lava lamp back.*

His response didn't happen immediately. And it was painstaking waiting for it to happen. I wondered what he was thinking. Had he not seen my text because he was still driving? Or was he mad? The red lava lamp I referenced was the one I had in college and had gifted to Finn at Christmas. It had been a symbolic gift, as in college he had teasingly called me Roxanne from the old Police song. He knew I was far from being a prostitute or a slutty co-ed, and that's what had made it funny. But that's also why I gave it to him six months ago—my search was over. I had found him. No more red light needed.

Finally, he texted back. *What is that supposed to mean?*

I answered how I was feeling. *What do U think it means? I'm starting to feel a little cheap. If this isn't what U want....*

I pressed send, letting the text deliberately hang mid-sentence. He did not respond...via text. My phone rang, ironically belting out the personalized ring I had assigned him—"Roxanne." I picked it up but didn't speak.

"How can you think that?" Finn's voice traveled across the line. "You know you're what I want."

"And how am I supposed to know that, Finn?"

"How do you *not* know that?" He sounded truly hurt.

I pleaded my case. "Because you're not here. You always spent the night."

His breathy frustration was audible even via a cell phone. "Do you want me to come back?"

"Do you want to?" I turned it on him, afraid I already knew the answer.

"Honestly?" And there it was.

"Well, that says it right there." My voice cracked on the last word. I didn't want him to know how much I was hurting.

"No, it doesn't, Lara," he said, exasperation evident in his tone.

"What does it say then?" I pressed on, curious how he could actually have an explanation.

"It says that I would do it if that's what you want...to show you...to prove—"

"But you don't want to." My voice rose as I cut him off.

"Lara, I'm almost at the penthouse." He spoke of his Manhattan cloud-reaching palace that was approximately an hour from my apartment. "If I thought you were upset about it—"

"Of course I'm upset, Finn. I'm confused. I thought we were *us* again." On that word, I broke.

27

"Fine, I'm coming over." His voice was quick, but I could tell he knew that he had hurt me.

"No, I don't want you to." I honestly didn't, because, even though I was still upset, I knew he was too, and he didn't need to be driving any more.

"Then wha—"

"We're both upset now, and I didn't mean for that to happen. I'm trying to understand. I just don't."

There was some dead air space before Finn spoke again. But when he did, it was pure honesty. "So much has happened. I feel like I've gotten the wind knocked out of me, and I don't know if I'll ever be the same."

When I had been contemplating texting Finn, a thought had crossed my mind. I knew it was, sadly, a realistic one. His behavior over the past week wasn't much different from what it had been prior to us splitting up—when he had stopped taking his medication. Finn was all over the place. What he said, what he did.... Changing his mind, wanting to be with me, then not.... Was that it again?

"Are you—" I started to voice my concern.

But he knew what I was about to ask. So the interruption was swift but kind. "Don't worry. I'm taking the meds. Look, Lara, I'm sad, and I'm angry about what happened, okay? There's only so much I can handle at once. I'm not a robot. I'm allowed to have feelings."

Oh man, that nearly broke my heart. "Finn, I know it's been a lot. I'm sorry. I just want to be there for you. It's all right. Go home. Get some sleep."

"You sure?" It wouldn't have surprised me if he was still contemplating turning around to appease me.

"Yeah. G'night. I'll talk with you later."

"All right. G'night."

I waited for his phone image to clear. I trusted what he told me. He was being as honest as honest could be. The problem was, I ached for more. I wanted us to be whole. I lay back in the bed, still naked and choosing to remain so.

I wanted to feel him with me as close as I could, willing things to be all right. The phone, resting now on the pillow next to me, alerted me to a text.

A little anxious, I picked it up and read. *Luv U, Roxy. Just give me time. BTW—the red light is extinguished.*

I stared at that phone, feeling the purest sense of relief. He had told me what I wanted to hear even if it wasn't verbal or formal. It was my "more."

My reply, I hoped, did the same for him. *That's all I need to know. Ditto.*

\*\*\*

The staff had the entire next day to clean out our rooms. Everyone had at least a dozen or more things on our to-do lists. So the good part of not getting enough sleep the night before was, I could roll out of bed, dress in any type of summery cleaning clothes, and still stop by Java Mug for a second cup of coffee.

Done with most of my work tasks by noon, I decided to text Finn. I had looked online to see that he had not won Video of the Year. So, in a way, it was good. The speech, whatever it might have been, did not have to be revealed. Before typing, I looked at his "Luv U Roxy" text from the night before and smiled. It gave me encouragement. It gave me hope.

Knowing that he had said he was getting together with his band, I texted. *How was practice?*

When I did not get an immediate response, I closed my door and went to meet some of my coworkers in the main office. Once we were all gathered, we started walking in a mob toward a local Italian restaurant for lunch. Everybody was talking at once, which suited me just fine. I didn't have to. I could just get lost in my own thoughts.

Just as I finished ordering my seafood hoagie, Finn's text came through. I grabbed my phone, excused myself, and scurried outside, wanting the privacy to read and respond. No one knew the current status of our relationship, and I wasn't willing to share until I felt on better ground.

His text read, *Just about done, but good.* And then a second one came in before I could even type a response. *U mad?*

Mad? That his practice was still going on? That it was a good practice? Did I not answer fast enough?

Confused, I texted, *No. Y?*

*Last night.*

Sadistically, I was kind of glad he was worried that I was still upset. It meant that he was thinking of me. And it probably meant he was sorry that things went the way they did.

I left him off the hook, though, with, *All good.*

I smiled when reading his response. *U R amazing.*

*Want to see U soon.*

My smile got even wider at his next correspondence. *For sure.*

That was the best part of my day. The worst was when I got back to work. I had agreed to help Gwen go through Wyatt's things in her classroom.

I glanced over at Wyatt's desk. It was in the front row, second from the left. Gwen couldn't bear to remove it or clean it out by herself. It was exactly how he had left it. Right or wrong, she had informed the grief counselors that Wyatt was going to be a part of her class until the last day. But the last day had now come and gone. And there we were with the desk looming in front of us.

Sitting in his small chair, I remained silent for a moment or two. I smoothed over the green name tag on his desk with my hand. He had seventeen "good work" stickers on it. He had only needed three more to get a new nametag and go "fishing" for a prize. Gwen said he would have done it too, before the end of the year…had he lived.

"Okay, Wy," I said out loud, knowing that there would be no response. "Help us through this."

Using my phone, I took a picture of his nametag and then watched Gwen peel it off in one clean swoop. She said maybe it was like the bandage saying—if you do it quickly, it might not hurt as bad. Everyone knows the removal always stings, regardless, though.

I opened up the top. His desk inside was fairly neat. Besides one loose paper—a list of names in the first grade club they created during indoor recess—everything was in order. Books were stacked and journals were put in correct folders. His "tool box" was closed and housed pencils, crayons, a couple glue sticks, a highlighter, and two pink erasers. There were also some math flash cards that Gwen said Nola or Will must have made for him to practice with in class. Dumping the writing utensils and putting aside the school property books, Gwen gathered everything else and placed them, along with his report card and his hallway artwork, inside a grocery bag.

I didn't cry. Although when Gwen pointed out his stuffed animal sitting solo on the bookshelf, it nearly brought me to my knees. He had brought in his well-loved, black and orange tiger to be his book buddy throughout the year. All the other kids had taken theirs home. The Bengal was all alone.

"Wyatt told me his uncle gave him the tiger—that it was his favorite football team's mascot." Gwen now held the stuffed animal close to her chest.

I semi-chuckled, knowing that must be the truth as Finn's favorite team was the Cincinnati Bengals. "Do you want me to call them…see what they want to do with his stuff?"

"Do you mind, Lara? I can do it. I probably should. But, you know, I don't know, especially with this pregnancy." She was in her first trimester. "I might just get all hormonal and breakdown on the phone, and they don't need that."

"It's fine."

"You sure? I don't want to pry, but…."

"We're okay," I said, knowing she was referring to Finn and me. But I didn't offer any more, because, really, okay was the extent of it.

"I have to pee. I'll give you some privacy." She handed me the stuffed animal and headed out of the classroom.

I called and left a message on Nola's cell phone, asking her to call me back. But it was Finn that I needed. He was not only one of a few people who would understand this pain, but he was the one who understood me the most.

*Having a rough moment @ work.* I texted, not wanting to interrupt if he was in the midst of any country music superstar business.

Finn answered me right back. *What happened?*

*Gwen & I just went through Wyatt's things.*

This time, it took him a little longer to reply. But he did. *What R U going to do w/ them?*

*Waiting for Nola to call me back.* I tacked on a sad emoji at the end. Again, it took him a minute or two, and I pretty much knew it had nothing to do with his career. *It will be all right. They'll want his stuff.*

*The stuffed Bengal tiger U gave him is here. Do U want it?*

*Don't want the memory. Throw it away.* His response crushed me.

I switched over and called him. "Are you all right?" I asked, omitting any usual beginning statement.

"Yeah." He answered with a positive word, but the inflection didn't mimic the meaning. "I'm not going to mess with my meds or hunt that old guy's family down." He spoke of the man whose deadly stroke while behind the wheel caused Wyatt's death.

"I didn't say that, but good. The thought did kinda cross my mind, though."

"I'm not going to tell you it doesn't hurt. It does. I know you can talk about him. It's just not the same with me. I'm just trying to get through."

My phone announced another call coming in. When I mentioned it was Nola, Finn insisted that I talk with his sister. I thought it was a tossup who needed me more at that point, but I reluctantly agreed, asking him to call me later.

***

Later came a little before noon the next day—my official last day of the school year. But it wasn't Finn who did the contacting. I did. I hadn't heard from him since that afternoon before. Not only did I not like how he reacted to Wyatt's things, but I didn't like that he hadn't called.

So, as I sat in a long committee meeting, I texted Finn. *Haven't heard from U.*

*Just a lot to think about,* was his text back.

Once again, I wanted to make sure to give him his space. I knew he had a lot on his mind. Certainly with his family and Wyatt. But also with his high-profile country music career. The re-worked summer tour was set to begin. And it was happening if Finn was ready or not. Some people need to jump right back in after such a devastating tragedy, while others need time to absorb solo. I believe Finn fell into the first category as his music was his self-proclaimed muse. But, regardless, he didn't have much of a choice—tickets had been sold months before and there was only so much rescheduling one could do without it being a major, catastrophic monetary expense.

Selfishly, I hoped I was on his mind too, but in a positive way. I would wait for him to let me know when he was ready. I just prayed it was sooner rather than later.

***

I was climbing the stairs of my apartment complex when my phone announced a text from Finn. I breathed in a deep breath of relief. He had contacted me this time. It wasn't the other way around. And it had only been a

33

couple of hours.

His message read, *What R U up to?*

I happily typed back, *Just getting in from walking. Had to cut it short. It started to rain.*

*It's raining there?* His text inquired.

*Just spitting now.* I answered.

*I'm supposed to meet Uncle Eoin @ his place.*

*Take an umbrella. Tell him I said hi.*

I liked Finn's uncle—his mom's only sibling. He owned a restaurant in Manhattan not too far from Finn's penthouse. It was where we had what turned out to be our first date.

Not hearing anything else from Finn's end, I decided to flirt a little. *Since I'm already wet, I'm going to slide into the shower now.*

Not missing a beat, Finn replied with a wink emoji and then typed, *How do your next few days or so look?*

Glad for the perception of an invitation, I texted, *Pretty free. Just having a Girls Day tomorrow—manis, dinner.*

*I'll get back to U. I have a lot of work, but maybe we can meet up…go somewhere or just hang out.*

I had to laugh. Due to Finn's celebrity, it was hard for him to go out like a normal person. While he didn't necessarily shy away from being out in public, I knew a lot of times he would prefer to stay in. And he knew I was good with hanging—just watching a TV show or whatever.

\*\*\*

I didn't hear from Finn at all that day though. Maybe it was because he knew I was busy. Or was it because it was the second week anniversary of Wyatt's death? Regretfully, I only realized that fact once I was home later in the evening. I felt awful that I had been so neglectful about such a crucial fact. It wasn't that I hadn't remembered. It was that I never forgot. One day was as devastating as the next when grief hung on like the heavy, cold rain.

I tried calling Finn the next morning after I had some coffee in me. When there was no answer, I hung up and texted him instead. For some reason, I despised leaving voice mail messages.

My text was simple. *Call me when U have a chance.*

The familiar rock sound of "Roxanne" belted out mere seconds after I put the phone back at rest on the kitchen counter. It slightly startled me. But then again, it didn't take much. After years of growing up with an angry, explosive, alcoholic father, sudden noises often had that effect, especially when I was already worn down emotionally.

Besides, I hadn't expected an immediate response from Finn. After all, he hadn't picked up when I had called just seconds before. Was he screening my call and waiting for the message before knowing if he wanted to return it?

"Hey," I answered.

"Is everything all right?"

"Yeah." I was thrown a little by the concern in his voice. "Why?"

"You called *and* texted. I thought something must be up."

"You didn't need to call me right back. I just wanted to make sure everything was all right with *you*. I haven't heard from you."

"Oh." Back to solemn-sounding Finn.

I wanted to remind him that I thought he was going to call so we could hang, but I refrained. So I did the inviting instead. "Would you want to do something?"

"Yeah. It's just I'm so busy right now. You cannot imagine how insane this is trying to rearrange all these shows."

And just like that he sounded more alive. Music or business I was realizing were safe topics. His feelings or family did not seem to be...at all.

"Plus, I'm supposed to do a radio promo. And then dinner tonight with Reese and other reps. We're trying to get the push back on the music and not…not the accident." His voice skipped on the last word. "Or whatever else they think they know." That addendum was full of hurt and spite toward the media who had incorrectly speculated that Finn had been back to using drugs. The fact was, the behavior that they had been witness to had actually been Finn being off medication. But since he didn't want anyone to know about his PTSD disorder, it was a double-edged sword, and obviously, something his team just wanted to brush under the carpet with good, positive press instead. "Then tomorrow is Father's Day," he continued. "Will and I are going golfing."

"Really?"

"I guess Nola thinks it will keep his mind off of everything. I, personally, just want to smack the hell out of some golf balls."

"What about Kels?"

"Dinner out afterward, but I don't know…not sure I'm down for all of that."

"It sounds nice," I said, longing to be invited to join them.

It used to be so natural that I was a part of their family gatherings. There had never even been a need for an invitation. It was just assumed. But all of that had changed. It had changed when we had separated. It had changed when Wyatt died. And although in some ways things had gotten better, it was far from back to normal. It definitely was not the same.

"If we get done early tomorrow, I'll let you know." When I left out more of a sigh than an actual word, Finn said my name, "Lar?"

"Yeah?"

"Just making sure you're good."

"Thought that was my line." I laughed, but it wasn't whole-hearted.

"I'm gonna go."

"So, today business and tomorrow golfing."

"Yeah."

"Bye, Finn." *I love you.* I thought it, but I didn't verbalize it. I knew it didn't matter, anyway, because the line was already dead.

\*\*\*

I tried to lose myself that weekend. And I did a pretty good job. I read an entire 400-page novel, wallowing in some poor star-crossed lovers' angst. I didn't bother to shower. I just stayed in my pajamas and read.

When Sunday evening rolled around and the book was finished—happy ending intact—I had yet to hear any word from Finn. And all I could think about was that our time was ticking away. He was leaving in days for a tour that would take him far away from me for months on end. And if we didn't get it right before then, it might never be.

As if sensing my distress, my phone's vibrations against the glass table helped. His text came in just when I decided to give up and go to sleep early. *How was your weekend?*

*Great!* I lied.

Finn's response wasn't much. *Good.*

*How is Will?*

*Dealin. Golfing went extra-long. We had a couple drinks, but I decided to skip dinner. I'm back @ my place—tired.*

I noticed a few things instantly just in his couple lines of text. Finn didn't want to give me any space to ask more sensitive questions about his brother-in-law or, for that matter, him. He had continued on with the text, changing it to logistics. And I noticed how he bailed on more intimacy with his family by skipping dinner, and more intimacy with me by alluding to the fact that he was ready to end the day…without me.

I decided to appease the subtext in his words by adding a bit of humor but not feeling funny at all. *Old man!*

He waited a few minutes and then went sentimental. *I*

*know it's Father's Day. I was thinking of U. Hope U talked w/your mom or bro.*

My far from perfect father had been dead for many years…almost for as long as I had known Finn. He was an abusive drunk all of his life. Or, at least, all of mine. He died like he lived—careless, senseless, and having one too many. He was not to be mourned, especially when you put it in the perspective of losing a seven-year-old child. But Finn's concern touched me.

*Thx. Honestly, didn't think of him much.* For good or bad, my concentration was on Finn. *How's your dad?*

*Still need 2 call.*

*Get going!!!* I admonished electronic style.

*TTYL*

I decided to make our text ending a little more personal. *xoxo*

He didn't exactly echo my sentiment back, but it was better than nothing. 😉

# CHAPTER FOUR

I made an impromptu decision the following day. A quick text to Finn told me that he had a busy day. It would be another one where I would not see him. But I decided that simply couldn't be. We needed to see one another. Before our separation, if Finn had been in the New York area, no matter how busy or what work he had to complete, we were together. We saw one another on a daily basis or something extremely close to it. What was going on now wasn't right. And I couldn't let it go. We were taking the proverbial two steps forward and one step back.

Knowing that Finn had told me the latter part of his busy day was going to be spent at the penthouse listening to tracks, following up on contacts, and packing for the tour, I took the transit into the city that evening and headed straight to his place. I only called him once I was in Manhattan. It was a calculated risk knowing he could potentially not be there.

"That okay?" I asked. "Me stopping in?"

"Sure. You can stop over my place any time," he answered. "I'll tell Graham to key you up." He spoke of the building's front doorman and the special access needed to get to Finn's penthouse floor.

"See you in a few then."

During the elevator's ascent, I ran my hands through my long, dark strawberry blonde hair that I'd partially pulled back in a barrette. I flattened my hands against my stomach, suddenly nervous and second guessing myself. Not that I wasn't sure it was what I wanted and what I needed. But I wondered how Finn would react, especially with so much on his mind.

The elevator doors separated, revealing the musician's front door. It was open, and Finn was leaning in the doorframe looking right at me. Wearing loose gray sweat pants and a worn college T-shirt, a pleased smile spread across his face, making him look as sexy as hell.

"Didn't expect your beautiful face at my door, especially this late," was his greeting.

"It's not that late," I challenged, although it *was* closing in on sunset.

I didn't move. I wanted him to give me a hug like he always had when he would first see me—a hug like he couldn't wait to feel me on him. But that hadn't happened since our split. That was one of the reasons I knew he was still holding back. That's the reason I was there and what the night was going to be about.

"No. Not late. Just—" he started.

"I know you're busy. Or"—suddenly, a horrifying thought crossed my overactive mind while watching Finn's body stretched across the entrance—"if you are entertaining—"

"Entertaining?" he asked with the most perplexed expression on his face. "No. Come on in."

He led the way as I followed him into his sleek and open living room underscored by multi-toned hardwood flooring. I could see papers splayed across his expansive granite coffee table. There also appeared to be a half-eaten container of Chinese food.

"And as far as being busy," Finn continued. "I'm just

fussing now. Gotta learn when to drop things and let them be. Get you a drink?"

"No," I answered, despite thinking I could really use one after having that insecure, absurd thought of Finn having someone else over. It was the touch of insecurity I still felt about our reestablishing relationship. I knew in my heart that Finn wasn't "that" guy. But I did need him to be my guy—"My Finn," like I had called him lovingly many times before.

"You're probably pretty warm with that coat on. Here, let me take it." He broke into my thoughts. "Why are you wearing one, anyway? It's nearly eighty degrees."

"Yeah, I guess I don't need it."

I brought my hands down to the black belt that encircled my pink wrap coat knowing exactly what was going to happen next. Unfastening the belt and letting the ends fall to my sides, I then slid my hands along the fabric of the center of my coat. When the jacket spread open and fell to the ground, the look on Finn's face was priceless…and just as I imagined. I was standing in front of him in nothing but small gold hoop earrings, a gold bracelet, and a lacy, black, strapless bra/panty combo. Oh, and heels, which I kicked off rather quickly.

"Oh, my God!" To his credit, his scan of my body was quick, before meeting my eyes and locking into them with adoration. "Roxy, you give a whole new meaning to that name."

"Finn, I miss you," I said honestly.

He tucked a not-loose hair behind my ear—an obvious ploy to be close to me. As his body closed in, he slowly and seductively kissed me…his teeth gently nibbling at my lower lip, his tongue licking mine. I brought my hands up and under his shirt, massaging his upper chest, liking the feeling of being caught between his muscular frame and the cottony fabric of our alma mater.

"Nice shirt," I said coming up for air.

"I miss you too, Lara. I think of you more than you

know." With those few words, he alleviated one of my greatest fears.

"Oh, yeah?" I teased, now more at ease. "What are you thinking about me right now?"

"I'm thinking, I can't believe how lucky I am, and I'm wondering why the hell the bedroom is all the way on the second floor."

I laughed openly. "Well, if you want to *get* lucky, we better start making our way to that stair—" Before I could finish "case," Finn lifted me into his arms and carried me up the glass and metal stairs. I wrapped my arms around his neck, nuzzling his shoulder.

Done in a steel color, just a little duller than the color of his car but mirroring his natural eyes, we entered the master bedroom. I slid down Finn's sleek body, letting my bare feet touch the coolness of the hardwood floor. I sat on the white bedspread of his king-sized bed.

"Even though I like that shirt, Cowboy, I think one of us is completely overdressed."

Finn put his hands on the bottom of his gray shirt and slowly lifted it over his head. He smiled as he softly tossed it at me. I caught it, taking in the scent that was uniquely, wonderfully him, and then put the shirt on the bed's edge.

"Come here." I pulled at his hands so that his body was inside my open legs. Putting my hands then on his waistband, I tugged his sweats down.

Never letting his eyes even blink away from mine, Finn stretched his long fingered hands on my shoulders to anchor himself. He started to wiggle his feet out of the rest of the sweat pants. As he did, I slid my hand beneath his briefs, cupping him securely in my grasp.

"Ahhh…Fuck, Lara."

"Yes, please." My eyes didn't leave his, and his were beginning to bounce. "That's the idea."

Finn pulled his briefs down with one hand and put his other on top of mine. "Your turn…the rest of your clothes," he said, nearly breathless from the feel of us working together.

I stood up, unfastened my bra, and shimmied out of my panties. Then I lightly pushed Finn down onto the bed. Slightly surprised and slightly amused, Finn watched as I climbed from the foot of the bed to plank directly above him.

We twisted and turned in nearly every way imaginable on that bed. The whole evening...the whole reason for surprising him was so that he couldn't deny or forget our connection. I thought that was accomplished. Or at least I hoped. How Finn reacted in those next few minutes or so was the real test.

I lay on top with him still snuggly inside me. With my head resting on his chest, I said, "My favorite pillow."

"You tired?" His voice vibrated beneath me.

"Aren't you?" I asked, trying to disguise the hope in my voice.

"Getting there."

"Are you staying?" The question...the fear.

"It's my place."

"So it is." I tried to keep it casual.

"That was the plan all along, wasn't it?" His chest seemed to harden a bit under my cheek.

"And if it was?"

It wasn't really a question. It was the truth. I did not want to or plan to take the train back home that night. It was, indeed, my plan all along—to actually spend the entire night together.

Weary, Finn's voice vibrated next to my still head. "Lara."

I adjusted a little so I could at least look at him directly. When I saw the hardened, yet sad, look in his face, I knew our fun was up, especially when he didn't offer anything more. "Then I have to leave?" I didn't let him answer, because I knew I couldn't emotionally invest anything more without breaking down. I had my pride. I had my emotional walls to protect myself. "I'm getting up."

Feeling me start to lift, he lightly pushed on my back. "No. At least let me…I—"

"No. Just let go." I said, realizing that I had never been the one to determine the timing of our disconnect.

We locked eyes for a few seconds. But when I shifted again, his hands relented and loosened so that my body was withdrawing from his. I hoped the emptiness that came because of it wasn't also symbolic. But I feared it was.

Lying on my back next to him, I immediately pulled the sheet up to cover my exposed body. Like a child scared of monsters under the bed, I needed the feeling of protection for whatever was going to happen. I covered my entire face with my hands and let them rest like that for a moment or two as I breathed in slowly. Beside me, I felt Finn move around. I was waiting—begging him in my mind not to get out of that bed…begging him to help us somehow turn the corner and become the two people we used to be.

It took him a moment, but he spoke. "I'm scared, Lara. I'm scared of loving you. I'm scared of loving someone so much again and for it to all go away. And it can go away just like that." He paused. "Baby, please look at me."

I was still covering my face, but it wasn't for the same reason. I was processing. I was finally understanding his hesitation—the moments where it felt like he was backing away from me and not being committed the same way. I took my hands from my face and saw that he was sitting with his back against the headboard. I scooted up to sit at his level but turned my body slightly to face him.

His eyes were the pleading, puppy dog ones. "Lara, promise, don't leave me."

I had left him. I had left him in April when he had been acting so erratically and gave me no explanation. I knew it had crushed him as it did me. But what I hadn't known then was how being left was such an emotional, traumatic trigger in his life.

I had left Finn, but there had been others. Audrey, Finn's fiancée from shortly out of college, blindsided him when she broke their engagement and entire relationship off. He had told me how absolutely shredded he had been and how, ultimately, that had led him on a momentary dark path of drugs. And it also led to the suppressed preschool memory of his grandmother leaving him in a park and being separated from anyone he loved for almost an entire weekend. His mom's mom had been the first to leave him—in the park and then dying—and then Audrey. But there also was Wyatt. Wyatt had essentially left him too.

Because of that, I wasn't the only one with trust issues. Finn knew how to build up walls to protect himself just like I had in the past. I had just been too self-absorbed with my own grief and need for him to be with me to notice his personal construction crew sawing and hammering away. I finally got it. Finn had decided to be the one to leave on his terms before risking the chance— the hurt—that I would leave him again.

The pain in Finn's eyes mirrored mine. I wanted to take it away for both us. But could I?

"Just don't keep any more secrets, even if you think you're doing it for me. Trust that I love you." I paused, and then said more slowly to drive my point across, "I love you, Finn." There, I said it. I gave in, but it was necessary and so true.

Finn's response was to take my hands and bring them up to his lips. He was good at keeping eye-contact. It was probably the performer in him. It found the romantic in me.

"And you know," I continued. "I'm scared of the same thing. I'm petrified of you leaving. God, we're just trying this again and you're leaving in—"

"Come with me," he said suddenly and confidently.

"What?" My hands were back at my side.

"On tour. Yeah...for the summer. You have the

summer. I need you with me. I can do this with you by my side." His eyes were wider, watching for my reaction. As I began to open my mouth to respond, he continued, "Please, Lar. I know you could find a million excuses, and I probably deserve most of them, but God, Beauty, I—"

"Shush. Give me a chance to talk. You're as bad as a kid," I admonished.

"Okay." He broke the little word into two slow syllables.

I hadn't had much time to think. His request came out of the blue. But I knew my answer just as succinctly.

"You want me to be your warm up act?" I let my fingers pretend to play an imaginary keyboard on his thigh.

"Really?" He seemed happily surprised by my creative "yes" answer.

"Yeah, if you're serious. I know you kinda just threw it out there. So, if not, I understand."

"Oh, God, Baby. Yeah, I'm serious. I can't believe it. God, Lara, yeah." His smile was enormous, wide, genuine.

"Huh? Wow. Yeah. I'm going on the road with you," I kind of repeated because his question and my answer went through a sort of delayed reaction. My brain was only catching up and comprehending what I had just agreed to. "That's nothing I ever expected to do in my life."

He was still beaming. "How about warm up act and encore?"

I answered with, "That can be arranged. But, just so you know, mine is a private, acoustic show."

His authentic laugh warmed my heart even more. "Mmm hmm." He began tracing his hand along the side of my naked body, starting with my breast. His seductive, caring touch made me instantly react by sliding into a more prone position and teasing circles on his hips, which I knew drove him wild. Finn may have started by kissing my stomach, but I don't think he missed an inch anywhere else, either.

Our love making Round Two was exactly that. We

made love. We were finally in sync, not only with our bodies but with our souls. It was the way we used to be…the way we were meant to be.

***

I'd like to say that I slept soundly next to Finn, but I didn't. We did fall asleep entwined with each other. But my sleep wasn't restful.

I found myself awake just a couple hours later. And I knew what had caused me to break slumber. My evil subconscious made me do it.

I adjusted my eyes to the darkness, which wasn't completely black because Finn had left a dimmer light on in the adjoining sitting room. It was something he always did so if I needed to use the restroom or get up in the middle of the night, I wouldn't bump into anything. The bed was empty in front of me and fear crept in.

But when Finn and I had fallen asleep, we had been spooning. So I turned around. Using his elbow, he was in bed propped up on his side simply watching me.

He read my mind just like he had always been able to in the past. "I'm not going anywhere," he said quietly, reassuringly.

"Me, either," I echoed in the stillness of the room.

Then he finally, as if waiting to see that I was, indeed, sticking, verbalized the words I had been so anxiously waiting to hear again. "I love you, Lara. Not once did I stop. I'm sorry that maybe—"

"Hold me, Finn," I interrupted, knowing his sentiment without him needing to relive it. "Don't let go. Because God knows, I would be destroyed without you."

His strong arms enveloped me into their embrace. I cherished their tenderness, comfort, and security. Those arms wrapped around me, felt like heaven…felt like love.

Who knows what would have happened to us if I had not gone to Finn's penthouse that night. Maybe being on the road and being back in the groove of the career that he loved would have naturally helped energize him and motivate him to find a way, somehow, to reconnect with me. But maybe not. Absence might not have made the heart grow fonder but torn us apart once again. I tried not to dwell on it and instead appreciated that things did happen the way they did.

\*\*\*

Finn would be playing at his first summer concert a couple days after I was at the penthouse. So there were a lot of arrangements that had to be made in a short amount of time to make my joining him a possibility. I had to talk with the post office, make sure all of my bills were ready to be paid online, make sure everything was off in the apartment, give my plants to a neighbor and pack, pack, pack. Finn was in charge of informing his "peeps" of my tour status. The short notice of my addition was probably not ideal. But everyone, from the band to food services to assistants to drivers, was welcoming.

The first concert stop was Boston. Finn was anxious that day. I'm not sure if that was typical of starting off a mega multi-city tour, or if it was because of all the extracurricular circumstances that had led up to the day. Noting this, I tried to give him as much space to himself and with his crew as I could. Prior to the concert doors opening, I grabbed my straw cowgirl hat and a book and found a solitary spot far off from the stands. Feeling the summer heat, I was rolling up my capris to form shorts when Finn collapsed down next to me.

"Geez, there you are," he breathed out. "Didn't know where you went. I tried texting you."

"I didn't want to get in the way." I took off my hat so I could get a better view of the handsome creature by my side. "Must have left my phone on the bus."

"Keep it with you," he said with a sense of command.

"I will," I agreed while registering in my mind that Finn's comment was rooted in his "don't leave me" fear. We were both going to have to work on that trust thing.

Now softer, he touched my nose. "And you're not in the way."

I smiled. "How you feeling? You were pacing like a caged animal when I last saw you."

"Just working out some nerves. Anxious to get back on stage."

"Yeah?"

"Yeah. Once that curtain rises, it'll all be good."

"You're gonna rock tonight," I said encouragingly.

"That's the plan." Finn rubbed my inner thigh. "I'm so glad you're here...that you decided to come."

My tongue lapping his was my response and thank you for inviting me in the first place. Even though I felt his desire back, I could also feel him pull slightly away. I looked in the direction he was to see one of his staff peering our way. "You need to get back?" I asked.

"Yeah. Sound check or something. Want to spend a few minutes with my girl first, though."

"I'm still your girl?" I asked, fondly remembering when he had first called me that and how much it meant.

"Definitely." He echoed the words he had used that day in January. With a hint of moisture in his eye, he then jokingly tossed out the other words he had said that day too. "But I believe my girl has to dance."

"Don't push it, Murphy!" I laughed while hitting him in the upper arm.

Knowing my detest for dancing, Finn grinned and swallowed me into his arms. "Fine. How about a picture then?"

"Just the two of us?" I asked. Photos weren't my favorite thing either, but with him, I didn't mind. There were a lot of things I let down my walls for when it came to Finn.

"Yeah. We could get one in every city." He wrinkled

his nose. "Too cheesy?"

"I love it."

Finn pulled out his phone and held it in front of us. "Say, 'Boston.'" He clicked and then turned the phone back around so I could see the image of our two faces mushed happily together. "Beautiful," he stated and kissed me as if it confirmed his statement. He pressed a couple buttons. "I just sent it to you."

"Thanks."

"There's something else I would like to do in every city too." He smiled slyly at me.

"Not on that bus full of bunks and band." I shook my head as a visual confirmation to my verbal one.

Finn had insisted that his personal bus had all bunks and a living area instead of a separate small bedroom area for him. He had wanted everyone to feel equal. It was good for morale—not so good for sex.

"Yeah, not as glamorous as the world thinks, huh?" he admitted. "We'll find some time for just you and me. I promise." He kissed me quickly and got up. "Listen, you need anything—anything—the guys know that you're gold."

"Gold?" I kidded. "I thought I was a platinum star."

Chuckling, Finn agreed. "You're a record breaker, Beauty," he said, placing the hat back on my head and tilting it beneath my eyes. "Some time, that hat and nothing else."

I felt my blush. "That's a different type of dance."

"Mmm-hmm." He smiled back and squeezed my hand. "I'll see you in a bit. Get your phone."

# CHAPTER FIVE

The next time I saw him, it was much closer to concert time. We grabbed a bite to eat with the rest of the crew before Finn went off to do the exclusive Meet-and-Greet and VIP acoustic pre-show in a back room. He wanted me to come along with him, but I didn't want to. I had seen how women acted during those events. It wasn't that Finn couldn't handle himself. I was afraid that *I* couldn't. Let him be in his element. Let him do his thing…his job. I could wait. I knew no matter how many butt grabs and overfriendly hugs by concert goers, I was his girl at the end of the finish line.

When he got back to the band's private area, he immediately planted a lengthy, determined kiss on my lips. "I love you," he declared freely and then said to the guys, "I need to shoot someone."

They laughed while I looked at him inquisitively, if not a bit concerned. But it was quickly explained to me that one of Finn's pre-show traditions was to play a war-style video game. It helped him get rid of the fake Meet-and-Greet business that I knew he detested but put on a good act for. And it helped him get pumped up for performing. A bunch of the band members battled it out video style while I sat with some of the other friends and family members who were there that night.

After a while, though, the warm-up acts were through and Finn's stage was set. Someone was yelling at them, with some urgency, that it was time to go on. Finn wasn't reacting with the same resolve, though. He didn't care if he was late. He never seemed to.

"I have one more ....Yes!" he yelled out like he was ten years old, not thirty. "Gotcha!" He had killed someone or something on the screen. The game was then shut off, and he submitted. "All right," he said. The group, well-trained and experienced in Finn's road rituals, silently and in sync formed a circle as Finn took my hand to join them. "Now, let's pray."

I looked at him in awe. He just went from "killing" someone to praying in the matter of a mere minute. And, although I had my doubts and issues when it came to organized religion, I respected Finn's views. I leaned my head into his shoulder as he made an eloquent speech about being thankful for all that they had and praying that their night and tour be a safe, magical, and rewarding one.

The crowd absolutely erupted when Finn eventually made his debut that night. It was a much bigger venue than when I had seen him perform in North Carolina in the springtime. It made me truly appreciate the level of Finn's fame. Of course I knew about his numerous hits, his multitude of awards, the demands on his time from agents, press, the label, fans, etc. But to watch it all culminate in one arena was amazing—amazing, overwhelming, and energizing.

It seemed to be all three of those to Finn that night too. The Boston crowd was well aware that they were now the first tour stop because of Wyatt's accident. So when he took the stage, they were appreciative of Finn's journey and his effort to be there. He tried a couple times to start his first song, but the audience was just too loud. I watched on the monitors from backstage and peeked at him live. He smiled at the crowd while placing his hands on his bended knees obviously overwhelmed by the moment. Just as I placed my steepled hands up to my face hoping that it would all go well, he sang—strong, proud, and full of emotion. It was the most beautiful thing I had ever seen. It was like watching a resurrection.

During planned elongated instrumental sections of select songs, Finn would run to the side to grab a gulp of water. The first time, he managed to ask me if I was all right and stole a kiss. The second time, he informed me that my song, the song that he wrote about me and for me, was up next on the set list. I kissed *him*.

Of course, my favorite time hearing, "Lara's Song" was the first time Finn had sung it to me on my birthday in the beginning of April. It had just been him and me, and the words had resonated so beautifully from his heart to mine. Now sitting on a wooden stool on this much grander stage, he managed to look at me a few times and even threw in a wink while performing my song. I knew, in that moment, that Finn wasn't just returning to the world of music, he was also truly returning to me. Sure, the grief was still going to be there. It would never fully go away. But neither was life.

\*\*\*

The next morning, as we were traveling to the second city, I watched as Finn got a bottle of water from the fridge and grasped a pill in his other hand. He wasn't hung over. In fact, the only thing he had to drink the night before was some celebratory champagne. To my delight, he had been on a natural high, jazzed again like that ten-year-old kid instead of someone with the world weighing on his shoulders. We hadn't stayed up late, either. Finn explained that he had a self-imposed curfew especially at the beginning of the tour.

The pill was his mood disorder medication. It was

what, in the past, before I knew of his condition, he had called his multi-vitamin. It was the first time since I realized what they were that I actually saw him take it. Somehow knowing that I was watching him, he looked at me while putting the pill in his mouth and swallowed it with a slug of water. His face portrayed a mixture of guilt and assurance. Guilt for not letting me know from the start about his condition. Assurance to let me know that he would not fail me again. Encircling his body with my arms, I rested my head on his T-shirt covered chest and held him securely for a moment.

And that was all we had before hearing one of his bandmates/boarders approaching. Finn's hand rubbed circles on my clothed back. He kissed the top of my head before pulling away.

"Personal...private. Just between you and me, right?" he said referring to not only the medication but the diagnosis itself.

I realized the risk to his career and the implications if that knowledge got out. "Without a doubt." I kissed him to solidify the pact.

*** 

Lunch break at an in-between-locations restaurant was a time to get off the bus, stretch, and discuss their opening day experience. I tried to just listen, but everyone was dragging me into the conversation, asking my opinion as a newbie. I was about to say something sarcastic just to get out of it, when Finn's phone started to ring. He looked at it and then turned to me.

"It's my folks. Do you mind talking with them for a couple minutes while we finish up here?"

Glad to not be a critic—they were going to force me to say a negative for every positive—I agreed. "Sure, I'm done, anyway." Purposefully rubbing his hand, I grabbed Finn's phone and said, "I'll be outside."

"Give me just a minute or two."

Walking through the door, I managed to answer the phone before it went to voice mail. "Hello?"

"Oh, um, I was looking for my son." Finn's father's voice sounded disappointed on the other end. "Who's this?"

"Mr. Murphy, its Lara."

"Lara?" Shock replaced his previous tone.

"Yeah. Hi. Finn asked me to answer. He'll be out in a minute."

Mr. Murphy practically cut me off with a much more jovial tone this time. "Lara! Hi, Darlin'."

"Hi." I leaned against the rickety front deck railing outside the restaurant.

"So good to hear your voice. I thought Finn was on tour. We were calling to see how the first show went. What's going on?"

"Yeah. He's on tour. Boston last night."

"You came to visit? Good. He needs—"

I realized Finn hadn't told his parents of my plans to join him on tour. Of course, everything happened so fast. They probably weren't even aware of how we stood as a couple. The last time I saw or spoke with Finn's parents was at the beachside memorial service.

I started to clarify. "Finn didn't tell you? He invited me on the first part of the tour with him. I'll be here until August."

"Oh. Hold on a sec." I heard him talking with someone on his end, presumably his wife. "It's Lara! She's with Finn….Yeah, on tour…for a while."

I was getting excited just listening to him being excited. And while I would have liked to have thought their joy was for me, I suspected it was because they knew my being with Finn would bring their son some happiness. They were good parents. I was starting to love them as if they were my own—maybe even more so.

As I was straining to hear what Mrs. Murphy was

saying to her husband, I felt Finn very softly rub the back of my shoulder. I knew he did it that way on purpose so he wouldn't surprise and frighten me. And I was thankful for his thoughtfulness. I placed my free hand on top of his before he wrapped both of his arms around me from behind.

"Your fan club?" He nuzzled his lips on my neck.

I set the phone a little to the side. "They're still yours. But you better watch out, I'm climbing the charts." I smiled and then spoke back into the phone. "Hey, Mr. Murphy, Finn's here now. I'm going to give you to him. I hope to talk with you again soon, though."

"Us too, Darlin'." His booming, jovial voice bounced across the line. "Yep, give me that son of mine."

"Here you go." I handed Finn the phone and went to walk off, but he kept me in his embrace.

"Hey, Pop," Finn spoke on the phone. "Yeah?...Yes...Yes." He laughed after both "yesses" causing me to wonder what they were talking about. "Yeah, the show went really well. It truly was one of the better openers. You know—perfect weather, awesome crowd. It was good...I know...It is good to be back, whichever way you meant it...I am." Finn's fingers tightened a little around my waist. Turning around, I boosted myself up to sit on the banister and then widened my legs so Finn could walk between them as he spoke. "Yeah, she seems to be. I hope so..." He smiled at me— the obvious "she" in the sentence. "Yeah, I know, Pop. Believe me." His mood changed slightly as he asked the next question, "How's Nola?" I looked more seriously in Finn's eyes as he continued, "No. Not really...Yeah, well, keep me posted, I guess...Yes, you can reach me on this phone. If I don't answer it, I'll...No!" he yelled laughing. "That wasn't what I was going to say!" He laughed again softly touching my face. "No, I don't think we have any watermelon. Don't need any, either." Before he had the word "either" completely out, I playfully smacked his arm knowing what he and his father were talking about—an embarrassing inside joke of watermelon having a Viagra effect. "Owww!" Finn jokingly yelled out and then swiftly pulled me into a standing position, sliding his hand inside the front of my pants. His finger was teasing and tempting the lacy part of fabric that separated my sensitive skin from his.

"Finn!" I strongly whispered while sucking in my breath and grabbing his sides.

"Pop, I'm…I gotta go. Talk to you later…Yep, see ya." He quickly got off the phone and gently released his hand from my pants. "I know it's not the most romantic situation, but the bus is ours for a little bit."

"Crap, I can't say 'no' now. I'm kinda a hot mess."

"Baby, you can always say 'no.'" He spoke with sincerity. He was always careful, recognizing that, pre-him, I had been in a situation that had been a "no" scenario.

"So how does this work? Is it like college? You put a tie around the door?" I joked.

"You didn't do that," he said, confident that he knew me back then. But the slightest doubt in his macho armor set in. "Did you?"

"Didn't need a tie. I had the red light, remember?" I teased. "You better get me to that bus to finish what you started, Cowboy."

\*\*\*

The tour and our time together absolutely flew by. Summers always seem to go fast, but those six weeks went exceptionally fast. There were times when Finn was performing three days in a row. There were times when there was a day in between due to travel. And there were other rare, cherished times when there were a good few days or so in between gigs. Sometimes, band and crew would take that time to make a quick trip back home wherever that might be, but Finn and I stayed. We explored whatever city we were in and checked into a hotel so we could sleep on a regular-sized mattress and take a shower in something that when you turned around you didn't have one foot in the kitchenette. Those times were magical.

We spent a night like that in the beginning of August, right before I had to go back to New York and work. When Finn and I had originally planned that date at the start of our summer adventure, it had seemed like a long time away. I was on the road with him for a month and a half. That was huge for me as an individual. I had been living on my own since after college. And now I had been with a group of people practically 24/7.

In addition, it was huge for us as a couple. Even before our temporary split, Finn and I only got to see each other for a few days in a row every couple weeks due to his career and life in Tennessee and mine in New York. On the road, we had been practically inseparable. And it had worked out okay—more than okay. I had been afraid we would get on each other's nerves. But, in general, that wasn't the case. I had plenty of time to myself on tour. After all, Finn was working. It was his job. He would focus completely on it, and that didn't just mean the performance itself. It meant prepping before each concert, additional meetings, and other aspects of his career that kept chiming in via his phone. I learned to explore the different locales on my own, as well as download a vast number of books.

I was so relaxed that, by the end of my time with him, Finn pointed out that I hadn't been grinding my teeth at night while I slept. It was a horrible, subconscious, continuous nervous habit that I had developed since adolescence. I never imagined that it would ever go away. But it did. And I'm sure it was because I finally, for the first time in my life, felt truly free and loved and safe. He did that for me...his continued presence and our devotion to one another.

Finn took me out that last night. It was a real date. We stayed at a hotel where we had dinner, drinks, talking, hand-holding, and winking across the table. We were a real couple, not two roadies who had been traveling together non-stop, eating some form of take out, and playing basketball with the gang. After we made love that night, we lay in bed talking. Neither of us wanted to give in to the night or what the next day was going to bring.

"I'll bring you back something," Finn said twirling my hair.

Sarcasm flew from my mouth before I could restrain it. "Preferably not a disease."

"Lara Faulkner!" he jokingly bellowed and then sat up, causing me to do the same. He looked at me seriously then. "You don't really worry about that, do you?"

I had truly meant it as a joke, but since the subject had been broached, "I'd kinda be a fool not to, right?"

"Lara…." His voice was a bit sad or disappointed. "Would you cheat?"

"Of course not!" I said, offended but knowing that my opportunities were much more limited than Finn's.

"Then why would you think I'm any different?"

"I don't," I answered honestly. "I meant it as a joke."

"I know you did, but it still crossed your mind."

"You can't deny all the stories of musicians hooking up on the road. I don't get it. Is it the proximity…the comradery…just because you can and you're away…or is it just the physical—"

"Lara, stop." He cut me off with determination but, at the same time, gently. "Listen, I know the stories. But you've been with us all summer. You know that's not me, and it's not a lot of us. Yes, it happens. But it also happens with business people and construction workers and any other profession. We talked about this before. Nothing has changed. You are my one and only girl."

I should have just appreciated that sweet and sincere statement. But since we were on the subject, there was something that had been tugging at me for a while. "What about when we were apart?" I cringed, because the question brought back such a painful time. "What about in the spring?" Before he could answer, I conceded to the fact that he would have been justified even if internally I would be crushed. "We weren't together. I told you it was over. I just need—"

"No." He spoke firmly while looking me directly in the eyes. "No."

"You had every right." Why was I trying to make him say otherwise? It was like I wanted to be hurt. Or was it that I was just used to being hurt?

"First of all, I had no rights." He gently touched the side of my face with the soft back side of his hand. "I had no right after how I treated you. And second, I just refused to believe that we were over. I know you said it, and you meant it, and it was, but I couldn't see that. No. The answer is 'no' and it always will be." When I didn't respond, he questioned. "Okay?"

"More than. And the same goes for me." I smiled and pecked him on the lips.

"Besides,"—he smiled back—"I'm pretty sure that would have fallen into the no omissions clause thing, right?"

I couldn't help but laugh yet be reassured that he took our verbal, total-honesty agreement seriously. "Damn straight."

"Hey, watch your musician mouth," he teased. "You're going back to enriching the lives of today's youth."

"I know. I'm sorry." I chuckled, glad that our conversation was more relaxed and there were no lingering doubts. I think we both needed that in preparation for the empty, alone days to come.

*\*\*\**

I'm not sure if it was the thrashing or the sound that

woke me up first. But both were equally disturbing. Finn was next to me, still asleep but in obvious nightmare distress—something that, in all the times we had shared a bed, I had never witnessed. It quickly became apparent what he was dreaming about and, most likely, what had triggered the onset.

"No!" he yelled out in his sleep. "Wyatt!" He moved as if he were reaching for something but in the opposite direction of me. He tossed some more and then yelled, "Don't go!" Tears, actual tears, were coming from his eyes.

I wanted to cry for him. He was screaming for his nephew—the nephew he couldn't save. Neither Wyatt nor the accident had been mentioned the entire time I was traveling with Finn and his ensemble. Those closest around him seemed to know not to. In the beginning, they asked Finn how he was doing in a way that alluded to the incident. Finn had claimed, generically, that he was fine and immediately changed the subject. From what I understood, at the first Meet-and-Greet, a fan had offered Finn her condolences. A band member told me Finn was polite but walked out. And from that point on, one of Finn's staff gave the fans a little precursory speech about what not to say before every session.

While I didn't want to shy away from the topic of Wyatt, there weren't, in all actuality, a lot of circumstances that brought him up. Only when Nola would call would the subject be remotely close. For the most part, though, Finn texted his sister instead of speaking with her in person. And there was the note that Wyatt had written to Finn wishing him luck and telling him he loved him taped securely inside Finn's favorite guitar case. Finn never mentioned it, but he knew I had seen it. And I knew the depths of what it meant.

"Finn?" I said gently while carefully rubbing my hand on his chest. "Finn? Wake up."

Uncharacteristically, he almost swatted me because I had startled him so much. I scooted a little away as he adjusted his eyes to me. "Lara? What's wrong?"

"Nothing. You were dreaming. And it didn't seem like it was very peaceful."

"Huh?"

"You were calling out for Wyatt, Baby."

"Oh." He was more awake now. He sat up and ran his hands through his hair. "Sorry, haven't done that in a while now."

"You were before?"

"Yeah…right after."

I realized it was probably another reason he kept leaving after we had made love back then. "You all right?" I touched his face.

"He was leaving, but he was on a plane."

"Hmmm." I was going on a plane that day. It didn't take a psychiatrist and a couch to figure that one out.

"I couldn't get the plane to stop. I was on the runway but…."

"Talk to me, Finn. I'm here."

He let me curl into his side, remaining silent for a little bit. "You're not gonna be."

I knew it. "I know, Baby. I've had an amazing…amazing time. We gotta find a different word than 'leaving.' I can't bear that. It's not like before. And it's not like Wyatt."

"Lara, there are times I still think that it was a bad dream. I couldn't do anything. I couldn't help him."

"That's just it, Finn. You couldn't. You couldn't. You did everything you could. Anything anyone could have. Everyone knows that. You say it, but you need to believe it."

I kissed him. Or at least I tried to. But he sort of denied me, still lost in his own pain.

"Finn?" I held his hand in mine. "I know you don't like to talk about him. But I worry about you bottling things up."

"I thought of trying to write something."

That made me smile. His heartfelt lyrics were as much a contribution to his success as his voice was...maybe even more so. His damn sexy physique didn't hurt either.

"Good," I said. "Maybe that will keep your mind off of me le..." I stopped on the bad "L" word and changed it to, "anxiously waiting to see you again."

"Good try." He half chuckled at my attempt. "And as if." He ran his finger down my nose and to my mouth.

I licked my lips in anticipation of his kiss which came soft and smooth. "I'm gonna miss you something fierce, Finn Murphy."

To add salt to the wound, Finn's schedule was jam packed the second half of the tour. Not only was there little to no downtime between venues and traveling, when there was, he had television appearances and recording sessions booked in the limited space. He had shown me his schedule before I left. There wasn't a thing we could do about it. We weren't going to see one another for at least two months. That was longer than we had ever been apart since becoming a couple. I just had to trust that the bond that we formed first as friends and then as so much more could hold us together.

# CHAPTER SIX

That first night back home, apart from him, silence surrounded me. It was so bizarre, so abstract, so lonely. Every day for weeks on end had been filled with either loud music or the commotion that goes with traveling with an insanely large and boisterous group of people. And now there was none of that—just my apartment walls.

Finn had insisted that I let him know when I got home. It was kind of a tradition for us—a final good night in a way. But it was also because he needed to know I was safe. And, admittedly, I didn't mind. I liked knowing that someone was looking out for me even though it was miles and miles away.

Figuring that he was most likely in his final preps before hitting the stage, I texted as soon as I got in. *Back home. Go break a leg.*

His response was nearly immediate and, with just a few words, relayed so much. *It would match my heart. I miss U already.*

My mouth hung open for a moment. It was as if he was speaking for both of us. So I texted back, *Ditto. xoxo*

Noting the stale atmosphere of my closed-for-months apartment, I opened the patio doors to let some fresh air in. I then grabbed one of the very few, non-perishable items that had been left in the kitchen—cheese-flavored crackers—and practically inhaled them. The soothing shower's water beads helped me relax my mind enough to start mentally creating a list of all the things that needed my attention that next day—restarting the mail, grocery shopping, and laundry topped the list.

While combing through my wet hair, there was a knock at the door. I glanced at the clock, but I pretty much knew what time it was. I knew because I couldn't stop thinking of Finn and what he was doing every moment. I had his schedule down pat after living it day after day. He was definitely on stage when that knock on the door occurred. That meant it was very late for someone to be directly on the other side of my apartment.

Walking softly and cautiously, I peered through the peep hole in the center of the door. A delivery man stood on the other side swaying from foot to foot and carrying a vase full of gorgeous red roses. Modest, I grabbed a jean jacket hanging in the hall closet and shrugged it on over my pajama top before greeting the stranger. After quickly exchanging my signature for the roses, I closed the door and buried my nose into the flowers. I knew they would be unscented as much as I knew who they were from. Finn knew about my allergy to anything strongly scented, and flowers topped that list.

Smiling, I placed the roses on the coffee table and flopped down on the sofa before removing the card embedded in the flower arrangement. When I opened it, I smiled again. His words never seemed to fail regardless if it was in his lyrics, in person, or in a simple note sent from miles away.

*You have no idea how much this summer meant to me. You make everything better. I love you.*

I held the card up to my chest, re-inserted my face into the roses, and...lost it. I just sobbed and sobbed and sobbed. When I managed to regulate my breathing and tears, I shook my head and silently cursed myself. Why was I such an emotional mess? Sure, I was tired and missed Finn. But it was unlike me to totally indulge in such an onslaught of tears.

I re-read the card, damp from me clenching it so long. And then I got it. I was finally grieving. Since rushing to the hospital after hearing of Wyatt's accident, I had been taking care of everyone else—making sure I was there for Kelsea, Nola, Will, Finn's parents, people at work, and, most of all, Finn. I needed to support him through the terrible tragedy of his nephew's death. And, in the process, I had shoved my own feelings of loss and grief far off to the side. After reading that card, I knew I had at least helped him find some kind of peace. But I needed to find my own. I let loose the tears for that sweet little boy I had known and loved too. And I let loose the tears for knowing that I could…for those last three words on Finn's card. Knowing that he loved me, gave me the security to grieve and love too.

***

A few weeks later and only a couple days into the student school year, the message light on my work phone was blinking. Anticipating that a co-worker had some sort of technology issue, I took a deep breath and punched in my passcode to begin listening to the message. Surprisingly, it was not from anyone on staff, though. It was not, actually, work related at all. The message was from Carter—the dark-haired drummer in Finn's band. Carter was the playboy of the group. He was single and took life as it came. He didn't seem like the tie-me down kind of guy, but was charming and considerate and kind to everyone he met.

Carter's voice was low on the message. He started by apologizing for calling me at work, but it was the easiest number of mine to find without asking Finn for it. And he couldn't do that, because Finn had no idea Carter was calling me. Carter explained that Finn had been "absolutely unbearable" since I came back to New York about a month before. And, in turn, he was starting to make everyone miserable around him. In fact, at one point, Finn and a guitarist almost got into a physical altercation.

That came as a surprise to me. When I spoke with Finn, he seemed to be doing fine. He told me he missed me and, God knows, the feeling was mutual. But we both were keeping busy with our careers. *I* wasn't making my co-workers miserable. And I certainly wasn't about to brawl with any of them. That was so out of Finn's character, I questioned the validity of Carter's word.

I continued to listen to the message. He wanted to see if there was a possibility of me coming to visit Finn. He had looked through the schedule to find something close by and on the weekend knowing that I couldn't, most likely, take a day off work. That's when I knew the situation was real. Carter, or any guy for that matter, putting that much thought into it?

"Finn," Carter said in the voice mail, "needs a Lara intervention. Actually,"—he turned the charm on—"we would all like to see you."

The date Carter had in mind was perfect. It was less than a week before Finn's September 11 birthday. So I could be there to celebrate that. Plus, it was a Saturday in Baltimore. And Baltimore was only a four or so hour drive.

After Carter and I texted back and forth a few times throughout the day, we had it figured out. I would be a surprise birthday gift from the band. I could drive down Saturday for the evening performance and still drive back the following day without missing any work. I asked Carter if I could bring a friend. I wasn't too keen on driving by myself that long to somewhere I was unfamiliar with. Plus, I was positive my co-worker/friend, Vanessa, would totally be game for a road trip, especially if it meant a backstage concert experience.

His typical single-guy text response was, *Is she good looking?*

I described Vanessa accurately. She was a single, average build but petite, twenty-nine-year-old with wavy brunette hair. She was pretty easy going and was always out doing something. Carter answered that they would take good care of her.

I texted back, *Not sure that is reassuring at all…LOL!*

\*\*\*

As expected, Vanessa was stoked to go to Baltimore with me. The road trip was a blast. We had the windows rolled down and nibbled on chips as we cruised down the interstate. We talked about everything from trashy books, to crazy things we had done, to bashing men. I had a hard time doing the latter since Finn and I were in such a good place. But when I suggested she might meet someone over the weekend, her attitude changed to something more positive.

And, of course, we listened to music. Vanessa insisted on just Finn Murphy tunes. She wanted to make sure she was on top of her game. But she didn't need to worry. She knew most of the words. It was yet another instance where I truly realized what a mega-star Finn really was. I simply saw him as my friend from college…my love. Oh, and he liked to sing.

It was hard for me not to go straight to Finn when we arrived. But it was supposed to be a surprise. So I continued along with the plan. Vanessa and I went to an outdoor restaurant for salad and sandwiches.

Right before we were ready to leave, I got a text from Finn. *What R U up to?*

I didn't want to lie, especially with our no omissions pact. So I didn't. *Drinks w/ a friend.*

*Drinks? Friend?*

*Jealous?* I teased.

*Curious…*

*It's Vanessa and soda.* I left him off the hook.

*I want to be the something in your hand—not the glass* 😊

I sent a blush symbol because I really was. *U getting ready for the show?*

*Yeah. Just have a few last minute tweaks.*

I decided to flirt back. *I'm sure you're on top of it. You're good when you're on top.*

*Ditto, Roxanne.*

Because I was feeling flustered next to Vanessa, who was trying her best not to be nosy, I decided to end our sexting. *Talk soon.*

***

Vanessa and I eventually made our way to the venue. As the opening band played, we bought margaritas and found the seats Carter had on hold for us at the gate. They were in "peanut heaven," so there was no way that Finn could spot me. By the time the crew was setting up the stage for the main attraction, I had a slight buzz on thanks to the combination of the late summer sun and the anticipation of seeing my love. I wondered if Finn could feel my presence as much as I could him.

Carter had given me the set list. Although I knew that pretty much by heart too. So right before "Lara's Song" was due up, Vanessa and I made our way onto the floor. As Carter had directed, we gave one of the security personnel the note that had been attached to our tickets. The bulky man smiled and helped Vanessa and me bully our way nearly to the front of the pit section. I kept sneaking glances at my man. Finn was just finishing rocking out to one of his most popular songs on the left side of the stage. Vanessa was singing right along.

The wooden stool was brought out for Finn to sit on as he started straight into singing my song. And it was as beautiful as ever. The crowd fell silent during the ballad, except for echoing the words. I smiled and did as planned. I took the *I ♥ U Finn!* sign I had made before leaving New York and started waving it in the air like I had seen so many young females do at Finn's concerts.

Vanessa kept bumping into me laughing. She seemed almost as excited as I was. Almost, because I was on Cloud Nine. I could feel Finn and I together as if our bodies were entwined between sheets. And he hadn't even spotted me or locked onto my eyes yet.

But my repetitive sign waving eventually got his attention. He smiled generically in my direction as I identified the blank performer in him. Then recognition slammed him square in the face. Still singing, Finn's eyes got wider at the second look. He got off the stool and walked to the edge of the stage, sitting down and allowing his feet to dangle. His amazing eyes, even though contact-performer green, remained shining on mine. Not a lot of people would notice, but I did, how he signaled backward for his band to continue playing instrumental so he didn't have to sing. When the pit fans started stretching closer and closer toward him, he put both his hands out to urge them to stop. He had to do it a couple times, but they followed his directive like good little soldiers. Finn curled and moved his finger signaling for me to come to him. I gave the sign to Vanessa and allowed the security guard to block the way. When I was able to be directly in front of him, Finn shrugged in a laughing way, pulled out his one ear piece, and leaned down to speak to me.

"What are you doing here?"

"Happy pre-birthday," I yelled.

"God, I...Wow! I'm...c'mon." He leaned slightly over, reaching out his hand for me and at the same time signaling for one of the security guards to help me onto the stage.

As I felt the muscular tone of the guard, dressed in black and fluorescent yellow, start to help me, I yelled, "No, Finn. Go and sing. I'll be here."

Finn nodded to the bodyguard again but spoke to me. "It's your song, Baby."

The crowd was loud but, yet, so attentive on what was going on with Finn and me. The band was starting to play another round of the instrumental section of "Lara's Song." I hated—hated—being in front of a crowd of people. Put me in front of thirty kids, I'm fine. Close to 30,000 adults? I was as nervous as hell. But I knew it was inevitable and didn't want to insult Finn.

So, before I knew it, I was on the stage with Finn holding my hand, shaking his head, smiling, and leading me to the wooden stool. Before I could even sit, a stagehand had another stool out for Finn to sit directly next to me. It was so loud, it seemed to counteract itself, and I almost went deaf. I didn't dare look anywhere besides his eyes. If I looked out to the thousands of concert goers, I probably would have thrown up. Finn smiled, rubbed my hand, and nodded to the band to continue.

It was a good thing I already knew the words. Because I'm not sure I heard anything coherently. It was like I was in a virtual reality. This was not part of the night's plan. He was supposed to see me, be surprised, and we would meet up after the show.

I dipped my head down a couple times during the serenade embarrassed by the attention. But at the same time, I was in awe that Finn had chosen to spotlight our relationship. He had always been passionately protective of his personal privacy.

When the song ended, he leaned over to say something in my ear that only I could hear. "I'm going to kiss you."

"You don't have to," I tried.

I knew his love. We knew our love. It wasn't something we needed to, nor did, put on display.

"Oh, but I do." He smiled and, before I knew it, his lips were on mine. It was quick but it meant the world. Standing up and taking my hand, he addressed the audience who were hooting and hollering. "Ladies and gentleman, give my special guest a round of applause."

As the crowd erupted, Finn guided me, with his hand on the small of my back, behind the stage. "Don't go anywhere," he directed.

I noted immediately that me leaving was still his concern. "Of course not," I confirmed. "But, Finn, I brought a friend. She's still down front."

He turned to one of his best friends and right-hand man. "Hawk?"

That was all he needed to say for Hawk to confidently declare, "Got it, Chief."

And with that, Finn kissed me and just as quickly ran back on stage. I watched as he nodded to the band to begin the next song. And when his main set was finished and the lights dimmed for the crowd to start chanting for an encore, I heard him yelling, "One and done! One and done!"

They only played one encore song, whereas, he would usually play four. I knew the reason. He wanted that extra time with me. He wouldn't say it, but everyone knew. Probably even the disappointed fans. But I didn't care. I wanted every extra second I could get with him too.

After signing far fewer autographs than he usually did for the fans who managed to squeeze up front, Finn came off the stage for the final time that night. His smile lit up when we locked eyes again. "Hi," he said softly.

"Set sounded real good."

In response, he kissed me and then looked to Vanessa who had made it backstage several songs before. "Hi."

"Finn, you remember Vanessa?"

"Great concert," Vanessa practically screeched.

"Thanks." Finn responded ever the host. "You girls being taken care of?"

"Yeah," she said.

Finn looked back at me. "I can't believe you're here." Someone handed him a towel, and he wiped his head and arms.

"It's my turn to surprise you." I smiled, alluding to the time in March when Finn had reversed roles and surprised me by flying in from Nashville.

"I'd say."

"I'm glad you saw the sign," I teased. "My next option was throwing my bra on stage."

"Oooh, I would have loved that, Roxanne." Finn saw my uncomfortable glance at Vanessa but continued. "Is it red like your light or just like your face?"

"Finn, stop!" I plowed into his arms, willing him to stop embarrassing me, but loving that he was in such a jovial mood. "Don't ask," I said looking at Vanessa.

"Never too much T.M.I." My friend laughed.

Finn's black T-shirt beneath my face was soaked with sweat, but I didn't care. "You're staying, right?" he asked.

"We have to go back to New York in the morning. But tonight you're mine." I separated a little from him so we could look at one another.

"Lara!" Carter called out my name, and I gave him a hug.

"Thanks for everything, Carter," I acknowledged, breaking from him.

He handed Finn a paper with the hotel info. "The room is under Lara's name. Gift from the band."

"Thanks." Finn grinned and looped his arm and hand with mine. "Everything good here, then?"

"Take off! What are you waiting for?" Carter answered.

"Uh…." Finn pointed a little awkwardly to Vanessa.

"Vanessa's going to stay on the bus. That's okay, right?" I asked Finn.

"If Vanessa's all right with it." Finn looked from Vanessa to Carter. "I'm sure we can get you a room."

"And miss a chance to sleep on a tour bus? Are you kidding?" Vanessa was serious yet funny.

"Carter…." Finn looked at his buddy using his warning voice. "This is Lara's friend."

"And Lara's driver tomorrow." I jumped into the conversation.

"I'll take care of her." Carter winked at Vanessa who smiled back. "It's covered."

"God, girlfriend, go get some. Quit worrying about me. I'm fine." Vanessa started physically pushing Finn and me away.

I took Vanessa's hands in mine. "Have fun. Get some sleep. You have my cell number if you need anything."

"Uh-huh." And she began pushing me again.

*** 

It took us quite a while to actually exit the concert grounds. Finn had to thank people for the evening's show, confirm some details, take a quick shower, and grab some of his things. But we eventually made it to the hotel.

The door was barely closed with the "Do Not Disturb" prominently displayed when Finn tossed me on the bed. I liked the instant possession...the instant desire. His shirt was off before I even had a chance to look up.

"What was that texting about earlier? Who's better on top?" He was getting out of his pants.

"I think it was a mutual admiration society." I smiled and then remembered, "Aw Finn, I left your birthday gift in the car." It was a McDonald's gift card like the one I had given him at college graduation and a digital picture frame uploaded with our selfies from every city on the tour.

"Baby, as much as I love gifts, can it wait? Besides, you are the best gift I could ask for."

"Start unwrapping then," I teased, drawing on my seductive side.

Just like he dismantled wrapping paper, he similarly, hastily removed my clothing, eager to get to what lay beneath. "Black and white. Mmmm-hmmm, almost as good as red." Finn's eyes were scrolling over my lingerie.

"Where were you when you sent those texts?" Curiosity was not only in his voice but in his roaming hands.

"If you look out the window, you'd probably be able to see the restaurant." As Finn shook his head, surely still amazed how differently his day was turning out, I asked the next provocative question. "And what was it that you wanted in my hands…a glass?"

"Ha…not exactly." He kicked off his briefs, slid his tongue into my mouth, and we let our magnetic bodies do the rest.

# CHAPTER SEVEN

We got an hour—maybe a little more—of sleep. Finn had set the alarm purposefully early so that we could have a little time together before both of us had to set off in different directions for over a month. The ringing of the alarm sounded more like banging until I remembered where I was and who was beside me after such a long absence.

I snuggled even harder into his side. "You awake?"

"Yeah." He switched off the alarm and turned to me. "Don't think I'm going to have to work out today after that night."

"Did I make all your birthday wishes come true?" I allowed my index finger to draw hearts on his bare abs.

"Yep. And all the ones from my teenage boy years too." He smiled.

"I bet." I kissed his chest. "Speaking of, when I'm gone, you behave yourself and play nice."

"I do." He laughed.

"I'm being serious, Finn. I don't want to hear about you getting in fights." My head was resting on his firm torso.

"What?"

"I heard that there's been some friction in band camp." I casually used a fun term for their group. "You're still taking your meds, right?" I started to raise my body when I asked the question but had to become completely inclined upon Finn's reaction.

"Christ!" He boomed and propped himself into a seated position in the bed. "First of all, everything is fine with the band. And second, Lara, I can't keep proving to you that I'm taking the medication. If we're going to make this work—"

Whoa! What? What did he just say? Stunned and hurt, I started to look for my bra and black T-shirt.

"If...?" I left the question hang while throwing my legs to the side of the bed and away from him.

"Where are you going?" He seemed like a dazed deer in headlights.

"I'm leaving." I was so upset that I didn't realize the detrimental "L" word was coming out of my mouth until after the fact. I felt bad for saying it, but it was, regardless, accurate.

Finn tugged at my arm urging me to stay. "Don't."

"Why?" I had the top in my hands. I didn't care about the bra.

He looked at me, realizing I wasn't messing around. The agitation that had been in his eyes was still there, but it was mixed with pain and fear. He didn't talk for a moment. I think it was because all of those emotions were colliding at once. I shook off his hand and put the black shirt over my head.

"I want you to stay," he said plainly.

"Are you sure?"

"Yes. Of course." We both took a breath, neither of us understanding how the conversation had gotten this way. "Why—"

I was calmer. Yet not patient. "You want me to stay? Then why would you say, 'if'... 'if we'? I didn't realize there was an 'if.'"

"You know that's not what I meant. You know how I feel about us."

"I thought I did."

"Why are you purposefully trying to pick a fight?"

His question only made me more upset. "I'm not." I punctuated each syllable.

Seeing my arms thread through the shirt noticeably upset Finn. "Lara, damn it! Listen. What I meant…I just need you to trust me. I'm not going off the meds. I can't be defined by this thing—this disorder. It's such a little part of who I am. And sometimes I wonder if that's all you see now." He had started out angry but finished hurt.

"It's not," I said quickly. That was the truth, and I needed him to know that without hesitation. I breathed in again, wanting to slow things down and not have the escalator of pain move as rapidly. "I'm sorry. I'm still working on the trust thing. You know I've always had issues with that." Between my father's alcoholism and the infamous night in high school when I didn't know what I drank or who I slept with…. "I never trusted anyone completely until you. And then when you hid your diagnosis…."

"…I broke your trust." He said it calmly, making me grateful that we were possibly coming back to a normal conversation. "I know. I get it. I deserve that. But please, please, Baby, don't ever tell me you don't trust how I feel about you. There is no *if*, okay?"

That helped. That definitely helped. Maybe it was just my insecurities that were failing us.

"Finn, I love you so much it scares me. And I can't help it." I put my hand out to touch his arm. "I worry about you. When I ask about you or your meds, I don't mean to interrogate you. I really don't. I just want to make sure everything's all right. I'm just going to be a little, I don't know…"—I searched for the right word—"quirky. Can you try to ignore it and just pacify me?" I wiped my eyes, which were burning on the verge of tears.

"Can you quit putting that shirt back on and let me?" he asked tentatively, trying to sound relaxed and joking. He brought his hands up to mine, first holding them and then wiping a straggling tear from my face. That act earned him his reward of removing the shirt again. "Lay down, Beauty," he directed. When I did so on my back, Finn clarified. "Other way."

I turned over, lying this time on my stomach. The heat of the sheet beneath my body was nothing compared to Finn sitting gently on top of the back of my legs. His strong hands kneaded into my shoulders, rhythmically massaging the kinks that had, unfortunately, taken hold. He was a good masseuse, and I had often joked that if his music career ever tanked, he definitely had something to fall back on.

My negativity was quickly eroding. "I miss you already," I admitted.

"Uh-huh," he said in an all-knowing voice behind me.

"What 'uh-huh'?" I questioned.

"Just pacifying you," he quoted my word back to me while still magnificently manipulating out the knots.

"Finn!" I admonished.

As I tried to turn around to face him, he rested his hands solidly, yet soothingly, on my back, willing me to stay still. "It's harder to leave this time, isn't it? I mean, compared to a month or so ago."

I mumbled an affirmative response. He had nailed it dead on. How did he know me so well…better than I knew myself? Because we were mirroring each other's emotions.

"It's harder for me too. This isn't long enough—it's just a tease," he said this time kissing my back where his hands had been. "But you know, I'm so glad you came. It's worth it. It was. I was miserable without you. But it was just missing you. Nothing else. No doubts, Baby, about anything, all right?"

He let me turn around then. It seemed as if Finn and I

had always had a connection even as originally just friends. But at that moment, it was magical. His eyes were moist from emotion and ever so lovingly peering into mine. He laced our hands together, pulling them above my head. His kiss was soft and knowing.

"I love you."

"I love you too." He smiled. "No ifs. You and me…forever."

His words, the meaning behind them, and knowing I felt the same way, made me emotional too. Being with him in that hotel room was the closest thing to paradise I could imagine…if I didn't have to leave. But because of our connection, I knew our hearts weren't leaving and that made any separation possible.

\*\*\*

The next month dragged by so slowly, it seemed as if it was sixty days instead of thirty. At work, there were always plenty of things to keep me busy. But the nights were lonely and empty. Finn and I couldn't always talk in person because of our nearly opposite schedules. So, often, we would rely on a few texts back and forth. I made a point of calling him from work on one of the first few days in October, though.

"Hey," Finn answered sounding a little worn. "You all right? I know it's practically taboo for you to call during the day."

"Just checking to see how you're doing. I know it was Wyatt's birthday."

His voice cracked across the line. "You…how did you remember that?"

"I had put his thank you card from the party last year in my October file. He drew a huge smiley face and made sure to write in it when his real birthday was. I'm staring at it right now." Wyatt's birthday was one that I would forever remember in my mind. How could I forget such a special day for such a special boy who ultimately brought Finn and me together? It was at Wyatt's pre-birthday party, after all, that I had opened up about my past to Finn—my teenage pregnancy, giving the baby away....

"Yeah?" His voice was full of melancholy. He still resisted talking a lot when it came to his nephew.

"I wish you were here. I miss you. I miss him," I said on this day to reflect.

"Yeah," was again his one word response, but that was enough to understand that the feeling was mirrored.

I resisted tears, knowing I had to be the strong one at that moment. "Have you called your sister?" I asked and partially shut my door as the change of classes meant a little more noise in the hall.

"Not yet. I don't know. She probably doesn't want to hear from me."

That idea was ridiculous. It was something that Finn completely built up in his own mind so that he didn't have to deal with the pain of talking with Nola. Without directly telling me, I knew he still felt the guilt of being with Wyatt when he was killed and not being able to do anything to stop it from happening. I hadn't needed to be witness to his nightmare to know that. Neither Nola, nor anyone, blamed him for the accident. But he couldn't see it. I ached for both of them. They were close siblings, and they needed one another to get through. I just hoped that in time Finn would allow himself to grieve completely for both of their sakes.

I tried to encourage him but not preach. "Today is going to be so rough on her. She won't be able to get him out of her mind. Not like she ever does. But today is a biggie."

"You can understand." He was obviously referring to the baby I gave up.

"What I went through—did—is not the same. I don't have that right." I meant what I said, but, regardless, there were some days more than others that I thought of that child. "Besides, it's *your* family we're talking about right now." Even though I had been candidly open and honest with Finn about my past, it wasn't something I liked to dwell on.

"But you have the right to feel what you feel. And that matters to me. You know that, right, Lara? You know I love you."

"Forever." I recalled the word he said to me prior to leaving Baltimore. It seemed an appropriate time to recite it back.

"Forever," he echoed with a smile in his voice while obviously remembering himself. "Yeah, exactly. Thanks for thinking of me...and Wy."

"I always think of you, Finn." I purposefully let that sit for a moment before adding, "You okay?"

"Yeah. Yeah." He was emotional but with due cause. "I gotta get some stuff done. What's your day look like tomorrow?" he asked, trying to get himself back to some semblance of normalcy.

"Might be a little long. I have a ton of copies to make and the superintendent is coming down to meet with me regarding some projects. Not too bad, though." Idle chit-chat.

"I'll talk to you tomorrow...sometime after work, then."

"Sounds good. Enjoy your last gig tonight." A body-wide smile spread through me. I was so happy that it was his final show after a stretched out touring season.

"Yeah. Then a few days in Nashville, and I can set my watch for the same time zone as you."

I smiled as he referenced the dual-time zone watch I had given him for Christmas. "Forget time zones. The same city is what is important." As he agreed, I wished him luck. "And call your sister."

"Yes, Miss Faulkner," he teased, using my formal name.

"I love you."

"Right back at you."

I hung up the phone and turned from the window I had been absently staring out of while talking with Finn. Vanessa's presence in what I thought was an empty room slightly startled me. Knowing she must have heard at least the tail end of my conversation, a natural blush spread across my face.

"Finny?" she teased.

"Yeah." After walking to my desk, I placed my phone back in my purse. "I had to talk with him for a sec. It's—"

"You don't have to explain to me, girlfriend. I totally get the musician thing." I put my purse in the closet, and Vanessa continued since I didn't offer anything else. "Finn ever say anything about Carter?" Her voice changed from confident to nervous.

I knew Vanessa and Carter hadn't completely hooked up that night in Baltimore. But they may as well have considering everything else they did. At the time, she was taking it for what it was—a fun night. But as the days went by, I could tell she hoped for more, and Carter texting her every so often encouraged that in her mind. I softly tried to remind her of Carter's playboy status and the probability of a relationship with someone miles away. In turn, she tried to reference Finn and me and our relationship. But it wasn't the same. Finn actually had a place in New York. Carter lived in Tennessee full time. And, most importantly, Finn and I had known each other a long time before getting together. It wasn't a one-nighter.

But for now, what I said was, "You know guys, they don't talk about that stuff. Finn and Carter don't sit around and talk about their outfits or gossip about girls."

Although, that wasn't exactly true. Finn and I had discussed the Vanessa/Carter situation. Finn said it seemed like Carter liked Vanessa but wasn't sure if it would lead to anything for the same reasons I had outlined to Vanessa. He wanted us to let them deal with it themselves and not get in the middle. I whole-heartedly agreed and hoped for the best but braced for the worst.

\*\*\*

The meeting with the superintendent went smoothly and the copier didn't break. So I was able to leave work that next day only forty-five minutes after my usual time. Slightly tired, but more exhilarated that it was the weekend, I looked forward to getting in the Jeep, driving home, and waiting for Finn's call. Just knowing that we were mere days away from seeing one another brought an overwhelming joy to my inner being.

When I approached my Jeep Wrangler, a suit-clad gentleman stepped out of the black town car parked next to it. "Lara Faulkner?" he asked.

After I leerily acknowledged my identity, he informed me that he had been sent by Mr. Murphy and was to drive me to an undisclosed location. I shook my head, amused by this surprise gesture of Finn's, and wondered what he was up to. But in the back of my mind, I also had the presence to question all of it. So I took a few steps away and speed-dialed the superstar himself.

"There's a man standing here wanting me to get in the back seat of his car. You know, I don't do that with just any guy," I teased while hoping, and pretty much knowing, that the car and driver were on the up and up.

Finn laughed. "Get in the car, Lara."

"So this is legit?" I asked, eyeballing the driver.

"It is." Finn laughed again. "Has he given you the drink yet?"

"The drink?" I started, but before the two words were completely out of my mouth, the driver handed me a tall glass. I took a sip and was delighted that it was a delicious margarita. When a favorite memory of the drink and the November before fluttered in my brain, I said to the driver, "Sir, you can take me anywhere."

"Hey!" came Finn's voice over the phone line.

"Well, it is tall, cool, and pure ecstasy," I teased as the driver, all serious, opened the back car door and I slid in.

"Quit messing with me," Finn groaned.

I put the glass in one of the cup holders so I could fasten the seat belt as the car began to move. "Finn, what's this all about?" I asked, finally secured.

"I just wanted to treat you," he answered. "You've had to put up with a lot. I know I haven't made it easy to love me, and it's been hard with me being—"

"It's always easy loving y—" I started deeply touched by his sentiment but at the same time opening up the white box next to me. "Are these chocolate chip cookies?" I interrupted myself.

Again, laughter. "Not just any chocolate chip cookies."

I bit into one—sweet and salty perfection. "These taste just like my mom's."

"That's because they are," Finn said matter-of-factly.

"They are not!" I shouted so abruptly. I was glad the driver didn't swerve off the road.

"Yes," replied Finn clearly amused. "They are."

"How?"

"I had her send them."

"You talked to my mom and asked her to send chocolate chip cookies?" As far as I knew, Finn had never talked with my mom besides when we visited at Christmas…when she served him chocolate chip cookies.

"Yeah."

"That had to be a conversation."

My mother, in a normal situation, is nosy. But with me, she can go to an extreme. Plus, when she had met Finn, she seemed down-right, embarrassingly star-struck.

"Oh, it was for sure," he admitted as I shook my head, wondering about the details.

I glanced out the window, recognizing that we were heading south and away from my New York suburb. "Finn, where am I going?"

"Just sit back and relax."

A thought crossed my mind. It was a good thought, yet an unrealistic one at the same account. "I'm not going to the airport, am I? I can't come to Tennessee this weekend. Not with work o—"

"No, Beauty, I know." He stopped me. "No, as much as I wish…this is just something special for you."

I was relieved yet sad at his answer. Going to Tennessee to see him simply wasn't feasible on a regular two day weekend. But, yet, I wanted to see him so desperately.

Quietly, because of my mood, and because I knew the driver surely had to be listening, I said, "I miss you."

"Me too," he echoed.

I changed the subject. "How did the show go last night?"

"It was hard," he admitted.

"I thought so. Want to talk about it?" I finished the cookie and took another sip of the margarita.

"Well, it's weird. We're all exhausted, beyond exhausted, when we come to the end of the tour but, knowing it's the last one, there's this boost of energy mixed with melancholy I guess."

"That's because you put your all into it."

"Yeah, everyone does—the guys, the crew, everyone…everyone. We're beat and want to get back to our girls and families and normal houses. But it's a rush hearing those fans and knowing how much they support us."

Since he didn't bring it up, I did. "Just before I left work, I saw a video online…."

"Yeah?" he asked, but I think he knew what I saw.

"Your encore."

I heard him breathe before responding with a reflective, "Yeah."

"Finn?"

I didn't want to pressure him to talk about it. But I wanted him to know that I was there for him. If he was able to do what he did during that encore, then hopefully telling me wouldn't be hard. It would be—should be—a release.

"Yeah," he said with a tone of introspective.

"That had to be hard but amazing. I don't know how you did that."

I was proud of him…of what I saw. He had dedicated the encore, the night, and the whole tour to Wyatt. Finn spoke about what an honor it had been to be his uncle and then was able to get through most of the songs. Although, there were moments when he got silent from emotion.

"I don't know either, Lar. The crowd? They helped me along. They sang when I couldn't." Finn spoke as I started to silently cry, knowing how deep his feelings ran. "But I needed to do it. It felt right. It felt good. He deserved so much more."

"I wish I could have been there for you," I said.

"Don't cry, please. Not when I'm not there to hold you."

"I'm not," I lied while quickly swiping away tears as if he could see me.

"You are. You have your sinus nose."

I shook my head. My nose did automatically clog up when I cried. "Sorry."

"And, Beauty, you were there for me last night. You always are. You're always in my heart."

"I thought you said you didn't want me to cry," I choked, full of emotion.

"Okay." He paused and changed his tone so that we were both in a more jovial mood. "Eat a cookie. That will help put that sweet smile on your face. Enjoy the ride. I'm sure I'll talk with you when you get to your destination."

"Not a clue?" I asked as curious as ever.

"Hmmm…just that it will be familiar."

"That's not much to go on."

"How about, 'I love you.'?"

"That is everything I go on."

"Good. Now I'm smiling. Catcha soon."

Just a couple more days. Just a couple more days and that statement would be 100 percent true. But until then, I just had to wait and figure out what surprise he had in store for me.

# CHAPTER EIGHT

When the driver wouldn't give even the slightest hint as to our destination, I relented to just sitting back and enjoying the ride. At first, I tried to busy myself with the work that was in my tote bag. But having just left the building, I wasn't ready to dive back in quite yet. That was usually a Sunday evening tribulation. So I started playing some games on my cell phone instead.

As I predicted, we were making our way into Manhattan. I contemplated the different scenarios that the city could bring as far as a specific destination. Could it be one of those ambush makeovers? I would be thrilled with one of those. Although I didn't see Finn going that route since he always seemed to prefer me au natural. Perhaps a spa evening or a night over? I couldn't imagine liking anyone's hands massaging my body more than Finn's. And that thought made me think neither would Finn. He could be sending me to a Broadway show. I didn't have a problem with attending something like that on my own. But I wasn't exactly dressed for a night on the town.

My continuous wondering came to an end as the car pulled up in front of the skyscraper that hosted Finn's penthouse. I thanked the driver and started for my purse only then realizing that I should probably tip the man. I was hoping I even had enough cash on hand since I relied mostly on my credit cards to cover my expenses. But it was a moot point. The driver was insistent not to take any money from me.

I grabbed my tote and light jacket that I had needed in the morning but not in the warmth of the afternoon and entered the building. The doorman, Graham, was at his post. That man never seemed to have an hour off.

"Good evening, Miss Faulkner," Graham greeted me.

"Hi."

"Mr. Murphy asked that you call him when you arrived."

"Did he?" I was amused.

When I started to pull my purse from my tote, Graham offered, "Here, let me hold that for you, Miss."

"That's okay. I got it."

"You shouldn't have to." Graham smiled, taking the tote from me nonetheless as I speed dialed Mr. Mystery Man.

"Hi, Beauty," he answered. "Are you there?"

"I'm in the lobby. What's going on?"

Ignoring my query, "Graham will bring you up on the elevator. He has a key to get you in the penthouse."

Oh. I was disappointed. There was a part of me, after pulling up to Finn's apartment building, that anticipated him being there. I should have known better. I did know better. I just had to hold on for a couple more days.

Not wanting him to know my sadness, I teased, "You trust me in your place alone? You might need to count the silverware."

"I'll do that." He laughed openly.

As I walked toward the elevator with Graham at my heels, Finn instructed me that once I was in the penthouse to go in the master bedroom. There was something to change into before my next destination. The driver would be there to pick me up in about twenty minutes.

"Where am I going?" I practically screeched.

"Have fun. I miss you," he said before hanging up.

"Ahhhh! Men!" I groaned to Graham who only smiled and motioned me into the elevator.

It felt weird being in Finn's place without him. I had felt strange being in his home in Nashville by myself the previous November, but at least I had known he was on his way. This was even stranger. The Manhattan digs seemed cold without him. Despite just talking with him on the phone, the emptiness of his abode made me miss him even more.

I did as directed and went to the master bedroom. On the bed was a garment bag. In it, I discovered the teal dress that I had worn at the CMA Awards—the dress that Finn had unzipped so masterfully that first night we had made love. I had loaned it to Nola just a week before, because she needed something for one of Will's formal business functions. Or so I thought, because there it was, beckoning me to wear it. Plus, there was a new pair of matching shoes in my size and a cosmetic bag with lip gloss, blush, eye-shadow, deodorant, and a brush.

I dialed Finn's cell, but he didn't answer...on purpose for sure. Not giving him the satisfaction, I didn't leave a message but instead relented and gave into my mission at hand. After all, I only had twenty minutes until the driver would take me to God knew where.

Now primped and polished, I made my way down the stairs to the main living area. My mind was going overtime as to why I was wearing such a nice dress. I settled on one of my original thoughts—a Broadway show. Something, though, was suddenly making me nervous. It was a good nervous, but nervous nonetheless.

Like he said he would, Graham called on Finn's landline to let me know he had sent the driver up to the penthouse. When the knock on the door came, I was wondering why I couldn't have just met him in the lobby. Regardless, I grabbed my purse from the kitchen's center island and scurried to the door. That's when I found out why my nerves had been on overdrive.

"Finn," I sang his name seeing him now just inches away.

"Speechless." Looking dapper in a gray suit with slightly darker tie and white dress shirt, he smiled, replaying the word he had originally used when he first saw me on CMA night.

"I love you so much."

I was so thrilled to see him. Surprised, but thrilled. As Finn's smile grew, an unexpected, happy tear slid down my cheek. I wanted to kiss him, but Finn had a thing about PDA because of the press.

"Go ahead," he said reading my mind.

"But—"

"Lara, we're in a private hallway. Besides, I think that smooch on stage in Balt—"

I put my hands on either side of his face, tipped slightly up and kissed him for all the days that I hadn't been able. Then I promptly hit him in the shoulder. "And that's for deceiving me."

He didn't miss a beat. "I love you too." He pulled me close to him humming "Lara's Song" in my ear.

"I don't understand," I said, pulling away slightly but never wanting to leave go. "I thought you were supposed to be in Nashville."

"Couldn't wait one more day."

"That's sweet, but you planned this." I was still holding onto his hands. "I mean Nola asked for this dress a week ago."

"I couldn't wait one more day a week ago, but I had to."

As I shook my head, Finn led us back into his place, closing the door behind him. "Will you tell me now where we're going?"

"We're not."

"What?"

"We're staying here."

"Oh." I said just a little shocked considering our attire. "That's fine with me as long as it is 'we.'"

"It is." He smiled. "Can you open up the wine? There's a bottle of white in the fridge. I'm going to fix dinner. It won't take long."

"Kiss first," I cooed, thinking how quickly my entire mood had been elevated. When Finn obliged, I said, "God, I am so glad you're here."

"Me too, Baby." And he kissed me again this time a little longer. "Now, before I can't stop...." With a sexy smile, he turned and went into the kitchen.

Going along with what seemed to be the theme of the night, our dinner consisted of chips, veggies, dip, kabobs, and potstickers. It was the same meal we had eaten my second night in Nashville. This time, though, we weren't in a hot tub. We were, instead, dressed formally and eating in the nearly restaurant-sized dining room underscored with dark hardwood flooring and painted in a deep blue with white trim. At the end of the meal, Finn informed me that there was still dessert.

"Oh, yeah?" I asked suggestively.

"Real food." He laughed.

"Finn, I don't need anything," I stated honestly. I was full on food and on life.

"Don't spoil my fun." He winked. "You don't have to eat it—just let me get it."

"Okay." My curiosity was definitely piqued. "Do you want help?"

"No. I got it. Do you think you can start the fireplace?"

"Yeah. I can do that," I agreed.

I went on my mission of starting the gas fireplace in the living room. Then I heard Finn re-enter the room. He was carefully carrying a bag that he placed on the coffee table. When he started taking out the contents of the bag, I laughed, remembering the dessert from hot tub night—s'mores.

"This sure is some homecoming," I said, taking a sip of wine and laying out the graham crackers, chocolate bars, and marshmallows.

"Well, I'm not used to being away from you this long." His eyes pierced at mine from above his wine glass. "We can roast the marshmallows in a sec. Feel like playing a little game?"

"A game?"

"Yeah. You'll recognize it."

"Um, all right. Sorta like everything else down memory lane tonight?"

"You've noticed." Finn smiled, proud of himself.

"You certainly have."

"Beauty, all of these things tonight—the margarita, the s'mores, the dress...," He paused. "That weekend last November...I knew I was falling in love with you. I mean really falling in love with you. How you took in everything with me...even that stupid Meet-and-Greet." His mouth twitched on one side before continuing. "How you were interested and wondered and wanted to know about everywhere we went and what it meant to me."

"Finn, of course. Why wouldn't I have?"

"Lara, people usually only want to know me for *what* I am, not *who* I am."

"And you thought I was one of those people?"

"No. Not at all," he answered immediately. "I knew you weren't. And that's why I never felt as free as I did that weekend, especially the day after the CMAs...and that night. That night at the hot tub and firepit, after we talked and made love...I felt it might be possible that we could actually get it right." He paused—his eyes passing their love directly into mine. "I think we have."

Oh, God! My nerves had returned like a tsunami to the shore. All of this planning...the details.... I didn't want to get my hopes up. But, with that beautiful speech, I was pretty sure.

"Yes," I spoke just above a whisper.

"Yes?" Finn asked. "Yes, we have?"

"Yes, Finn. No matter what, the answer is yes."

The butterflies in my stomach were like acrobats in Cirque Du Soleil. I wasn't expecting a proposal, but I was pretty confident that's what it was. I was even more confident of my answer.

"Lara," Finn, now seeming a little nervous himself, half laughed and half shook his head. "you have to wait for a question."

He put his finger up to my lips and asked me to sit on the sofa with him. I happily obliged, not knowing if I was even able to stand any longer. *I have to wait for a question.* His words pretty much confirmed my suspicions. I'm not sure where the paper and pencil came from since I was such a bundle of nerves, but suddenly an upside down paper was in front of me on the coffee table.

Speaking so genuinely, Finn held and caressed the top of my hand. "You make everything seem possible…right…perfect. You are the reason for all that is good in my life. I let you slip away once. Well, twice. And I can't imagine my world without you. I've had to live it, and I don't want to do that ever again. Your love, your heart, your understanding, make me the most blessed person in the world."

As if I wasn't already about to cry, looking at Finn's own misty eyes intensified my strong emotions. He turned the paper over on the coffee table to reveal a BINGO board. It appeared similar to the computer version I used at work. Finn had helped the first grade class play the game the first time he had visited the school. The blocks then were filled with basic high frequency words. But on my personalized version, the words were all significant to my relationship with Finn:

*College, Roxanne, Forever, McDonalds, Wyatt, Java, Cookies, Jeep, Ice-skating, Pumpkins, Carolina, Eoin's, Bookstore, Thanksgiving, S'mores, Margaritas, Baltimore, Tour, CMAs, Love.* But going straight across the middle were the words: *Will,*

*You, Marry, Me, Lara?*

"Oh, my God," I whispered, wiping the tears that, as expected, were escaping my eyes.

"I love you." I had never heard him say it so emotionally.

"Oh, my God." I couldn't say much more.

Finn handed me the pencil and a tissue at the same time. Once I was as dry-eyed as I was going to be, he started with the first word, "Will."

I looked at him for an extended moment before taking my pencil to that word. This game was going to change my life. This man had changed my life. To show him exactly how much, I chose to draw a heart around the word "Will" instead of crossing it out.

Finn smiled at my choice and continued calling out the words, pausing between each as I encircled those also with a heart. "You…marry…me…Lara?"

When he said my name and bent down on one knee, I may as well have melted. We both knew my answer. Yet, you could physically feel the anticipatory nerves as we were mere inches from one another. I paused, soaking up the significance of the moment. Then looking at the love of my life, I drew a double heart around my name.

"Dude!" I managed to squeak out the fun word I had the kids use instead of the word "Bingo."

"How about now you say, 'yes'?" He looked at me, wanting no doubt that I was going to be his wife.

With tears actively flowing once more, I resorted to the phrase I had just been able to let go. "Oh, my God." And then tacked on, "Yes. Yes."

Before I knew it, I was in his arms and being twirled around. It was completely an out-of-body experience. I was trying to savor every second yet still attempting to process that it was even happening in the first place.

"S'more?" he asked, setting my feet back down on the floor but rubbing my arms.

I had forgotten all about dessert. That was nearly the

farthest thing from my mind. But if that was what Finn wanted, I would go along.

"Um, sure," I managed to get out.

Finn smiled, went to the stereo, and turned on some instrumental music. He returned with a poker for the marshmallows. When I went to grab it, he steadied his hands on mine and cautioned, "Careful."

What? I wasn't about to impale myself. It wasn't hot yet. Then I saw why. Finn may have wanted to have s'mores eventually, but that wasn't why he gave me the poker. Resting gingerly on top was an absolutely gorgeous ring. A cushion-cut diamond took center stage flanked by a mixture of brown diamonds and a unique light green stone that I instantly recognized.

"God, that is so beautiful. Is that our...?" I was afraid to even touch it.

"Sea glass." Finn confirmed my suspicions of the beach treasures we had found in North Carolina in the springtime. "Yeah. And chocolate diamonds. It reminds me of the s'mores." When I didn't speak because I was still taking it all in and in such awe, Finn asked, "So, you like it?"

"It has to be so exp—" I started thinking about the cost of a custom made ring when I was interrupted.

"The question was, 'Do you like it?'"

"Are you kidding? You put so much thought into all of this."

"Then it's worth it. And," he said before I could interrupt again, "I've been thinking about it for a while. I just had to make sure everything was right. That *I* was right," he clarified looking down for a second.

"It's perfect. Everything is perfect," I reassured him.

"Here, then." As he slid the ring onto my finger, I noted how his own hand was shaking. "Well, that went on a little bumpy."

"But it ended up beautifully. That's all that matters." I smiled, looking from the ring to him and thinking the ring-fitting summed up our relationship to a T.

"God, there's nothing that makes me nervous any more. But you—"

"Good nervous, I hope." As he touched the ring and my hand, I continued, "I never want the butterflies to end. And, Finn, I didn't need any of this. You being here? That's all I want."

He brought my newly crowned hand up to his lips and kissed it. Not letting go of that hand, he rested it on his chest and pulled me in closer. His kissing was intimate, and I never felt safer.

Even though our lips eventually parted, I looked down at our hands to note that they hadn't. I smiled, seeing the unabridged, genuine happiness in Finn's eyes as he looked at our entwined hands. He felt safe and loved too.

"I'm guessing your sister knows since she tricked me about needing the dress," I said in reference to the proposal.

"Yeah. She bought the shoes and insisted on the cosmetic bag too," Finn acknowledged.

"Thinks like a girl." I smiled. "But when you called my mom about the cookies—" Did he tell my mom?

"I actually visited your mom."

"What?"

That shocked me. Not only that he had physically seen her but the fact that my mother had somehow managed not to tell me about it. I had even spoken with her two days before. No wonder she got off the telephone so quickly. I knew she could keep secrets, though. She had kept my deepest one for over a decade.

"Yeah, when we were playing in Pittsburgh a couple weeks ago. I drove over so I could, you know, get her permission to ask you since your dad isn't around."

"That is so…." I struggled emotionally for the right word.

"Last century, Bingo dude?" he teased.

"Well, yeah, but sweet—very, very sweet." And for his

thoughtfulness I pecked him softly on the lips.

"I told her, her cookies were one of the reasons we got together."

"Finn!"

"Well, it doesn't hurt to charm one's future mother-in-law." That broad smile would not leave his face.

"Especially when you do it so well." I rubbed his chest with my free hand.

"So she insisted on packing up a box." His eyes changed mid-sentence to something more sensual. "When do you think I'm going to be able to help you out of that dress?"

"Where did it fall in this grand plan of yours?" I let go of his hand so I could put both around his neck and press up snuggly against him.

"Right…" His lips paraded across my neck. "about…" I felt his hands move the zipper down the back of my dress. "now."

# CHAPTER NINE

His fingers slowly and softly circling their way around my breasts and then onto my stomach was what woke me that next morning. I savored the tantalizing touch for a moment or so. When they ventured to my legs, I smiled a serene, wide, closed-mouth smile and finally opened my eyes.

"What are you doing?" My jovial voice barely broke a whisper.

Propped up at my side, Finn didn't move his hands but said, "Good morning" and pecked me on the lips.

"Morning." I smiled even more genuinely.

"I can't stand these long times away from you." He shifted so he was more in line with me as he took my face in his hands and gave me a longer, more passionate kiss. "Lar?" Just my name alongside that kiss was all that was needed to understand the desire in his question.

"I'm still asleep," I semi-murmured, trying in mock to reclose my eyes.

"I could wake you up."

I slightly chuckled and re-opened my eyes with a smile. Glancing at my gorgeous, thoughtful engagement ring, I said, "I'm glad it wasn't a dream."

He brought my hand up to his lips and kissed the ring. "You're going to marry me." His prideful grin surpassed his cheeks.

"Yeah."

"We could wake up like this every morning."

"Now who's dreaming?" I tried not to sigh out loud. "You would need to be in town."

Finn *did* sigh. "I know."

"There's something to be said about anticipation, though." I wrinkled my nose in a suggestive way to get us back in a lighthearted mood.

"There is," he agreed, and then turned to his phone that seemed to be vibrating like crazy on his nightstand. Grabbing it, his eyes seemed to brighten when he paused on the screen.

He handed me the phone, revealing a text message from his sister. *Well, did she say yes?*

"Can I answer it?"

"Go ahead. The question was about you."

As I texted, Finn watched. *This is Finn's fiancée. She (I) most def. said yes! Thanks for bringing EVERYTHING to make it special!*

"I just wrote fiancée," I giggled to Finn like a teenager.

He laughed. "That's what you are."

As he started playing with my hair, Nola's return text came in. *Congrats. We R so happy for U both! Tell my bro it's about time.*

I showed the phone to Finn who promptly took both the phone and me in his arms while texting back. *Let me & my girl have some private time already—geez. Luv ya.*

He pressed "send" and placed the phone back on the nightstand. Next to being elated over being engaged, nothing could have made me happier than seeing the positive, carefree exchange between Finn and his sister. We all needed happiness.

I snuggled into his chest, which was even more sculpted due to the nearly daily exercise of performing on stage. "You don't have to go anywhere today, do you?" My tenuous voice was trying hard to lead his answer in the direction I desired.

"No. But…."

When he hesitated, I looked up. "What? What's wrong?"

"Nothing. The phone…it keeps buzzing. People did expect me in Nashville, and I gave a lame excuse to be up here. I'm going to have to answer some of these."

"Okay," I said, a little disappointed but realizing the sacrifice that had been made.

"Listen," He kindly pulled me a little to his side so that he could look at me more directly. "Reese," he said, referring to his publicist, "should put out something about the engagement before there's speculation."

"Does she know?"

"No. No one knew except for Nola and your mom. I'm pretty sure Graham might have some suspicions, though." He air-chuckled.

"Really? No one in your, um, entourage?"

He laughed at my choice of words. "No. You know I try to keep my personal life separate."

"Yes, almost to a fault, I might add."

"I know, Beauty, and that's the thing. I don't want you to have to put up with it."

"Finn, I think the secret is out of the bag after being pretty much inseparable this summer."

"Loved that, by the way." He took his finger and ran it down my nose before resting it on my lips.

"Me too." I captured his finger in my mouth.

"Dating someone with summers off definitely has its advantages."

"Um, dating?" I corrected.

"Being engaged to…even better." He traced his finger down my throat toward my breasts. "So if I tell Reese, she'll probably give minimal details. No date, no where, no how…. Maybe about the ring?"

"Yeah. But I'm pretty sure my mom is going to want details, though."

"Okay." He laughed.

Now my mind was on wedding. To be honest, I hadn't even really given it much thought. I was too wrapped up/ecstatic just about being engaged. Knowing that we had that commitment, even though I didn't need a ring to prove it, was my focus. But there was an actual ceremony to consider. And Finn was right. With his celebrity status, we had to plan carefully.

"When are you thinking?" I asked. "For the wedding?"

"The sooner the better as far as I'm concerned. But I know you girls like the planning and shopping and all the parties and things that go with it."

When Finn said "you girls," reality suddenly slammed me head on, and I wasn't sure the seatbelt was going to hold. Finn had done this before. He had been engaged right out of college. And even though they didn't go through with it, he had done all of the color choices and registries and food samplings, etc.

I pulled back a little and said quietly but confidently. "I'm not Audrey."

"What?" His brows furled. "I didn't say—"

"All right," I used an authoritarian tone. I wanted him to know that in no way did I want to be compared to her. I realized it was probably my own irrational fear, though. So I quickly let it pass starting with a more jovial tale. "When I was young, I mean Barbie doll playing young...." I paused and ran my hand along his cheek and chin so he knew I wasn't angry. "I used to dream up my ideal wedding—a white, battalion-like frilly dress with each bridesmaid dressed in a different color of the rainbow. The flowers would match their dresses and—"

"Really?"

"Really. Yeah." I tried to look still enamored with my six-year-old dream wedding, although nothing could have mortified me more. But I couldn't pull it off. "Don't worry. That was a long time ago—not a chance."

"Oh thank God." He jokingly covered my face with his entire hand.

"Simple. Please, let's do simple," I said, stating what I guess was my true self. Because after my experience post high school, I never once dreamed again about being married and having a wedding. Now, with Finn, I realized I felt as if we already were married. "And yes, I don't want to wait. I think we've waited long enough."

"I knew there was a reason I loved you," he teased.

"Cute!" I countered.

"Yep, you are." He kissed me. "You sure, though? Simple?"

"Yeah. I'm not doing granny pearl necklaces and all that. But you will *not*," I emphasized the last word and poked my finger into his chest, "show up in cowboy boots."

"Damn it," he joshed. "I think that may be a deal breaker, Roxanne. I already bought a green pair to match my contacts that day," he added, knowing how much I hated those fake contacts. And for that, he got a back-handed smack on his upper arm. "Christ, Lara!" he called out but laughed all the same.

"You show up with those damn contacts in your eyes, and that was nothing. Nu-thing!"

"I love you, Baby." He smiled that irresistible grin of his.

"I love you too. Now, talk with Reese or whoever you need to. I'll go make some breakfast. But we are not leaving this bed. Got it?"

"Wouldn't dream of it." He ran his hands on my bare back and bottom as I sat up and searched for the temporary clothing of my bra and panties.

\*\*\*

Finn was able to fly back to New York once during

that month. It was a quick trip with him coming in late one Thursday night and leaving Sunday. I called off sick on Friday, because I didn't want to use my personal days since we only received three each year. We spent most of our time confirming wedding plans, which involved buying our bands and making a few phone calls.

Our wedding, taking place between the Christmas and New Year's holidays, was going to be at our alma mater's chapel in front of just immediate family. The press would only find out about the ceremony after the deed was done. In fact, no one would know, except for the few invitees. We didn't want any possibility of leaks happening. Plus, I didn't want any showers being held. I had absolutely no desire to be the center of attention while opening up gifts. God, the fuss my coworkers made just over the engagement ring was insane. Besides, what more could I need? I had Finn.

The engagement news, however, was all over the media. There were pictures of Finn and me on entertainment television shows and on the internet. Both Reese and Finn had warned me not to read any of the comments, but I couldn't resist.

I knew people could be cruel without even knowing the individual they were hurting. But it took a whole new meaning when you were the one they slammed. Some wondered how long the marriage would last. Sidebars were practically betting. I think the most years we received on the one page was eight. There were also comments about Finn's past drug use. And people stating that I wasn't good enough for him. After all, I was just a techie. There were women who wanted Finn to marry them instead. And there were men who requested the same. There were also comments about my physical appearance —from my teeth to my body frame.

But there were also many congratulatory posts. Some posters from Baltimore commented how in love we were on stage that night. There were a couple comments about how country boys always chose right.

For the first time, I truly got why Finn tried to keep his personal life separate. He had chosen this life...this business...this world. His family hadn't, and I hadn't. So I decided not to tell him that I had read any of the comments and, like a smart gambler, finished while I was ahead. I never did click on or read another engagement article. I knew the truth and, God, was it a good one to be living.

\*\*\*

Vanessa flew to Nashville with me for the CMA Awards held the beginning of November. Carter had asked her to be his date. She was beyond excited. I told her not to overthink anything. They hadn't seen one another since the concert in Baltimore in early September. From what I knew, they only texted every so often. She claimed she didn't care. She was going to the awards show if nothing else. I was happy for her and glad to have a companion for the flights back and forth, as flying was not my favorite mode of transportation by far.

It was hard to believe it had been a year since I had first stepped into Finn's home in Nashville. So much had changed in twelve months. There were new people who had entered my life and, sadly, people who had been taken from it. I first arrived as a friend and now was a fiancée.

Finn was still closely protective of me as we made our way through the pre and post parties, as well as, of course, during the awards ceremony. His hand was continuously interlocked with mine if it wasn't showing off the ring. When he won the Single of the Year award, he called his entire band up on stage and acknowledged every one of them, only leaving a second for him to personally thank anyone himself.

"For my family and my fiancée. I am forever grateful." And he threw in a wink in my direction.

Vanessa, who had scrambled forward to momentarily take Finn's seat, took some pictures on her cell phone and said, "I think we'll both get lucky tonight."

"You better hope you do," I teased. "Because I know I am, and I'm counting on you staying at Carter's place and not with Finn and me."

"Don't worry, girlfriend, I plan on getting my hands and other things on that man's drumstick tonight."

"Vanessa!" I cried out, but laughed, all the same, at her creative, musical pun.

***

Despite his win, Finn's mood seemed to change as the car approached his house after the big night. I wouldn't say he was upset. He was more internal. When we entered the ranch, I unthreaded his already loose, silky, silver tie and wrapped it around my hands, gently swinging it at his all black ensemble.

"What's bugging you?" I tried to brighten his mood.

"Nothing." It wasn't convincing…at all.

"Finn, c'mon…."

"It can wait." He put his hands on the beaded waist of my floor length black and white halter dress.

Perplexed and concerned, I decided to play my hand— "I guess I'm going to sleep, then."—and started for the stairs.

"What?" That shocked him.

I knew what he was expecting. Heck, I was looking forward to making love with him too. But I didn't want to do it while something was bothering him. He needed to tell me.

"It can wait." I echoed his words, but *I* was referring to sex.

"Lara…," he said as I took another step toward the stairs. Men weren't so different than little kids. "I just…I don't want to do this on our…our anniversary."

I turned around and smiled. Neither of us had called it our anniversary, but I guess we were both thinking it. It was the place and date of the first time we had made love. For all due purposes, this would always be one of our anniversaries.

"I want to know," I said. "No omissions."

Remembering what he had promised the night of Wyatt's memorial service and how lies of omission tore us apart before, he said lightheartedly, "You're going to put that in the vows, aren't you?"

"Hmmm...I hadn't thought of that." I smiled to reassure him. "Finn?"

"We need to talk about a prenup."

My stomach dropped. I don't know what I had expected. But it certainly wasn't to talk about a prenuptial agreement. The whole atmosphere in the room seemed to change in an instant.

My words came out in a whispery cry because I was so stunned and hurt that it was a thought, nonetheless a discussion we were going to have. "I don't want your money."

"Lar—" He started to reach out for me, but I backed away.

"Oh, God. What? No. No. Why would you think that?"

"I don't, Lara. I don't. Calm down."

But I didn't. "Finn, if that's what you think, I.... Oh, my God." I was actually pacing with an occasional glance in his direction.

"Lara, Baby, calm down. It's not.... I know you don't."

I finally stopped and turned in his direction, but I didn't know what to say. The subject matter was a complete curve ball in our evening. "I—"

"Oh, Lara." I allowed him to rub my shoulder with his knuckles for a moment. "It's my...what did you call them? Entourage?" He attempted a smile to get me to do the same, but I was stoic. He tried to explain a little more as I took a step away. "They're insisting. That's who I was talking with when you got here today. Remember?"

What did it matter if I remembered the tail end of a phone conversation or not? "No." I had just been excited to be there.

"Well, I wasn't happy. I don't want a prenup. But I guess in this industry, it's a necessary evil. Listen,"—he continued straight away—"divorce is not an option for me. We get mad at each other? Then there are different rooms. We go and cool off. We try another day. If we split? I'm done. There is no me. I think you know that. You can have it all. It won't matter."

"For me either, Finn," I said, glad to be calming down and not having to go into those different rooms. "I know my family wasn't all *Leave it to Beaver* like yours. But my folks did love one another, and they stuck it out in their own way."

"Things aren't always as they seem, Lara. We both can attest to that." He paused, and I waited, wanting to know what he was alluding to. "My parents...there was a time I was convinced they were going to be another statistic. When I was like eight or nine, I was in the basement of our house, and I heard my dad upstairs yelling at my mom, 'If you don't like it, then leave.'" He acknowledged the shock on my face before he continued, "He didn't really mean it, but they were both upset, and she left. She marched right past me into the garage and took the car and left...for a few days or so." It was another time and another person who had left Finn unexpectedly.

"I'm sorry. I know what that's like. But see, that's my point. I'm agreeing with you. You fight and you fight for your love. But if I have to sign something for your peeps," I used a silly word to break the tension but, yet, remained adamant with my statement. "I am signing that I don't want a damn thing. No money, no houses, no cars, whatever."

"You wi—" he started.

"Finn, you hurt me more than I ever thought possible this past spring."

I knew that stung him. But it was the crux of what we were, unfortunately, discussing. So it needed to be said.

"I know," he admitted quietly.

"And yes, I thought it was the end. It had to be. And it would have been. But not once, not once, did I think, wow, I'm missing out on the monetary perks. I missed *you*." When I exaggerated the last word, I started to cry. Tell that to your "people" I wanted to say.

Finn couldn't stand it when I cried. And it was one of those times he knew he was pretty helpless to do anything about it. "Look, I don't know why we're arguing about this. I'll do whatever you want, because it won't matter."

"No." I shook my head back and forth and tried to smile. "It won't."

"But—" He stopped himself.

"What?"

Geez! What else could there be? *But* wasn't good.

I found out, though, when he spoke in a quiet tone, "The lawyers want to add a clause about future, well, kids."

Ah! Kids. Well, that was a whole other.... All of this was so heavy for what had started as such a festive evening. Finn and I had once talked about having kids. But it was a pseudo scenario. And it was a long time ago...before everything changed.

Part of me was pissed. Lawyers and music personnel should have absolutely no part in if or when I would bear Finn's child. But I recognized Finn's angst. So I relied on the calming, yet sarcastic, part of me.

"God, we're not even married yet. What's this? Like Rumpelstiltskin? Are they going to take my firs—" I got caught on the word.

Any babies with Finn would not be my first-born. My first-born was given up for adoption many years before— before I even met Finn. It was *my* reason to hesitate about having kids.

"I know," he said empathetically. "It'll just state that I will monetarily take care of any children. But that's the thing...." He swayed from side to side. "You know, I'm not sure about the kid thing. Being a father...being responsible.... I don't know. I guess maybe we need to talk about that."

None of this conversation had been good. We, Finn and Lara, were good. The outside forces were not. I was bound and determined not to let our pseudo anniversary be marred.

I took a breath before responding. "I know what happened with Wyatt scared you...changed you. Something like that, losing a child, it makes you question everything. I completely, completely understand that. And, Baby, I feel the same way. So I want you to know, kids or no kids, I'm with you, Finn. I'm yours. Rich, poor...gray eyes, green eyes," I smirked. "College co-ed, rock star...I'm yours." I meant every single word. When he squinted his eyes ever so slightly and didn't give me a verbal response, I questioned him. "What?"

"Wyatt's part of it. But it's not just that," he answered almost methodically.

"No?" That threw me. "What then?"

"I don't want our kid to have to deal with...with...what I have to."

"Oh." I saw the mental disorder diagnosis rear its ugly head as Finn dipped his down. "You don't know that would happen." I went to touch his face but he sort of brushed me off to meet my eyes instead.

"Lara, it might." His tone was matter-of-fact, as if he wanted to scare me.

"Your parents don't have it. You didn't get it from them. You had something terrible happen to you."

"But I was preconditioned. I could pass it on. It can happen." Before I could interject, he continued. "I looked into it"—he paused—"before. It was one of the reasons I went off the meds." As he looked down again with regret,

I thought again about that conversation many months before. He wanted to know if I ever wanted children. But he hadn't told me the underlying reason behind the questioning and how my answer affected such a big decision in his life—going off meds.

"Oh, Finn…." Guilt crept in, even though I knew I couldn't have possibly had any idea of the implications from that past conversation.

"Like I told you, I thought I was good. We were happy, and I wanted to just confirm that maybe it wasn't really a problem. All I needed was to be truly happy and that way there wouldn't be anything to pass on."

"God, why didn't you tell me that part?" I wasn't mad. I just felt bad that he had been holding that inside all that time.

"Because, then Wyatt…Wyatt happened and, you know, I haven't wanted to even think about kids. So it was a moot point. But this prenup crap came up and, Beauty, I know it's unfair to you not to talk about it. If you decide—"

"Stop," I demanded but in a kind tone. "I decided to love you. That's what I decided—a long time ago in fact." I smiled. "And you told me in Baltimore not to have this condition define who you are. And I haven't. I don't, because you don't. You are in control. So I certainly won't let it dictate, just like I won't let your lawyers dictate, any childbearing decisions that *we*"—I emphasized the word—"might make. Because neither of us is going anywhere. We decided that too, right?"

When he didn't answer, I got a little worried. Was he doubting my words? Us?

"Finn?" I tried.

"Sorry. It's just 'I love you' doesn't seem like enough for the overwhelming amount of affection and admiration I have for you. You are my very breath, Lara."

"Forever."

"Forever."

# CHAPTER TEN

The rest of the weekend, thankfully, went a lot better. The next morning, after he did some meditation and I showered, I went with Finn to the studio so he could re-record a track that needed some additional work. It was inspiring to see him in that atmosphere—surrounded by people, yet all alone in the booth with his music. I could see the true musician in him— the perfectionist wanting to make sure that his tone, breathing, and sound were just right. He had his eyes closed for most of the takes, totally mesmerized by the words and music. And when he would open them, it was like he had awakened from a most wonderful, long dream.

Following a round of high fives from all those at the recording, Finn smiled in my direction. I took a sip from my iced tea and walked over, handing him my cup. After a hearty gulp, he hugged me into his side and kissed the top of my head.

"Whatcha think?"

"Are you kidding me?" I answered. "You could see how excited everyone was."

He pulled me slightly away before taking my hands and meeting my eyes. "I want to know what *you* think," he said.

"Honest."

"It was so unique. I mean…a little more edgy for you, but then the chorus was so soft. I liked that. I can picture the cell phone lights swaying."

"Exactly! Like the chorus has a whole new meaning with the ballad style thrown in. That's what I wanted to re-do."

"I don't think it would have had the same impact if you would have gone all rock. It makes you really think and wonder what's going on. It's another song of the year for sure."

"Yeah?" he said now with more confidence while starting to walk us toward the doorway. "Speaking of, can some of the guys come over tonight? I know it's last minute, but I thought since the win, we should celebrate."

"Of course. It's your house. You do whatever—"

"Ours. It's our house, and it's our life. You get a say. And I always want to know what it is."

I stopped mid-stroll. Despite our impending marriage and our discussion on prenups, it hadn't quite sunk in yet. This *was* my life. More importantly, this was my love—both of which dreams were made of.

***

It was fun playing "hostess with the mostess" and celebrating with the band that night. But I even more appreciated the next day—my final day in Tennessee—because it was just the two of us. After sleeping in late, we strolled through some of the local shops and had lunch at one of the off-the-beaten-path restaurants. Then we totally escaped. Finn chartered a private boat from a friend, and we soaked in the stillness of the river despite it being early November.

"When is your rent up?" he asked.

It took me a second, because renewing had become so automatic since I moved to New York. "July."

"Oh. All right. That's fine. If you can get out of it early…but it doesn't matter."

"Why?"

"Well we're not going to live in your place, right?"

I guess it was another way that I hadn't given our soon-to-be new life as a married couple any thought. We would just keep going like we were, right? But that really didn't make any sense. Did he think I could live in Manhattan and commute? As much as I loved the penthouse, that wasn't logical.

"Well, there are two bedrooms," I teased with sass while referring to my tiny abode. "You'll have to have the smaller one, though. All of my stuff is already in the master."

"Ha! Funny girl." He flicked some of the water he had in his cup at me. "No, I thought we'd look for a house. I have someone researching info on houses near where you live now."

"What about your place in the city and the house here?"

"We'll have those too," he stated without a care. Finn sat up a little straighter so his feet were on either side of his chaise lounge, and reached for my hand, causing me to sit up on my adjacent chair. Rubbing my ring finger, he said, "Look, I haven't asked you this because I think I pretty much know your answer. But I'm going to do it now."

"Okay…."

"You know you don't have to work, right? We can just live here. Keep the place in Manhattan and live in Nashville."

Again, it wasn't something I had given any thought to. But as he pointed out the day before, my response was honest. "I can't be like your mom, Finn. I don't have the happy homemaker, stay-at-home-wife gene in me. Not that there's anything wrong with that."

He laughed boisterously. "No, Baby, I don't think you

do. And, believe me, I'm glad you don't remind me of my mom." He touched my nose and added, "Besides your caring hearts."

"I want to work," I continued. "I love my job…most of the time."

"I know. That's why I never asked. I get that. I love my job too," he said, paused, and then suggested tentatively, "You could try to get something down here." When I wrinkled my nose as if I smelled something rotting, he concluded with, "Uh-huh."

"It's just, I have friends in New York," I started to explain. "and my co-workers. You're gone so much—"

"I know. It's okay."

"I'm being selfish. It's too much for you to commute like this."

"Not to toot my own horn, Beauty, but I'm pretty much on top of my game right now. I'm going to make New York my more permanent address. Not that I won't have to be down here sometimes. But if they want me, they're going to have to know where to find me."

I definitely knew where to find his lips. Meeting his with mine, I couldn't help but feel so blessed to have such a wonderful man in my life. But I still wanted to make sure. I knew the scenario he had laid out couldn't be his ideal world. "Are you sure?"

"As sure as your eyes are that brilliant turquoise."

"Finn…." I didn't need complimented or coddled. I needed to make sure it was the best decision for both of us.

"Your eyes are a fact and so is my love for you and so is my decision about the house in New York," he said with heartfelt determination. "I gave the realtor both of our e-mails. She said there will be some listings in our mailboxes tomorrow."

"All right." I sighed, but it was one of contentment. It was feeling that things were almost heavenly. If only I didn't have to get on that plane the next day to head back home. But that's exactly what buying the whole new house would remedy. It would be our home and our future together.

***

I noticed those real estate listings in my e-mail inbox shortly after dinnertime the next day. I had just gotten back to New York and, after texting Finn of my safe arrival, I was exhausted. It was only after taking a shower, starting a load of laundry, and getting things ready for an early work alarm in the morning, that I got to opening up the e-mail.

Hours later, after tossing and turning in bed, I was still awake with an acidy burning feeling in my stomach and esophagus. If that wasn't bad enough, my mind was on overdrive. And the only way to get rid of both symptoms was to face the culprit head on.

With that in mind, despite it now being late night, I texted Finn. *U home? Can U call me?*

When "Roxanne" belted out almost immediately, I picked it up just as readily. "Hey," I answered softly.

"Hi…." I heard the cautionary tone in my fiancée's voice. He was surely wondering what was prompting the late hour correspondence. "You all right?"

"Where are you?" I knew he had a late dinner business meeting, and I really didn't want this conversation to be in the midst of clanking wine glasses and deals being made.

"I'm at the ranch," he spoke of his home, but it was still with a sense of caution.

"How was the dinner? You weren't sleeping were you?" Relieved at his location, I tried to ease into the conversation-to-be.

"It was fine. I'm up writing," he said just as succinctly and then questioned, "Lara, what's wrong? You should be asleep."

"I couldn't."

"Uh-huh." His voice was leading and requesting an explanation. "Why?"

"Finn, I…." The stress that I had been holding in escaped with an audible sigh. "I can't do all of this." I expected him to say something, but there was silence from the other end and almost eerily so. "Finn?"

"Switch to video chat. I need to see you." His voice had quickly become terse.

Exhausted from Nashville, the flight, and stress, I couldn't be bothered. "Finn, I don't—"

"Lara, look," he interrupted. "I'd jump on a plane right now so we could talk in person, b—"

"That's ridiculous," I said, knowing he probably would.

"Baby, I love you and whatever is wrong, we can work—"

"They're too expensive," I blurted out.

"What?" Confused.

"The houses. I know you—"

"This is about the houses?"

"Yeah."

"God." I heard a tremendous cleansing sigh followed by, although only two syllables, a much more relaxed next word. "Okay."

I forged on. "I know you're going to say 'our' and 'we' and 'us,' but there is no 'us' and 'we' on something like that. My share wouldn't even be the front door! And I don't want you going into debt having a house here."

"First of all," his voice, now bordering on light laughter, had changed once again in contrast to mine, which had remained stressed the entire conversation. "I'd live in a tree house, or a box, or a barn just as long as you're still with me."

"Of course," I answered slowly, only then digesting what he thought I initially meant about not being able to do *this*—the dreaded leaving. "Oh, Finn, you didn't think—"

Deliberately not letting me ask, he cut me off as I

thought *can you feel me sending the vibes that I'm sorry for scaring you?* "Second, my priority is making sure you're somewhere safe and that we have some privacy."

"I know," I agreed. "I understand what that means to you, but they're too—"

"I kinda forget what it's like to be thrown suddenly into this life…this amount of money. I went from college loans to financial planners in the blink of an eye. Baby, I can afford any of the homes. Believe me."

"Re—"

"And we have plenty of money saved," he continued as I noted the word *we* again. "I am still my parent's child. They are logical and prepared and sensible and conservative to the core. They trained me well from getting a college degree to finances. And you don't see me overspend, do you?" My mouth was starting to open, but he couldn't see that. "Eh, before you say it, that Jeep was a necessity and seriously not even a blink in the account." My car—my over-the-top Christmas gift from him the year before.

"Get out of my head!" I bellowed through laughter.

"But it's such a beautiful one." I heard the smile in his voice. And before I could argue the Jeep or my physical attributes, he continued, "Listen, I want to sit down with you and show you everything, anyway, so you know you don't have to worry about money. Most likely when we do the…now don't scream…prenup." He paused between words, once again knowing me too well. "It'll kinda come up, anyway. You all right? No more worries?"

"Just so you know, I'd live in anything with you too." I was glad that we hadn't been on a video chat as silent tears were starting down my face. Even though they were tears of relief…of love…I knew Finn would be concerned if he had seen them.

"Well, about that…I'd really prefer a colonial or contemporary over the box situation," he jested before double-checking my status with sincerity. "Lara? Okay?"

"Yeah. I just got overwhelmed, I guess. I want to put money down too, though."

"Sure thing, Beauty. You can buy that door."

"Don't expect a knob with it," I continued the banter, glad that our conversation was now relaxed.

Laughing, he said, "So which houses did you like?"

"Well, I didn't really look after I saw how much they were."

"Get some sleep," he said in a way that I was sure he was shaking his head. "Ignore those numbers with the dollar signs in front of them and look tomorrow. Then let me know so I can set up some times for us to see them. And Lara?" he tacked on.

"Yeah?"

"I am madly in love with you." Jesus hell was that ever sexy.

"I think I'm gonna be able to sleep now." At least dream. "Thanks for talking me down."

"Any time."

"I love you madly too."

\*\*\*

Finn wasn't back in the New York area again until Thanksgiving. It was the first major family holiday where Wyatt wasn't around. And, as expected, Thanksgiving wasn't the same. The venue, for one thing, was moved. I don't think anyone wanted to cook or see Nola having to deal with the empty spot around the dining room table. Finn's parents flew in from Louisville, Will's parents flew in from Boston, and we all joined Nola, Will, and Kelsea at an Irish restaurant, of all places, for Thanksgiving dinner. We had a secluded table in the back and it was near my apartment instead of Manhattan. So it wasn't terribly busy, nor did we have to deal with a Finn Murphy fan onslaught.

It definitely wasn't the same, but it somehow worked. And I think Finn's and my engagement helped bring a happy banter to the table. I already felt like part of the Murphy family but didn't forget to call my mother and brother at their respective locales—Pennsylvania and North Carolina—to say how thankful I was for them too.

Finn managed to score us private box seats to the Jets football game that evening. They were playing Cincinnati, which was the team that Louisville natives cheer for since they don't have a hometown team. So Finn's parents, Finn, and Nola were super excited to change into their black and orange jerseys and cheer on their team. I thought they looked like Halloween and teased them unabashedly. Will, as a native Bostonian, hated the Jets but refused to cheer on Cincy. So he remained neutral. Since Will's parents took Kelsea home and babysat, that only left me in a Jets jersey cheering on my adopted city. Oh, and, of course, the majority of the stadium.

"Who Dey?" the Murphy clan chanted, ganging up on me once we took our seats.

"We Dey." Even though not much of a football fan, I knew the Bengals rhetoric. "We dey the ones who are going to fly like jets right over your asses." I tossed a peanut shell like a jet airliner at the four of them.

Finn's father roared laughing. "Lara, girl, I love your spirit. You're going to lose, but I love your spirit."

"Not a chance." I shook my head.

"Control your woman, son." Zak Murphy laughed again.

"If only." Finn tousled my hair. "You are going to lose, though, Baby. Cincy is on a roll. Every year, they are getting better. The Jets have no identity."

"Do you want to bet?" I recalled the hockey bet we had made at the coffee shop right after we had first met up again after so many years.

"Really, Rox? You want to take me on again? You are a glutton for punishment," he said, knowing the outcome the last time was in his favor. "What are we betting?"

I thought for a second. What I really wanted was, "If I

win, you have to stay in town an extra day. Leave on Monday instead."

"I can't." We both knew it was unrealistic. He had to be in Vegas for an awards ceremony that Monday night. He wasn't presenting or performing, but he was up for a couple awards. "I'll see you in two weeks. And we still have a couple days."

"I know. But it's not like I don't miss you." As he leaned his forehead onto mine, I recanted. "I have my bet."

"Yeah?" He broke slightly away.

"The Jets win and I get one of those famous, long Finn Murphy massages."

"Deal. And if Cincy wins," he whispered so that only my ears, thankfully, could hear. "I'm sticking with our original chocolate theme. I get to lick chocolate off every part of your luscious body."

The blush rose to my face instantly. Before I could counter or react, though, Will interrupted. Already buzzed from dinner, he had another beer in his hand. He sloppily pointed out the image of the six of us on the jumbo-tron, unofficially announcing that the country superstar was in the crowd. Will slid more than sat in his seat as Finn cursed and got on his phone, wanting to make sure that we could exit peacefully at the end of the game.

I proved to be the victor of our little sports bet that time. So I treasured Finn's methodic hands later that evening as they worked their magic. As he kneaded his knuckles into my shoulders and back, I felt some of the stress of the day fade away, not only for me but for Finn. It had been a day to celebrate, but it had also been a day to remember, and I knew it had affected every one of us in our own way.

\*\*\*

The next day everyone in our Thanksgiving group was

off to separate functions. Will's parents headed back to Boston. Finn and Nola's parents were going to lunch and seeing a Broadway matinee. And Will and Nola had a grief counseling session to attend. So to Finn's chagrin, he and I were taking Kelsea to the local children's museum.

Finn was grumpy, and it wasn't just because he didn't get enough sleep the night before. Although he wouldn't openly admit it, he really did not want to be responsible for Kelsea. After all, in his mind, Wyatt had been under Finn's watch when the little boy was killed. Finn tried to find an excuse to get out of going to the museum but finally relented, knowing that I was going to be with them the whole time.

Kelsea really seemed to like the water play area and the caged area where she could climb forever. It was at the puppet stage, though, where she and I put on a princess play for Finn, that her uncle started to finally loosen up. We heard him laughing as the sole member of the audience and then clapping when we came out to take our bows.

When we were in the art room, I decided it was my opportunity to make my move. "Take Kels with you," Finn tried after I made an excuse to go to the bathroom.

"No. She just went. Besides, it's, you know, female things," I said and hurried off before he could question.

Finn knew it wasn't my time of the month. And I knew that he knew. I also knew that he wasn't going to be happy when I returned. But I had to give it a shot. I had to give him this opportunity to be alone with his niece. He needed to see that it would be all right. She wasn't going to break. She wasn't going to die. She, in fact, would probably flourish.

I dawdled for as long as I could within reason and finally returned to the art room. I ignored Finn's icy glare and sat down next to Kelsea who was molding something with clay. "Did you and Uncle Finn have a good time without me?"

"Yeah!" she exclaimed.

"Good," I started to say as Finn got up to walk away. I cautioned Kelsea to stay right where she was. "Finn," I grabbed his arm only a few steps away.

"Don't do that, Lara." He was stone cold like I had never seen him.

I countered with the only thing I knew would make him stop. "Don't walk away. I know you don't want a scene."

In his greasy ball cap and nondescript, nonperformer clothes, he had remained, miraculously, unscathed at the museum. The gray of his natural eyes seemed to darken as he seethed at me for making the comment. "I know what you were trying to do."

"I know you do." I tried to remain the rational adult, but I felt more like a little child, afraid and seeking Finn's approval. Nonetheless, I trudged on. "She's your niece. She adores you. She needs you." I paused, and then said my closing remark, "Don't lose her too."

"That's cruel."

I felt sick knowing how Finn was feeling about me at that moment. But I loved him too much not to try. "That's the truth."

"Uncle Finn, come here. I made this for you," we both heard Kelsea call out.

"She wants you," I stated the obvious.

I got a menacing look before the performer in Finn put on a happy face and sat back down next to Kelsea. After complimenting her on what would best be described as an awkward snowman, he let her play for a couple more minutes, leaving me, probably on purpose, swaying awkwardly near them. When he informed Kelsea that it was time to go, she ran up to me and grabbed my hand, holding Finn's in the other. She wanted to swing between us. Finn went along with it for a couple times before letting go. I feared it was because it was too much of a connection to me.

He leaned down to Kelsea and said, "Stay here with Lara. I'm going to go get the car."

When Finn left for the car, I probably would have collapsed if it weren't for Kelsea. The tension between us was so thick. In that moment, I wished Kelsea wasn't there and that we weren't in a public place because at least we could talk and get things out.

And the confinements of the car didn't help matters. I kept peppering Kelsea with questions about her favorite things at the children's museum, and luckily, like her brother before her, she was a talker. Finn kept his eyes on the road and his mouth shut. His silence said more than any words, unfortunately, could.

# CHAPTER ELEVEN

.When we pulled in front of the Jamison abode, Finn threw the car into park and walked immediately down the driveway, disappearing behind the house. I had just gotten Kelsea out of her car seat when Nola came out to greet us. Kelsea bounced into her mother's arms and started to verbally revisit nearly every moment of our day with her.

Creating a purposeful conversation stopping point, Nola instructed Kelsea to go in and tell Will all her museum stories too. Watching her daughter safely enter the house, Nola then turned to me and said, "I'm guessing it didn't go well." Nola and her family knew of my strategy for the day.

"Kelsea had a good time," I tried.

"He's in the back yard. Do you want me to go talk with him?"

"No. No, I need to. It's my cross to bear. It's me he's mad at."

I don't know whose sigh was bigger, mine or Nola's. I ventured down the driveway, trailing my hand along the low concrete wall, recalling how it had been the place where I had opened up to Finn about my past. We had talked so freely then. Would we be able to now?

He was pacing near the swing set. He watched me approach the entire way and, with only a few feet between us, said, "Damn it! Damn it, Lara! I can't believe you did that."

"I'm sorry."

"Are you?" Every part of his body—his hands, his face, his voice, his stance—spoke of his anger.

"Yeah. I'm sorry that you're so upset."

"You don't think I have a right to be?"

"Well—" I mean, I expected him not to like or agree with me forcing him to be alone with Kelsea for, geez, ten minutes. But I guess I underestimated how much fear he actually had.

"Don't you ever threaten me with that 'I'll expose you crap'," he loud-whispered in a simmering way.

Oh, shit! It was the double whammy! I probably would have been all right with one strike, but it was the second one that did me in. He couldn't handle more than one thing to deal with at the museum. He had already not wanted to go in the first place. Then he had to be alone with her. And then he felt like I was selling him out with my "don't want a scene" comment.

"God, Finn," I said, and he turned from me. "You know I would never…I'm sorry. Really. You were walking away. You were leaving, and I couldn't…But I never would have made a scene."

On the word *leaving* he slowly turned back around. Deep down, he had to know that I was committed to him and to us. But deep down, the pain and the fear also still resided.

"I just wanted you to spend time with Kelsea…to see that it's okay."

He spoke methodically, "You have to let me do that in my own time."

"The thing is, your sense of time is different than a preschooler's. Everything seems longer at her age. I know how much I miss you after just a couple weeks. For her, months seem like a lifetime. She doesn't understand."

"I don't want to hurt her," he said simply.

*Yes, I know.* "You can't. You can't."

Finn left out an audible, frustrated exhale like I couldn't possibly understand what he was feeling. He interlocked his hands behind his head and turned, once again, from me. I saw the constriction of his back muscles underneath his dark gray shirt. He was tense for sure, and I didn't know what else to do about it.

"Finn...," I tried once again and waited. When he didn't respond in any fashion after a minute or two, I asked a question that I didn't want a *yes* answer to. "Is this one of those 'go cool off in a different room' times?" I asked referencing the comment he made when we had talked about the prenup and being mad instead of divorcing. "Do you want me to get Will or Nola to drive me home?" That would be my other room, I suppose.

He turned back toward me and recited an answer I hadn't expected, "I don't know, Lara. Maybe."

That answer emotionally crushed me so bad, I began to cry. "I did it because I love Kelsea, and I love you," I said in between sobs.

Not taking a step closer to try to comfort me as he usually did, Finn was instead admonished by his father. "You want to be mad at someone, you be mad at the rest of us too. This was not just her doing."

I hadn't seen him approach, and I'm pretty sure Finn hadn't either. We were too engrossed in our weighty conversation. I turned around to see both of Finn's parents and Will. Mr. and Mrs. Murphy must have just gotten to the Jamison residence from the theater. We were all supposed to meet there and decide on what to do for dinner.

I quickly rubbed my arm against my face, not wanting anyone to see how truly upset I was. Although I am sure they probably heard or saw the tail end of it, anyhow. "No. No, it's okay. It's me he should be mad at." I looked at

Finn's parents but not at Finn. Then I turned to his brother-in-law. "Will, would you mind driving me home?"

"Um," He looked from Finn to me and awkwardly agreed. "Sure. No problem. I'll get my keys."

I could feel Finn's eyes on me as I turned to his father and gave him a hug. "Have a safe flight," I said, acknowledging that I wasn't going to see them again before the next morning when they were set to fly home.

"You should stay, Darlin'."

I ignored the comment, too emotional to respond to a foregone conclusion. I turned to Mrs. Murphy next. Her hug was softer but just as loving.

"We'll see you in another month," she said, referring to the wedding.

"Uh-huh," I managed to spit out and somehow look at my fiancée, hoping beyond hope that it was still the case.

I started to walk away and Finn sidled up to me, meeting my stride. As Will was pulling his car out of the garage, Finn stopped and turned to me. "I need to talk with them. So this is probably best."

I responded with a one-syllable word, although I did not necessarily agree with it. "Yeah."

He did not kiss me goodbye which he always made a point of. And he did not shut the car door behind me. He simply turned and retreated back toward his parents and the backyard.

It was a twenty-minute ride from the Jamison's to my apartment. Will was respectful enough to remain quiet through most of it. I was thankful they had a toddler and, therefore, had plenty of tissues in the car. Even though I had stopped crying, the tears had caused a mascara landslide down my face.

When Will pulled into the parking lot of my apartment building, he joked with me, "Hey, thanks for bailing and leaving me alone with the in-laws."

"Not mine." I had meant it to be funny, but it came across quite melancholy.

"They will be. Take it from a guy—the fact that he is so emotional with you about all of this...he cares...." He trailed off and then said, "I wish his sister had some of that fight in her."

I found his comment about Nola kind of odd. I had always seen Finn's sister as a bubbly, no-holds barred kind of gal. But I had too much on my own plate to further dissect Will's statement. Instead, I entered my apartment building alone.

***

For nearly two hours, I sat stationary on the sofa, running through every millisecond of the day, wondering which step had been the fatal one. I replayed and I replayed. When I exhausted my brain, I started expanding the timeline and thought about the day before and then even the year before. And it all made me sad. Sad because there had been so much happiness.

There wasn't much else for me to do, though. Finn had, actually, chosen for me to walk away in that driveway. It didn't feel right at all. But us fighting wasn't helping either. I tried to trust the cooling down option, Mrs. Murphy's confidence, and Will's insight. But as the minutes passed, I felt less and less confident of a favorable outcome.

When my phone announced a text, I literally jumped. It was a good thing I had my thin cross-body purse that day, because I was wearing it more than carrying it. And with everything that happened after we arrived at Will and Nola's, I would have forgotten it if it—and consequently my phone and keys—had not been on me.

I dug the phone out of my purse. I knew the text was from Finn. But I hesitated looking for a moment, though, not wanting to see the worst.

*Still okay for me to come over?* It read.

I hovered my suddenly shaky fingers over the phone's

keys to respond. Of course it was all right for him to come over. He was supposed to spend the night. But he was asking permission. I wondered what had transpired on his end during the past couple of hours. Did his family have it out with him? Did he with them? Did he just go somewhere by himself? Was he calm? Or was he even more angry? His question didn't give away much.

So my answer didn't either. *Door is unlocked.*

I didn't get a response back. But it was probably because he must not have been that far away. I heard my front door creak open about fifteen minutes later. Looking weathered, Finn entered, carrying a restaurant food container. He found me in the corner of the sofa with my knees drawn up to my chin and my arms wrapped around them.

"Hey," he said quietly—probably because no other ice-breaker was appropriate. When I didn't get up to greet him or say anything in response, he forged on, "My mom ordered you a dinner—some kind of pasta," he explained the white container in his hand.

"Hmmm…comfort food." *Such a mom thing*, I thought. "I'm not hungry, though."

"No, I didn't eat either. Just got your meal and came over here."

"It was nice of her to think of me." I felt like I was making small-talk and walking on delicate egg shells.

Seeing him made my heart skip just like it always did but, yet, a little bit of me let anger slide in. Not anger. No, not anger exactly. It was the towering walls of Lara. I was afraid they were rebuilding. I was afraid of being hurt.

"Yeah. Well, they think I'm being an ass," Finn said, referring to his family. When I gave him nothing as far as facial expressions or verbal feedback, he placed the food container, his phone, and his keys on the coffee table and tentatively sat down on the sofa next to me. "Look, Lara, you knew I was anxious about the whole day in the first place."

I was so scared of what the day had turned into and the potential collateral damage that could come from it that suddenly, as if possessed by the little girl I used to be and hadn't seen in so many years, I said anything to stop what I was fearful of. "I'm sorry. Don't be mad. Please don't be mad. I know I shouldn't have pushed. It's my fault." I dipped my eyes from his. "And I deserve whatever...hit me or you can...." I started to claw my top off wanting him to know that I was his and he....

"Stop! Lara, God, stop!" Finn's hands were firmly but kindly wrapped around my wrists urging me to discontinue my actions and words. "I.... Oh, my God. I don't want to hurt you. Oh, God. Oh, Baby." He carefully let go of my hands, which dropped like lead to my sides, and he gently brushed my face with his fingertips.

"Don't be mad," I pleaded.

"I'm...I'm not."

"But you let me go."

My emotions were on overload again. All of the angst built up in my body started to release, and I started to cry. I brought my hand up to my eyes and tried to squeeze them into submission. But it wasn't doing much good.

"Hey...," Finn said scooting closer to me. "I would never let you go. And if I ever lay a finger on you in anger, I want to die. You understand me? I will die first. Do you honestly think I would do that?" he asked with obvious hurt in his voice.

I didn't. "It would have been...I deserved—"

He stopped me cold. "No one deserves that, especially...especially you. Oh, God. God, Lara. I.... Yes, I was upset. But some of that was because I know you're right about being there for Kels. I needed some space to sort it out...to calm down. I know that about myself. And when it all becomes too much, you need to let me do that. I know that's hard and you probably don't understand, but it's part of me. It's part of...of me." He paused, and I got it. Without him saying the actual words of his disorder, I knew what he was talking about. "And, I *don't* want to hurt you."

I let my legs uncurl and stretch to the floor beside the sofa. The sobbing would not stop. I brought both of my hands up to my face to cover it and felt Finn pull me into his chest.

"Lara, I would never leave you."

"I'm not used to you being mad at me." I pulled slightly away, thinking how, since as far back as I can remember, I cringed at the thought of someone having even the most minute conflict with me.

"You're not easy to be mad at." He shook his head, not letting his eyes leave mine.

"I'm glad you went with us, though. That meant so much to Kelsea."

"It was fun," he said with a glimmer of a smile before letting it fade as if he didn't want to admit to it.

"Kelsea needs to know that she still has her uncle." I looked up at him, my tears drying. "She's already lost too much."

"God, you're like a dog with a bone." He didn't laugh, but he didn't seem angry, either.

I was glad, because as soon as the statement had left my mouth, I worried that I had made it too soon. "Maybe I shouldn't have said that."

"No. You should have." He brought me arm's length away, but I was still in his arms nonetheless. "Listen, I hear you about Kelsea. I do. But, Lara, if you want me to do something or not do something, just ask me. Don't con me. I may not like it. But, you know, there is very little I wouldn't do for you."

"How about forgive me?" I tried.

Finn brought his hand up and slowly touched the corner of my face, letting his index finger trail at the end. I had to assume that was a "yes" because, before he could actually verbalize anything, his phone chimed a single beep on the coffee table. "Sorry," he said looking at the screen and then at me. "It's an e-mail from the realtor. Wants to make sure we're still on for tomorrow."

"Are we?" I both asked and looked tentatively.

"That was the plan," he said referring to visiting a couple of the houses we had selected. "Or we could do it on Sunday."

"You have to leave on Sunday." I reminded him why Saturday had been the only day to do it…if he still wanted to.

"I told you, I listen, Lara. I moved the flight to Monday," he said plainly.

"Oh, Finn, you didn't need to do that. I feel bad that I even brought that up."

"It's already done, and it's very early Monday morning. It'll be okay." It was one of the many things he would do for me. "So, stick with tomorrow?"

"To find our house…our home? Nothing sounds better." I smiled.

Emotionally and physically exhausted from the day and night before, Finn and I must have fallen asleep in each other's arms on the sofa. I woke up once to see his phone vibrating and the food container still lying innocently on the coffee table. I thought of getting up and putting it in the refrigerator, but I was wiped out and didn't want to leave the comfort of my fiancée's arms. If spoiled food was the only casualty of the day, we were definitely ahead.

\*\*\*

We looked at three houses that next day. The first two were in the same area. We liked the first one instantly— from the sunny window walls on. With the second, we didn't even bother to go beyond the first floor. It was a nice home, but we couldn't get past all the updates that were needed. The third one was a bit farther away from where I worked but manageable. We started imagining how we could enhance the neutral décor. But Finn worried about the setting and security. There was property with it but neighbors were close. He wasn't used to that in Tennessee. Everything was closer in New York, even if you didn't live in the city.

So we drove back to the original house that we initially liked and fell even more in love. Not only did it have more property with towering pines, but it was also in a gated community. Plus, the owners had already moved out. So it was in move-in condition pending a home inspection.

When Finn asked the realtor to give us a couple minutes alone to explore and discuss, she walked outside and instantly lit up a cigarette. I think he made her nervous. We started to tour the house again from the beginning. The hardwood foyer with built-in seating was the perfect place to kick off your shoes and stretch out with a good book. We both didn't like certain elements of the powder room. But they were pretty easy fixes. I didn't care for the color scheme. Finn thought we could add some brown to it and replace the mirror with a larger one. The sleek kitchen and dining room were ideally up-to-date.

We walked up the stairs to the loft underscored by hardwood flooring. There was a single bedroom done in a neutral décor. Then there were two more bedrooms connected by a bathroom. Painted in blue and white stripes, the rooms had most likely been for little boys and/or Yankees fans. Neither of us said anything, but I am sure we both knew those would be the first to be repainted.

We trekked back down the stairs to the great room. It reminded me a lot of Finn's place in Tennessee with its wall of windows and French doors. Adjoining that was the first-floor master, done in a neutral décor. It had access to the spectacular back deck. And below the deck was a full screened-in party/gathering room. Finn wanted to finish it off a little more so that he could make it his studio and exercise area.

I was looking out the great room's windows to the vast

yard and patio surrounding the elongated pool when Finn's voice sailed into my thoughts. "What do you think?" he asked.

Trying not to think of the price, I teased with a sarcastic answer, "I'm thinking about that pool boy already."

"You better not be!" Finn joked right back while playfully pushing me with his hand. "Seriously, Lar, yeah? You like it?"

"I do. It feels like home, you know? It feels like us. What about you?"

"Yeah." He smiled. "She sold me at 'soundproof master suite'."

I laughed. "I can't believe she called it that!"

"I don't think she was kidding, either. It's the carpeting. And a good idea. You're entertaining guests out here, want a quickie, slip into the bedroom...."

"I don't think that's why!"

"But it will be," he said, this time pulling me closer.

I snuggled into him, glad there wasn't any residual awkwardness from the day before. Neither of us had mentioned it since waking up. But I suppose there wasn't much else to say. We were both passionate people, especially when it came to those we loved. There would be times when we would argue, but it didn't mean the end of us. Standing in that home, I knew it was nowhere near the end. It was just the beginning.

# CHAPTER TWELVE

The next couple of weeks kept both Finn and me busy, albeit in different parts of the country and working on different things. Finn flew out to Vegas for the ACAs and collected three awards from the fan-voted ceremony. When I called to congratulate him, he, as usual, didn't boast or gloat over such an accomplishment, but I could tell he was excited. He never expected three, and it clearly proved that he was on his way for the major awards at the major events. He did gossip a little, though, telling me that Carter was flying in to see Vanessa over Christmas. I was impressed that Vanessa had managed to keep that bit of info a secret from me. That was until five minutes after I got off the phone with Finn. Hers was the next number to light up my phone.

In the meantime, I continued to work and occasionally work out. My spare time, however, was filled with doing house stuff. I dealt with the home inspection, making utility inquiries, picking out paint swatches, and going online to look for furnishing ideas.

I took a day off work in mid-December to fly out and meet Finn in West Virginia. It was a long weekend rendezvous near our college town and the location of our wedding. We wanted to confirm all the details as it was only a couple weeks away at that point. There wasn't much to do, but it was nice to be there in person just to see that everything was going to be perfect. It was also the last time the two of us would be alone together before the holiday and the wedding. And since we made the silly pact of not sleeping together after that weekend and before the wedding, we got in every second we could.

Our plan was to spend Christmas Eve and Christmas Day with Finn's family in Louisville. Then, the day after, we would all drive to West Virginia to start the wedding festivities. My mother was a little upset that we weren't going to be at her place for the holiday, but compromises had to start being made. Plus, she had my brother Lane and his wife, McEllie, there for Christmas.

A few days before my arrival in Kentucky, I sent a hand-written letter via snail mail to Finn at his parents' home. We had never corresponded through written letter. It had always been texting and telephones. But, somehow, this seemed romantic and right to me. The letter read:

*I'm sitting here watching* It's a Wonderful Life *and wrapping your gifts. I have this overwhelming desire to hear your voice. But I want to write this down too. I want to write down this feeling—this feeling that it* is *a wonderful life. Finn, you have made me so happy. I am so excited to become your wife. There are times when I still can't believe that we are in this moment. I love you.*

***

Struggling with the loud and pushy masses in baggage claim, I paid no attention to the man who was suddenly standing next to me. That was until he held up a sign in front of my face. It read: *It is a wonderful life.*

Although disguised with the cover of a cap and scarf, there was no mistaking those gorgeous steel-colored eyes of his. Nola was supposed to be waiting outside. This—he—was a complete surprise. I instantly forgot about everything else and threw my arms around his neck.

"What are you doing here?" I glanced around, but, luckily, everyone was too busy with luggage and the holiday rush to notice us.

"This." Finn pulled out the letter I had sent and quoted a line from the movie about giving the heroine everything she desired. When I told him to kiss me instead of talking—another obvious reference to *It's a Wonderful Life*—he obliged. Thanks to the busy holiday season, his rare PDA went unnoticed by the numerous passengers but not to me. "That letter was the most beautiful thing I have ever received. And this is just one of many moments, Baby."

"Finn." I tsked, thinking his statement was ridiculous. It was just my thoughts.

"That was sweet that you finally saw the movie," he said, speaking of the holiday classic he had told me his family watched every year when he was growing up.

"I was imagining you and your family watching it at the same time I was."

"You are my family," he said concretely. "And next year, we have a standing date to watch it together." He smiled, taking my suitcase from where I had haphazardly laid it at my feet. "C'mon, before I get noticed."

***

By the time Finn and I arrived at his parents' place, Finn's Aunt Joy had already gone. Still single and the youngest of Zak Murphy's siblings, she currently lived in California and had come to Kentucky for a few days but was headed to Florida. Mr. Murphy's other sibling, his brother, lived in Florida. It was near Finn's grandparents who alternated their Christmases every year between Florida and Kentucky. This was Florida's year. Having a small, intimate gathering suited me just fine. None of the extended family were invited to the wedding as we were truly keeping it a secret. So it was easier to speak freely with the family that I already felt a part of—Mr. and Mrs. Murphy, Nola, Will, and Kelsea.

Of course, the last time I had seen Finn's parents was the ugly moment in the back of Will and Nola's home. Mrs. Murphy had not wavered in her faith back then, and she didn't waiver in the generous hug that she gave me upon entering the towering foyer of their three story house. And Mr. Murphy's bear hug was one a doting dad would give to his daughter.

I took in a large inhale of their home. That was exactly what it smelled like—home. There was a sweet scent lofting through the air.

Finn's mom noticed my serene smile at the scent and said, "Made sure not to burn any of those candles. Hoping you're not allergic to Kentucky homestyle cooking."

I smiled at her thoughtfulness. "Most certainly not. It smells divine."

Just as the grandfather clock in the corner rang out half past nine p.m., we made our way into what the Murphys called the parlor. As I scooped up Kelsea who dove into my legs, I noticed the fake smiles on Nola and Will's faces. As if Thanksgiving hadn't been emotional enough, this was the first Christmas without their little boy. This was the biggie. I could not imagine the internal hell they were going through. Everything on the outside appeared perfect except…except that one, precious, loved thing was gone, and it would never be the same again.

I started to say something, but Nola interrupted me, explaining that the Murphy clan had a Christmas Eve tradition that they needed to fulfill before we all made our way to Christmas Eve mass. I knew about a lot of their traditions through the stories Finn had related to me. The Murphys always put their whole heart and being into everything they did. But this one I did not know about.

They only opened one gift on Christmas Eve. Everyone's names were put into a basket and whoever's name was drawn, they got the gift that night. That sounded good until it was my name that was picked.

"Oh, pick someone else," I protested. "I'm not even—"

"Stop it." I was surprised by Mrs. Murphy's insistence although kind. "Don't even say it. We don't need a piece of paper in a few days to tell us that." As I looked to Finn, who raised his eyebrows in an I-told-you-so fashion, Mrs. Murphy continued, "Besides, I would love to give you my gift."

Oh, boy! Now I was really on the spot. Not only was I the only one to open a gift that day, but it was from my future mother-in-law. Talk about pressure.

As Mrs. Murphy started to grab for a typical clothes-shaped box under the enormous tree, Finn said to me, "You'll love it. Mom gives the best gifts. She really knows how to pick for a person."

Okay. Good, I thought as Finn and I sat down on the white-and-yellow striped high-backed sofa. I could totally see Finn's mother being the perfect gift giver. She was incredibly thoughtful.

Gift in hand, I started to pull at the ribbon and unseal the tape with my fingers when Mr. Murphy yelled out, "Just rip it, girl. It's Christmas! Have fun."

"Huh! That's where you got it from," I said thinking of how Finn tore into every gift I gave him like an impatient little boy. Whereas, I had been taught not to—my mother always tried to recycle the wrapping paper and bows to cut costs.

"Where else?" Finn said proudly looking at his father. "C'mon. Open it, already."

When I saw what was in the box, I wished I would have stuck to my original thought and taken my time. Although, why prolong the inevitable? The gift was, indeed, clothing. And it appeared to be homemade. I pulled out the winter pajama set. The bottoms, unfortunately appearing to be in my correct size, were done in a—no other word but "ugly" best fits—tree pattern. The top, a solid black color, had the words "La, La, La, La, La, Lara" embroidered in red on it.

With all eyes, especially Mrs. Murphy's, staring at me, I put on an act. "How festive!" I exaggerated. "I'm sure they'll…" I started to say. I wasn't sure how I was going to finish, but I needn't have worried because Finn stood up next to me and started unbuttoning his pants and taking them down. "Finn!" I yelled out embarrassed and astonished all at the same time. "What are you…?"

That's when I noticed everyone in the clan was doing the same thing, including precious little Kelsea. Underneath their tops and pants, each member of Finn's family had their own personalized pair of pajamas. There was Pop-Pops's pj's with penguins, Noel Nana with reindeer, Naughty & Nice Nola with ho, ho, ho, Wassail Will with Santa, and Candy Cane Kelsea with candy canes. It was obviously one of the Murphy traditions. I stood up hitting Frosty the Finnman who had snowmen on his bottoms. And then I hit him again still not liking to be in the spotlight.

"How come I get hit?" He flinched, but as a joke, not in pain. "I didn't do it."

"You could have told me," I accused light-heartedly.

He turned to his parents. "This is what she did the night we got engaged."

"What?" I yelled not having any idea what he was referring to. "I did not."

"When you first saw me at the penthouse…when I surprised you. You hit me." He smiled in a knowing way.

"Yeah, well, I think I kissed you too," I said, remembering.

"So?" Finn tapped his finger to his lips demanding a repeat performance. After I obliged with a quick kiss, Finn pulled me into something a little deeper and sensual.

"All right! Wait for the wedding, you two," came Nola's voice.

With my head buried into the side of Finn's chest, still embarrassed with the attention, I heard Will tease, "Hey, at least you got your…"—he paused looking for the right, yet sarcastic, words—"lovely ensemble before the wedding. I got mine after. You still have time to run."

I'm not sure if it was my imagination or not, but I swore Finn squeezed me a little tighter at that moment. Just in case, to reassure him, I squeezed right back. When Mrs. Murphy dragged her husband into the kitchen to help get eggnog for everyone, I whispered to Finn, "Does your mom realize she gave your sister bottoms that are calling her a prostitute?" I referenced Nola's Ho! Ho! Ho! pajama bottoms.

"Jealous, Roxanne?" he teased.

"Do you really have the tradition of opening one gift?" I asked.

"What do you think?" He smiled his incorrigible smile, which earned him another smack. Taking the box from my hands, he started across the room. "I'll put it back under the tree, but it is truthfully a tradition that we all wear them for Christmas morning when we open gifts."

"Well, I think our pact will remain intact with you wearing those tonight."

"What pact?" Nola's question was interrupted when her parents reentered the room.

When Mrs. Murphy first handed Kelsea her cup of eggnog, the little girl asked, "What was on Wyatt's pajamas, Nana?"

Upon hearing Wyatt's name, everyone in the room froze as if we were outside in the chilly winter air instead of inside in the warmth. Wyatt had not been mentioned up to that point. It wasn't a situation where the family didn't talk about a deceased loved one. They did on occasion as warranted. Although Finn still shied away. But it was the fact that Kelsea asked about her brother. It had been seven months since his death and, in Kelsea's short life, the memory of Wyatt was surely fading faster than the others in the room. It was probably odd for her now to be the only child in the family, and I am sure she felt very lost around all adults most of the time.

I looked to Finn who was now across the room from me. I tossed him a quick wink wanting him to know my love. He shot me a half smile back.

Nana Murphy answered Kelsea as Will tossed his daughter into his arms. "Oh, Sweetie, he was Winter Wonderland Wyatt. Do you remember the snowflakes and hearts on his pj's?"

"Uh-huh." Kelsea agreed, but I'm not sure she actually remembered. She could tell the mood in the room had shifted.

I saw Nola turn from her husband and daughter and blankly stare out the window. By that point, I had made it to Finn's side. I rubbed his back in soothing circles similar to the way I had at the hospital that tragic evening.

"I remember him randomly belting out the 'Batman smells' version of 'Jingle Bells' in the middle of our club class last year," I offered trying to lighten up the mood but yet give that precious boy his due.

Nola started to laugh surely just conjuring up the image. Will said that he was a motor mouth even in his sleep. And Finn left the parlor. I stood still, wondering if I should follow him or let him be, not knowing exactly what he needed or exactly his destination. Then, just a moment later, we all found out. A couple notes sounded out from the baby grand in the foyer. They, of course, were being played by Finn who also sang the accompanying beginning words to "Jingle Bells." His family quickly, yet silently, gravitated to the piano to join in the singing of the tune. Sitting down on the bench next to him , I rested my head on his shoulder simply soaking in the true meaning of Christmas, love, and family.

On the very last beat of the song, Kelsea yelled out, "Now, Rudolph!"

\*\*\*

The Catholic Christmas Eve midnight mass was an experience like no other. It was something that I had not been used to and, quite frankly, was a little apprehensive to attend. I had gone to Sunday church with my mother and brother—my father was a devout atheist—during our adolescence. But when it became my choice, post high school, I didn't step in a church again. And besides that, my mother's church was Lutheran. Catholicism seemed like a whole other beast with rules of kneeling and offerings and communion.

But it was an amazing, breathtaking evening. The moment we stepped into the church, an overwhelming sense of serenity filled my soul. There seemed to be a special, calming stillness in the air. Snuggled next to Finn, who, despite the massive number of people, was not treated differently for his celebrity status on the holy night, I listened to the preacher preach and the choir sing. It was the same choir that little Finny Murphy had made his humble singing debut in as a child. Toward the end, not out of boredom or disrespect, but because of that peace, I must have fallen asleep. Thankfully, it went pretty much unnoticed as I was on the end of the pew farthest from the center of the church.

I heard my fiancée whisper, "She's sleeping."

Mrs. Murphy, who was sitting on the opposite side of Finn, replied with, "Poor thing, bless her heart. She's probably exhausted. I was just picturing the two of you up there at that altar. I don't see why you couldn't have gotten married here."

"Drop it, Mom." I heard Finn's directive to his mother and then felt his lips on my forehead.

"Hey, Beauty, the service is over. You awake enough to walk? I guess I could carry you, but—"

"Sorry." I looked up at him. "You mind if we sit here for a moment or two? We won't get kicked out or anything?"

"No. The church stays open. We can stay a bit." Finn turned toward his family who were all standing up in the pew we had taken over. "Lara and I will catch up with y'all at home," he said, knowing that we took two cars to get there so it wouldn't be a problem.

Nola bent down to say something to Kelsea who ran over to Finn and me, causing me to sit up a little straighter. "Merry Christmas, Aunt Lara!" She threw her arms around me, calling me by my unofficial name for the first time.

I smiled a little misty-eyed, feeling so blessed to be becoming part of this family. "Thanks, Kelsea. Don't forget to put those cookies out for Santa."

"I will!" she exclaimed and then barreled into Finn, giving him a hug too.

"Merry Christmas, Squirt," Finn acknowledged, hugging her back.

After Finn's family left and the church was nearly empty, I twined my leg with my fiancée's and said, "Sorry I fell asleep. It's just been a long day."

"I know."

"Your mom mad?"

"About you falling asleep? No." He semi-laughed.

"No," I clarified. "About us not getting married here—not doing the whole Catholic thing."

"You heard her?"

"Yeah."

"No. She's not mad. She's just a mom. She's never going to get to throw that big wedding. Neither of her kids went that route and she kinda feels like it's a mom's rite of passage."

"Wait. Nola and Will didn't do the whole big wedding thing?" I guess I had just assumed. They would have gotten married when Finn and I were in college, but I didn't remember him mentioning it back then.

"No. I never told you?" he asked but didn't wait for a response. "They eloped."

"Oh, wow!"

"Yeah. So, Rox, we're like golden compared to them." He smiled.

"Why did they elope? Too much family pressure with planning? Just decided to screw it?"

"Ha! No." He was moving his guitarist fingertips around the top of my hand. "They had been living together. Will was in grad school and Nola was working some entry level job. They were talking about getting engaged. Will actually already had the ring, when, well, Nola found out she was pregnant with Wyatt."

"Oh." I didn't know that.

"They flew to Vegas and did it right then and there. Not a word to any of us."

"Huh. What did your parents say when they found out?"

"About which part?"

"I don't know...either...both. What did they know...when?"

"Nola and Will told them immediately after coming home and just said everything at once."

"And?"

"And they were shocked and wished it had happened in a different order, but they liked Will. And when Wy made his entrance, well, who could even remember the circumstances?"

"God, what they would think of me." I blanched, putting my eyes down, reflecting on my life pre-Finn— the life of a knocked up teen who gave her baby away.

"Oh, Lara." He pulled me into him, resting his head on mine and understanding what I was referring to. "My parents simply adore you."

"But they don't know."

"Do you think there will be a time when we can tell them? I understand if you don't want to, but I promise, Baby, nothing is going to change the way they feel about you," he said reassuringly.

"Yeah." I couldn't help but feel a little bit melancholy. It was never an easy memory. "Maybe."

We sat for a couple more minutes, just staring ahead and lost in our thoughts. The sanctuary of the church gave us time to reflect. So much of life is by chance. I am sure that might not be the religious perspective. But fate intermixed with the choices we all make affects us, there is no doubt. I looked at the replica of baby Jesus, lying in his manger near the altar. It reminded me of the boy I gave away, as well as the one Nola had not. Although Nola and Will had been in a different place in their lives and relationship, they could have made a different choice. But then Wyatt would have never been at my work and Finn and I would not have reconnected. Possibly when Kelsea would have started school, but that was still years down the road.

I slowly got up and walked to the votive candles racked up along the wall. Finn followed me silently. He curled his body behind mine as I slowly lit two candles—one for each boy who profoundly changed my life. Those glowing jars in the dimly lit room reminded me that no matter how dark and dusty some days may seem, there's also light and warmth ready to be embraced.

# CHAPTER THIRTEEN

Christmas morning was really all about Kelsea. And the three-year-old didn't disappoint as she opened each gift with more glee than the last. Donning our personalized pj's, all of us adults nestled around her and the gigantic, beautifully decorated tree. I noticed the ornament with my name on it that Finn had made for me the year before. It dangled next to all the other family ornaments, including Wyatt's. There was not, however, a string of popcorn and cranberries. That had been Finn and Wyatt's tradition—one it appeared that would not last.

We took a break after Kelsea's gift-opening extravaganza and had a light brunch. Then we went to a local homeless shelter to volunteer—preparing food, setting tables, serving, and, of course, singing by one particular family member. The Murphys liked to help others and would usually go on the holiday to a children's or veterans' hospital. But no one had it in them that year to be in any kind of hospital.

Once we got back home and had a late dinner ourselves, I called my mom and brother to wish them a happy holiday and confirm some of the wedding details. Then it was time for the adults in the Murphy crew to open their gifts. Finn and I somehow managed to be last giving our gifts to one another.

"Just so you know," my fiancé started. "I listened. I got you a card. Well, two." He was referring to my insistence that he just get me a card in lieu of an elaborate gift like the previous year's Jeep Wrangler.

"Thank you," I said too quickly because, of course, they weren't just cards.

Inside the first one was a beautiful Claddagh necklace with the stone of December planted solidly in the center to remind us of not only the holiday but of our wedding. Along with it was a paper detailing the history behind the Claddagh symbol. I loved the necklace instantly simply because of its aesthetic quality. But after reading the story behind it, I realized what a personal touch Finn had put into his gift. It made me forget the hundreds of dollars spent.

The story states that a young man gave the Claddagh ring to his lover but then was kidnapped by pirates. She waited for five years. Then, one day he escaped, made a fortune, and returned to her to live happily ever after. Because of that, the Claddagh is a symbol of friendship, eternal romantic love, and a commitment of forever.

I was obviously touched by the parallelism to our story. Finn had been kidnapped in his own way…by the demons inside him. And yet, he had returned to me fortune in hand. Forever.

Because I was surrounded by Finn's family, I made light of my response. "Five years? That's all I had to wait? Geez, Cowboy, it's a good thing I'm patient and gave you seven."

"Had to get those pesky pirates off my trail," Finn chimed in with me.

"Oh, brother," Will growled in a way that told me I had been counting an excessive number of mixed drinks in his possession.

Ignoring Will, Finn handed me another card. Not

knowing what to anticipate for sure, I opened up the envelope. Inside were two tickets to Ireland for a just a few days away.

I looked at my fiancée not quite understanding. "I thought we were just doing the cabin." I spoke of our honeymoon plans in Maryland.

"It is. Cabin…cottage…same difference. But just across the pond. I want to really get away…escape…go somewhere neither of us have been and experience it together. And what better place for an Irish bride?" he added. "You good with that? We don't have to. We could put it off for later."

"Finn, that's…wow." I was touched by his sentiment but overwhelmed by the same account. I had to process the alteration of our plans on top of Christmas and the wedding. But I was learning to get better at sudden changes, especially if they were the good ones.

"Hey, I put them in cards," he teased.

I shook my head in mock disapproval while pushing him lightly. "You did. I'll give you that. I will have to be much more specific!"

He smiled his brilliant, confident smile. "Ireland's good, then?"

"Ireland's good," I said, then quickly added a humorous addendum, "But only if you wear a kilt."

As Finn started to protest, Nola burst out laughing. "Oh, yeah, that's a must. Make him wear the kilt with cowboy boots and a hat."

"Uh…no," he admonished his sibling. "Don't give her any ideas."

"What's a kilt?" Kelsea spoke up.

"It's a sissy skirt for Irish boys," Will gave a sloppy answer to his daughter who just looked confused.

I distracted Kelsea by having her give Finn his two gifts from me. "One sentimental and one practical," I stated having set the precedence for my gift giving the year before.

"I'm going sentimental first this year," Finn replied.

"Really?" I was surprised since he chose opposite the year before.

"Yeah," he said confidently.

"Big box, then."

Finn, with the help of his niece, tore open the skinny, elongated box. I bounced an ever-growing Kelsea in my lap, afraid that if she touched the gift, she might get hurt. Finn carefully pulled two long s'more pokers out of the box and looked at the engraving on each—"almost as sweet as you." One had my name and one had Finn's name.

"What are those...the captured pirate swords?" Will was the only one who laughed at his own joke, because it was obvious at that point that he was, indeed, drunk.

My fiancée gave me a sweet but quick kiss as we watched Will walk off toward the kitchen. Everyone had heard the s'more part of Finn's proposal, so there was no need to explain the gift. Therefore, moving on and ignoring Will, Finn opened the second, smaller box. On discovery of the simple chain necklace inside, his face took on a perplexed look.

I started to explain as Finn let Kelsea twirl it in her hands. "I figured when you're performing you can wear your ring around your neck, under your shirt...whatever."

That perplexed look changed to a slightly different variation. "I'm not taking my wedding band off." He stated matter-of-factly...almost offended.

With the room suddenly quiet around us, I explained. "I'm not asking you to. I'm asking you to keep it next to your heart." I continued, "I know with the amount of energy you use performing and the different temperatures depending on where you're at, that ring is either going to swell like a vice on your finger or fall off."

"You sure?" he asked, still a little tentative.

"Yeah," I replied and good-naturedly pointed my finger to the collective members of his family. "But I have witnesses. I said 'when you are performing.' All other times, it better be proud and prominent on this handsome finger right here," I said stroking his ring finger.

"Good God, if that's what you do with a finger," Will had re-entered the room with a new drink in his hand. "I can just imagine how you fuck him."

My eyes grew wide at the crudity. At the same time, Finn's father rose from his chair and bellowed Will's formal name. Finn clasped my hand extra securely, tensing at the awkward situation. He got up, dragging me and Kelsea, who was still on my lap, with him.

Nola reached out for her daughter's hand. "C'mon, good girl, let's go upstairs and try on some of those new clothes. We can have a fashion show with Nana."

Oblivious to the drama surrounding her, Kelsea jumped from me to her mother. "Yay! I want the sparkly shoes!"

As Nola, Kelsea, and Mrs. Murphy began to exit, my future father-in-law turned to me. "Lara, Darlin', you should probably go with the gals."

It was like a scene from a mob movie. The men needed to square off. The women folk needed safeguarded. I expected Finn to agree with his father. So, therefore, I was surprised when it was his dad that Finn wanted dismissed.

"No, Pop, go ahead. Will owes Lara an apology." Finn was speaking to his father but his stare remained evenly on Will.

"Will, son, get it under control." Mr. Murphy pointed a warning finger at his son-in-law, but I knew it was underscored with love.

What Finn had revealed to me in the church about the Murphys always liking Will was evident every time I witnessed them together. Will was ensconced into their all-American lifestyle whole-heartedly. And he was treated no differently than one of their own—with respect, love, and the blunt truth if it was warranted.

I'm not sure where Finn's father exited to—most likely

to the mock fashion runway. But it wasn't my concern at the moment. My focus was on Finn—his protective, tight hand in mine, and what he would say to the man whom he considered a brother.

"Listen, I get it," Finn started. "But you will not...*not*," he emphasized again. "speak to her that way."

Despite his eyes being semi-glossed over, Will looked straight at me and said with sincerity, "I'm sorry, Lara. I don't know why I said that." His pause was only slight. "I just can't stand that he's not here." The "he" obviously being his deceased son. "It's just wrong."

My heart broke for Will in that moment. He had been the one so strong in the hospital room when our worlds were falling apart. He had been the one to think rationally in an irrational scenario. And now, months later, the merriment of the holiday did him in. I knew his comment wasn't really directed at me. And Finn knew that too. That was why he didn't lay into his brother-in-law as much as he would have if the circumstances were at all different. Not many other people, besides Nola, truly knew the depth of pain that suffocated those two men standing in the living room next to me.

I embraced Will, holding him for an extended second, hoping that a hug would be enough...at least for that moment in time. I didn't know what to say. There really wasn't anything to say in that situation.

"It just gets to me some times," Will said breaking from me. "Don't you just see him in every memory? My heart aches."

Quietly, Finn acknowledged his brother-in-law's pain. "Things will never be the way they were." Then he asked, "Are you and Nola still doing the counseling?"

"Yeah, but it can't work when your sister acts like Miss Merry Sunshine, happy-go-lucky all the time. I don't understand how she just moved on."

"Did you hear what you just said?" Finn rationalized for his sister. "'Acts.' She acts. That is her coping mechanism. She hasn't moved on. God, how can any of us ever move on?"

I rubbed Finn's back knowing no truer truth had ever been spoken. Finn had healed in some ways from his nephew's passing, but it didn't take a deep blade at all to uncover the pain. I was proud of him for putting his own sorrow aside and, instead, empathize with Will and forgive his crude words toward me.

Will patted Finn on the shoulder in that rough way that drunks do. "Yeah," he said, but it wasn't convincing.

"Will?" I questioned in general.

"I'm gonna grab some coffee and go walk the neighborhood for a while," he replied, obviously noting the concern in my voice.

"Want company?" I offered. Maybe a Murphy in-law like himself would be the best option at this point.

"No. No. I need to clear my head. And, no offense, but you two are just too happy for me."

"Wi—" I started, but I wasn't sure how I was going to defend that. Damned if I wasn't happy. I was days away from marrying the love of my life.

"You should be. I remember that. I'm not that big of a jerk. It's not been that long," Will acknowledged. He forced a sad smile onto his face before grabbing his phone and walking through the dining room toward the kitchen.

Finn looked at me—the only sound being a large inhale and exhale from his nose. I closed my eyes, taking in the same after-moment as my soon-to-be husband. With the click of the back door, we knew Will had left.

I looked once again at Finn. "I'm worried about him."

"He's…he's fine. The neighborhood's safe. It's Christmas. There won't be a lot of cars out. He has his phone and—"

"No, not that," I interrupted. "His drinking. Every time we've seen him lately he's been drinking…a lot." I tagged on the last two words for emphasis.

After pondering or reflecting for a second or two, Finn

finally offered, "I don't know. Maybe. But give the guy a break. He has a high-pressure Wall Street job. And it's the holidays. He's allowed a drink or two."

"It wasn't—" Didn't he see what I saw?

"People can handle drinking, Lara. Just because your dad drank and you—"

It was my turn to interrupt again. "Okay. Stop. All right. You don't have to"—God, bring up that—"I'm just concerned."

"You don't have to be."

I wasn't sure I believed that, but I also didn't have a chance to vocalize any more of my opinions or thoughts as Kelsea bounded into the parlor. "Where Daddy?"

"He went for a walk. He'll be back," I answered.

"Mommy says I can wear my new shoes at the wedding!"

"Oh?" Finn said as we both looked down at the glittery purple sparklers on her feet.

"I did not," Nola corrected entering the room herself. "I told her to ask you." I started walking toward my ringing phone as Nola continued. "And I told you to tell them good night. It's way past your bedtime, little girl."

"It's Vanessa," I acknowledged the caller to Finn. "I'm gonna take it upstairs." He brushed my hand as I kissed the top of Kelsea's curly blonde head and answered my phone.

I talked to my best friend for a while in the comforts of Finn's childhood bedroom. Vanessa needed a distraction for a bit after being with her boisterous family for so long. Plus, she was anxious, waiting for Carter to show up the next day. I had to admit I was curious about how their holiday rendezvous was going to go too.

After I hung up, I stripped down to my panties and a tank top and laid on my stomach across Finn's bed. His parents had kept his and Nola's rooms similar to when they both moved out post-college. Although there was some memorabilia like grade school lunchboxes intermixed with more modern photographs and newer sheets and comforters.

It wasn't the bedspread, though, that brought me comfort. It was the dip of the bed and then Finn gently lying on top of me. He tickled my rib area, causing me to laugh and smile and squirm—a much needed release from the day.

When I turned around to face him, he spoke. "I hope you're good with purple sparkly shoes. I couldn't say 'no.'"

Of course he couldn't. He was a softie with all things with his family. It was just one of the many reasons I loved him.

"It's fine." I sat up, causing him to also. "Whatever makes her happy."

"I'm sorry about before. I didn't mean to come down on you about your dad. I was just frustrated."

I appreciated the genuine apology but understood my part in it too. "Finn, you know I'm bringing my own baggage into it. I'm probably preconditioned to only seeing the bad when it comes to alcohol."

"I think I'm preconditioned to loving you."

I slightly shook my head and smiled. "That sounds like a song title."

He chuckled. "It does. But it's just my heart."

When I kissed him my thanks, he reciprocated. Our kissing started turning into the open-mouthed, erotic, sex-starting kind. I wanted him. I wanted him because it had been a couple weeks since we had been together. I wanted him because I needed to forget any sadness that lingered from earlier. But most of all, I wanted him because I was so in love with him.

But we had made a pact. And if we went any further, that pact would be broken. I slowed my kisses down and pulled away.

When I started getting out of bed, Finn, puzzled, inquired, "Where are you going?"

As I slipped on the pajamas Mrs. Murphy had made

me, my words staggered out, "Bathroom. Cold water. It's either that or I'll have to kick you out of bed," I joked. "We made a pact, Cowboy."

Finn flopped back on the pillow exasperated but smiling. When I returned, he was under the covers. Instantly, though, I noted the line of pillows splayed alongside him from head to foot.

"What's this?" I asked.

"Your side and mine," he jested. "Hands off."

I shook my head in mock disbelief and, instead of walking around the bed, I slowly climbed on top of my fiancée, freezing with a smile before rolling over to my side of the bed—the one farthest from the door just as Finn knew I preferred. Settled, I sat up slightly to peer over Ft. Finn. "Kiss good night?"

"Night, Lara." He leaned over and pecked me on the lips, smiling extra wide.

I stretched back out but moved my body up against the line of pillows, sort of like those movie clichés when the couple mirrors their hands to each other's on opposite sides of glass. I couldn't bear not to physically touch my man, though, so I slid down a tiny bit and wiggled my foot across the "line" so it would meet Finn's.

"Lara…," Finn said in a warning yet kind voice.

"G'night back," was my answer.

I felt his foot poke me back in a loving way before I allowed myself to drift off to sleep. Somehow, not surprisingly, when we woke the next morning, the pillows were haphazardly lying in all areas of not only the bed but the floor. In our collective sleep, we had managed to find one another despite the barrier. Our bodies were entwined but our pact was intact.

\*\*\*

The Murphy/Jamison clan and myself met up with my mother, Lane, and McEllie that next afternoon in West

Virginia. We had booked a collection of hotel rooms for the entire merging group. After our parents and siblings were introduced to one another, we enjoyed dinner in a private room at a Japanese restaurant complete with theatrical fire displays and food tossing.

Then it was on to the night's activities. We girls were doing a bachelorette-like night with cabs and to-be-determined bar/s. Well, girls, meaning myself, McEllie, and Nola. Both the mother-of-the-bride and the mother-of-the-groom took the opportunity to babysit Kelsea and get to know one another better. I was a little apprehensive leaving my mother with Finn's. Not because I thought she would tell any deep, dark secrets, but just that she could rattle anyone's ear off. However, the alternative of having my mom join us while we talked boy talk and drank didn't seem any better. So Mrs. Murphy had to fend for herself.

The guys were having poker night in Lane and McEllie's room since Finn didn't want to be seen any more than necessary around town. We had done a great job thus far not giving away even the slightest notion that the wedding was that week or that we would be in town, and we wanted to keep it that way. Some things, like your one and only wedding, should be sacred after all.

Hours into our girls escapade and three bars in, I realized the inevitable had happened. And it was all right. But the one person I wanted to share it with wasn't there. So, sitting on a bar stool, I pulled out my phone, glanced at McEllie and Nola who were on the dance floor, and pressed Finn's speed-dial number.

I couldn't hear exactly how he answered because the pulsating music was too loud in the bar. Walking a few steps away, I called into the phone, "Baby?"

"Hey, Beauty." This time I could hear his melodic voice that sounded so smooth even when he wasn't singing.

"I think one of your dreams came true." I held onto a pole near the entrance of the bar.

"Hmmm…is it a wet dream?" he teased, although quietly, as he was surely in the presence of the other men in our lives.

My voice was quite the opposite as I spurted out, "I'm drunk. I'm pretty drunk!" And on the vocal confirmation, I began giggling.

Finn's laughter across the line outdid mine. "Where are you?"

"I don't know," I said, noting that Nola and McEllie were now at my side. Turning to them, I asked, "Where are we? I need to tell Finn."

Nola grabbed the phone and spoke to her brother using the nickname she had christened him with in childhood. "Munch, never mind where we are. This is girls' night."

"No, Nola, no. I want to see him," I pleaded and took the phone back. "Finn?"

"Hey, Rox."

I loved hearing his voice. I loved how he said my name. I loved that he had special, meaningful names for me. I loved how he listened to me and was there for me and protected me. God, did I love that man.

"Your sister is being mean," I joshed, sticking my tongue out at Nola in a way Kelsea would.

"Yeah, try growing up with her," he jokingly answered back and then tried again with, "Where are you?"

"We're ah…," I looked around, knowing that I knew the place from when Finn and I had attended college there. But it just wasn't clear in my alcohol-induced fog. "W…," I started again, and then it finally clicked. "Aaaaa Frat Boys!"

"You're with frat boys?" His voice changed slightly but was still filled with humor.

"No, no, no," I clarified and at the same time slurred. "Fat Boys!" I remembered—that was the name of the bar!

"Geez, Lar. Okay. Shhhh! You're talking really loud." He laughed. "Glad you're not far. Want me to come get you?"

"Yeah." I smiled. That's exactly what I wanted—his prince to my Rapunzel. "But—" I started, knowing that the whole idea was for him not to be in public.

He interrupted. "You're within walking distance. I'm on my way. And get ready—I'm buying you those shots."

"What?" I didn't understand. Nothing was clear but the fact that he was on his way.

"Never mind." He chuckled again before hanging up.

# CHAPTER FOURTEEN

Finn entered Fat Boys just as his sister and McEllie went into the restroom. Donning a leather jacket, he searched the room briefly before catching my eye. When he acknowledged me with a wink, I tried to be seductive by pointing my finger to the empty bar stool next to me. Finn shook his head in a joking manner, but took the offer. He then parenthesized my face with his hands and sucked in a strong, passionate kiss. The mix of his desire and my beyond buzz caused my breath to almost be taken away.

"So much for ananiminity," I managed to spew out.

"So much for what?" Finn held my hands in his and smiled a silly grin.

"Animosity," I tried again, knowing that it sounded like the wrong word choice too.

"Animosity?" It was clearly the wrong word, and he was clearly amused.

"You know what I mean!" I exclaimed, slightly frustrated yet able to laugh at myself.

"Anonymity"—he said slowly to reinforce the correct word—"be damned. This is so worth it! Besides, there's no one here. College bar," He scanned the area. "all home for the holiday."

"Finn?" I leaned a little more into him while trying to stay balanced on the stool.

"Yeah?" He held on.

"I'm drunk. This," I said, making an imperfect circle with my finger in front of my upper body, "is drunk."

"It sure is." He could not stop being amused. "And I am taking complete advantage."

"What? What do you mean?"

He tugged me off the stool. "C'mon, we're dancing."

"No. This isn't slow," I whined, detesting fast dancing because I wasn't good at it, and I knew I looked like an idiot.

Finn knew how I felt but didn't quite understand as a masterful musician with an abundance of rhythm. "Come on." He did not take "no" for an answer and led me onto the dance floor. "This isn't any different. And you dance to my music. You just refuse to call it dancing."

Before I could counter, he had me encapsulated into his body, which was moving to the beat of the base. I had no choice but to follow his lead. He moved his hands up and down my body and also forced me arm's length away so I had room to move on my own. But he never let go. And, admittedly, it felt so free and so sexy. Although that was after a couple drinks.

"Damn, it's like a recurring nightmare. This one keeps popping up everywhere." Nola, who was suddenly at our side, pushed her brother jokingly, yet in a drunk, rough way. "If it's not in person, it's on TV or on the damn radio. Should have appreciated those couple of years as a toddler before baby bro came along."

"Love you too, Nol." Finn clasped my one hand while also seeing if Nola was steady on her feet. For confirmation, Finn walked us over to McEllie who was at the bar. "Who's worse?"

My brother's wife laughed. "Hard to say. But, Lara, here, is the happier of the drunks."

"I'm the happy drunk!" I bounced like a toddler who had just been proclaimed the most wonderful eighth dwarf.

"I'm glad, Baby." Finn kissed me quickly. "Thanks for dancing with me."

"How'd you get her to do that?" McEllie questioned. "She's been refusing all night."

"It was his wedding gift," I teased.

Shaking his head, he asked me, "You okay for a couple shots?"

"Uh…" I was a happy drunk—not a black-out, not-remember-anything drunk. I wanted to keep it at that level.

But in the second that I hesitated, McEllie spoke for me. "She's fine. She's a lightweight. Just had a couple foo-foo drinks."

Finn took that as his answer, which happened to conveniently correspond with the one he wanted. "Four blow-jobs." He ordered the shots from the bartender.

"I am not"—drunk Nola sounded a little bit teeny-bopperish—"having a blow-job with my brother. Where's Will?"

"He's fine." Finn shook his head quite amused by his sister's behavior. "He's just had one rum and Coke."

"Really?" Her one word sounded hopeful and sober.

"Really," Finn confirmed. "*We're,*" he emphasized the word jokingly, "staying sober. But I'm sure he would like to have more the way Pop has the stare on."

"Good."

I saw Nola's face relax with her response. I was glad that she was out with us and able to unwind sans her husband and child. She needed that release. And Will had behaved himself since the Christmas Day outburst. Even though he was a little bit in the doghouse with his father-in-law, and the way he chose to get his feelings out was not right, he had needed it too.

"Both of your hubbies, by the way," Finn said looking now to McEllie. "are too busy cleaning out the old man at poker to come and join us. Plus the Cincy game was on. Pop lost that too."

"I'll do the shot," was Nola's response.

"Cincy lost?" I chimed in my delayed reaction with a smirk considering our Thanksgiving bet.

"Yeah forty-one to twenty-three. Too bad you didn't lay down a bet huh, Rox?" Finn smiled knowingly.

"I think it should be ongoing," I slurred.

"Oh, do you?" Finn was so amused. He leaned into me so that only I could hear. "I'll give you that back massage, Baby, but then I can't guarantee I can live up to our pact." He nibbled on my ear and then suddenly pulled away, facing my sister-in-law. "McEllie? Shot? You're in, right?" Finn asked.

"I'll do the drink version and later I'll do the Lane ver—" She started but was talking about my brother.

"Ah! Ah! Ah!" I bellowed, still turned on by Finn's comment and holding my hands to my ears cutting McEllie off. "T.M.I. T—M—I!"

The four of us did the blow job shots as was customary with our hands behind our backs and picking the glass up with our mouths. I hesitated, which only made the whole scenario worse, because Finn got to watch with pleasure as I tilted my head back and drank. It wasn't pretty, but it was fun.

Finn immediately brought his mouth to mine sucking up any excess alcohol and then sensationally doing the same with my tongue as if he were giving mouth-to-mouth. I kissed him back with equal intensity. It felt like we were the only two in the room and, luckily, the others there were either family members or didn't care as to what was surely a regular display on campus grounds. We had lucked out.

Finn broke our action. "Another?" he asked referencing a shot.

"Finn…."

"Totally up to you."

He knew that the last time I got really, truly drunk led to a disastrous, life-changing incident—the conception of the child I gave up. And, hence, the reason I had been resistant of too much alcohol since then— the reason why Finn had never seen me drunk before. But then I remembered something else. Right before Finn had graduated, he had told me he would line up shots just to see me drunk. That's what he meant on the phone. That's what he was finally doing now. I smiled. I knew he was remembering too. And I knew I was in safe hands.

"Okay," I conceded. "One more. But none of this hands-free business and…I love you."

"I love you too." He kissed me softly and reassuringly.

Finn ordered another shot for the two of us as McEllie and Nola decided to call it a night and headed back to the hotel. After the shot, Finn paid off the tab, grabbed my red coat, helped me into it, and encouraged me to lean into him as we made our way out of the bar. I felt warm and toasty from both the alcohol swirling inside me and Finn's protective embrace. Letting my ears re-adjust to the sudden quietness of the evening, I spotted a bench not too far from the bar. Finn complied to my request to sit, although I am sure he thought I was completely nuts considering the cold December West Virginia air.

"I just want a moment alone with you. We've been with everyone for days now. I miss you and me time," I semi-pouted.

"I hear that." He sat on the bench first and then boosted me onto his lap.

I touched his cheek before unzipping his jacket just enough so that I could lean my head against his gray and black cotton shirt. "I love this shirt." I rubbed the side of my face against it.

"Mmm-hmm."

"I love this place." I spoke of our alma mater.

"I have a feeling you're loving just about everything right now." His chest moved with his slight laughter as we watched three co-eds stagger down the walkway.

"Well, the dancing is still up in the air." I was not about to give in on that. "But I do love everything right now...this is everything...," I cooed, "that I have ever wanted."

He shifted a little to make sure that his arms were around me as warmly as they could be. "What made you drink tonight? I mean, I know y'all were going out, but I've seen you milk a beer for hours or simply drink diet soda. At the most it's one margarita or one glass of wine."

"You," I said simply as I poked him in the chest with my index finger.

"Me? I'm not sure how to take that."

"You." I lifted my head and waited for his eyes to gaze down onto mine, which they did instantly. "You make me feel safe...like I can drink and not worry. I trust that you're always going to be here. You'll make sure I'm all right."

His kisses felt like ocean waves softly, steadily lapping onto the smooth shore. "I've got you. You know that. You're my forever, Lara. I won't let anything happen."

We kept up our pact. Not only did I not sleep with Finn that night, but I stayed in my mother's hotel room. It was nice camping out girl-style with her. She seemed more content than she had in quite a while. I assumed it was because she was finally truly single. She had been jumping from one bad relationship to the next for quite a few years and now it had been months since the last loser. When I questioned her about it, she admitted that she did, indeed, feel more free and happy simply being herself and not somebody's woman. But she had also started taking a drug for anxiety to help her get to that point. I wasn't going to question it. She was happy. And so was I.

\*\*\*

December 27—our wedding day. I had slept soundly

the night before and, amazingly, woke without a hangover. But the in-room coffee my mother already had brewing for me definitely helped. She went down to the lobby to get me some breakfast. As tradition stated, I wasn't supposed to see Finn until the ceremony, and my mother was bound and determined to keep it that way.

When my mom re-entered the room, she was carrying an individual-sized box of cereal and a banana. But she also had a red rose, a folder, and tears streaming down her face. I was on my laptop checking e-mail but scurried to close the computer and take the flower she handed to me.

"What's the matter?" I questioned.

"Nothing. Nothing. I just love that young man of yours." She wiped her tears and put the food near the gurgling, aromatic coffee maker.

"Too bad, Mom," I teased. "I saw him first." I sat back down on my bed smelling my non-scented flower and thinking of Finn, the obvious flower giver.

My mother sat down next to me and handed me the folder. I gingerly opened it and pulled out a large piece of paper. Once unfolded, I instantly recognized that it was a replica of the sign that I had made for Finn in Baltimore. Only this one said, *I ♥ U Lara!* On the bottom, Finn wrote me a short note:

*You are not only one in 30 thousand…you are my one and only in 30 million. I love you and can't wait to see you on our special day.*

I smiled, expecting nothing less from this magnificent man who was going to be my husband. I picked up my phone and sent him a text. *I ♥ U 2.*

\*\*\*

My mother and McEllie came along with me for my beauty appointment. There really wasn't a need for one since we were doing everything so simplistic, but it did seem like the thing to do on one's wedding day. I watched as my hair was pulled back on the sides and up to a fancy back bun. And my make-up was neutrally photo-ready despite our photographers being family.

As we made our way to a private room above the college chapel, the snow appeared to be dancing more than laying, making the day even more beautifully white and pure. Taking my dress out of the bag hanging on the door, I slipped into the form fitting white gown. I straightened the straps and made sure the built-in bra was adjusted the right way before catching a glimpse of my bare back in the mirror. It wasn't a dress I would have ever thought to pick. But I had tried it on a few weeks before on a whim and knew that it was the one. I hoped Finn would feel the same. For that was yet another tradition we maintained…the groom was not going to see the gown until the day of the wedding.

My mother, in her silver, long sleeved top and white skirt offered me words of encouragement. And McEllie, who wore a lavender dress, gave me a hug before she opened the door to let Lane in. The women were going to take their places in the chapel, giving me that final moment with my brother before he would accompany me to the moment I had been dreaming of.

Lane stopped mid-stroll when spotting me and said, "You've come a long way from blue jeans and big wheels."

"We both have," I admitted.

It was only being alone with him that the reality of the day started crashing in on me. I had moved away from home after high school and never really did go back for any extended stay. I had dealt with things at a young age that I shouldn't have had to, and it had forced me to grow up faster than most. I thought of myself as independent and pretty successful. But suddenly, in that room, at that moment, I was a little girl again…maybe for the first time an innocent little girl. And now was my time to truly get it right.

I held onto my older brother—my only true peer in life—and thanked him for not only being with me on that day but for being born in the first place. I wondered if I would have even survived if it hadn't been for Lane. He had been my protector from our abusive father. And eventually, I learned to protect myself...even if part of it was shutting down emotionally. But now I didn't need to. Now, I was safe and loved and protected and free.

Lane escorted me into the chapel to symbolically, if not verbally, hand me over to Finn. The rest of the family and the minister formed a circle around us. I smiled at my soon-to-be-family, trying to take it all in, knowing that most brides don't remember their wedding due to nerves and/or too many things to think about. I gave Finn's mother a hug as I approached. Adorned in navy blue, she was already dabbing her eyes. Looking like a bride herself in a frilly pink dress and those purple, sparkly shoes, I gave Kelsea the diminutive yellow flowers I was holding. She giggled and tried to smell them but, of course, they were a non-scented variety due to my allergies.

And then there was Finn. He was in the center like it was his own mini-stage. His black suit with white top and straight black tie made him look down-right dashing. His smile was so genuine, and he appeared as relaxed as I felt. Reaching out his hand for me, he took his time and punctuated every word individually. "You are so beautiful."

"Oh, wow, this is really happening," I said, now holding both of his hands in mine and gently rubbing my thumbs on his palms.

"I hope so." My soon-to-be-husband breathed a relaxing exhale. "I feel like I've been waiting for this moment my entire life."

"Me too." My soft whisper matched my smile.

His eyes, natural gray and adoring, would not leave mine even as he said to the minister, "I know it's not time yet, but can I kiss my girl?"

Out of the corner of my eye, I saw the clergyman tilt his nod in my direction, giving Finn his permission. But

I'm pretty sure it wouldn't have mattered. Finn was already leaning in and melting his soft lips delicately on mine.

My fiancé's smile spread serenely across his face before saying, "I promise to always let you have the far side of the bed and the seat against the wall."

I let out a soft chuckle having not expected a personal vow but appreciative of its humor and sincerity, nonetheless. As reciprocation, I adlibbed my own. "I promise to let you drive and dance with you."

He squeezed my hands then and became serious. "I vow no omissions, Lara. I vow no omissions ever again."

From the moment I had said that to him all those months before, he had taken it to heart. And even more importantly, he had lived up to it. Now Finn had officially made it part of our vows—our private pact was vocalized as part of our marriage promise. It most likely didn't mean much to those gathered in the semi-circle around us, but it meant the world to me.

"I love you," was my response.

"Forever." He snuck in another magical kiss.

"I'm not sure I'm even necessary here," the minister jokingly interjected causing light laughter from our collective family.

Finn turned to the actual person in charge of the vows and said, "Sorry. Let's do this."

To me, though, everything else was a formality. Finn's promise to love, cherish, etc. was in his kiss and that special, heartfelt vow. And his willingness to forsake all others was in the way he looked at me.

\*\*\*

After a fancy catered lunch, Finn and I headed straight to the airport. It was only then that I realized why he had insisted I have my passport when I left New York. We had an early evening flight that would have us eventually arriving in Ireland the next morning. So our "official" wedding night was spent in first class, thousands of miles high in the sky. While, by far, flying was not my favorite activity, the international flight seemed to be so much smoother than the shorter US flights. So I managed to fall asleep for most of it and only clung onto Finn because of love and not because of fear.

Once we landed in Dublin, we got our rental car and attempted to make our way to the private, countryside chalet Finn had rented miles from the city. It wasn't driving on the opposite side of the road or the narrow bridges or the sheep crossing that did us in…although those were a joy. It was the fact that the GPS mechanism wasn't behaving at all. It was taking double the amount of time it was supposed to, and we even started down a one way street the wrong way on two occasions. I was starting to feel anxious and irritated at the same time. Anxious because it had been a long flight and busy couple of days. Irritated because Finn wasn't helping the case. He refused to stop and ask directions despite us passing a couple people. Eventually, he pulled over and we went in a market to get the correct directions.

"Well, it didn't take you long to truly become a wife," Finn stated as we were finally back on track to our destination.

"Huh?" I said more relaxed.

"Nagging me about directions." He shook his head in a semi-joking way.

"I just don't like feeling lost. I'm kind of surprised," I paused thinking maybe I better not say it but had already started. "that you are okay with it…with what happened with your grandmother all those years ago."

"Baby, I'm not lost as long as I'm with you."

I knew he meant that very seriously, but it was also damn sweet. I lightened the mood further by reversing his initial comment on to him. "I think you were just trying out the stereotypical husband role and refusing to admit you were lost and stop."

"I was too distracted with your hand on my leg." He smiled.

Rubbing his thigh, I teased, "If we would get there sooner, my hand would be a lot more places." I then leaned over to flirt some kisses on his neck.

"Geez." He gripped the steering wheel harder when the car had swerved ever so slightly upon my lip action.

"You're fine." I laughed.

"I call 'uncle,' Lara!" He laughed back, but he was also semi-serious because he started to accelerate the car.

"It's only another five miles or so," I stated looking at the now back-on-track GPS.

"Yeah, well…." Before I knew it, he maneuvered the car to the side of the deserted road.

"Finn, what's—?"

"Baby," He moaned, tossing his dark sunglasses off and leaning over to draw me into a passionate kiss. "It's hard enough being away from you weeks on end. But to be next to you for days and not be with you? There's only so much a man can handle."

"Oh," I acknowledged, trying not to laugh and then turned serious. "Finn, I don't want our first time as a married couple to be in the back of a rental car."

"I—"

"Do you want me to…?" I asked, purposefully letting the question fade, because blow jobs, even with the love of my life, weren't my favorite, and I still didn't want that to be our first intimate act since tying the knot.

"No," he answered solidly. "I told you. Not that…you…in the back of a car. No."

Ah yes, his wicked rock-star past. He felt it was demeaning considering his memories of how he treated women back then. And he held me to higher standards, which I adored him for.

"I—" I started.

"I love you," he said, I'm sure just to nullify anything that was racing through my mind.

"Oh, my God!" I screeched looking past him and out the car window. "What is my mother doing here?"

Finn swung his head violently fast in the direction I was looking, but he saw nothing but mountains and grassy fields. "What are you talking about?" He turned back to me.

"Did that help?" I laughed.

He only paused for a half second and then burst into laughter himself. "Uh…yeah."

"Let's go. Cottage. Now."

His answer was to purposefully place his hand on *my* inner thigh. When I squirmed and shook my head, he kept his eyes straight ahead and pulled the car back onto the road. His grin was broad and teasing. "I think it's just another few miles."

# CHAPTER FIFTEEN

Finally, we arrived at the house, which was more estate than cottage. While Finn laid our suitcases near the bottom of the steps leading to the second story, I took off my gray wrap jacket. The warmth of the cottage felt good compared to the crispness of the outdoor Irish air. I sat down on the sofa to admire the coffee table that hosted a dozen unscented red roses and a bucket with chilling champagne. Without a word, Finn took off his dark baseball cap and sank onto the sofa next to me. His mouth met mine as his hands traveled under my white mesh sweater to find my black tank top. Even though it was mid-morning and we had been traveling all night, this was the true beginning of our honeymoon. And I was a girl.

"I got something special to change into."

"Really?" he said, toying with the strap of my bra. "You don't have to. You look gorgeous just like this."

"Thanks." I smiled, not believing, and got up. "Let me change. You'll like it. I promise."

"I'll bring your bag up." He stood too.

"Nah, it's light." I kissed him quickly, holding onto his hand. "Just meet me upstairs in a few." He drew my hand up to his mouth before letting me ascend the stairs.

\*\*\*

Finn didn't notice when I came out of the bathroom now wearing white lingerie trimmed in blue. His back was to me as he was turning on the stereo to something instrumental. I approached him from behind, covering his eyes with my hands, snuggling up against him, and stretching on my toes to nibble the back of his ears.

As he slowly turned around, I let my hands drop, allowing him a full view of my attire.

"My wife looks so damn hot."

"Yeah?"

"Baby, I can't wait to be with you." Finn handed me a glass of champagne while holding one of his own. His gaze locked into mine even more securely. "To all new firsts."

"To forever," I added, clinking his glass to mine.

Taking my glass and his, Finn placed them on the nightstand and then, using his masterful hands, quickly and tightly harnessed me to his body. I laughed, loving the feeling of possession and how I felt snuggled up against him. I kissed him as I started to take off his sweater curling it from the bottom up. Finishing, he tossed it to the ground, grabbed me in his arms, and carried me to the bed. We cascaded haphazardly onto the partially pulled down sheets and helped each other shed our remaining clothes. Naked, my head dangled slightly off the bed while Finn was planked above me kissing my neck.

"God, you're like pulsing," he half said, half appreciatively moaned.

"Shut up, Finn and make love to your wife."

"That turns you on doesn't it?" He smiled. "That word…'wife.'"

"You turn me on." I propped myself a little more onto my elbows and then went a little more sentimental. "But, yes, I never thought a word would mean as much as that one does."

Amazingly, it did. Despite knowing our already solid, loving bond, that little piece of paper made everything just a little better. It made things seem more safe, secure, confident.

His hands traveled back up my torso and his body became more parallel to mine. "Me too." He softly touched my face and let his hand rest on my lips.

"Finn, seriously, I can't be this close. I need you now." I ached, feeling our bodies flirtatiously touching one another yet still not being completely together.

"Wow! This is like our first time." He adequately recalled the first time we had ever made love and my similar need with his body teasingly near mine.

"But better." I kissed his newly adorned ring-fingered hand.

"I love you," my husband said in such earnest that the pause in action didn't matter at all. The sincerity and meaning of those simple words meant the world.

"I love you too," I echoed, feeling a loved tear form in the corner of my eye.

Whether it was the extended wait over the holiday week or the fact that we were committed like never before as husband and wife, our first time as a married couple was amazing. Our bodies, which naturally always seemed attuned to one another, were even more so. And my heart? Well, it overflowed.

Cuddling afterward, Finn spoke with his lips near my ear. "Glad we waited?"

"Ah, yes…no…all of the above."

"Ha!" He chuckled lightly. "Way to be decisive."

"The end result made it worth it, but I don't want to have to wait again," I clarified.

"I think this honeymoon is going to be making up for lost time." Finn moved his body so that he was able to cup my breasts and kiss me on the lips.

"Just these past few days or the years we missed?" I smiled.

"Now you're thinking, Beauty."

***

Our time in Ireland was the most amazing time I ever remember experiencing. I felt like I was truly free. I imagined it was what childhood should feel like—carefree, happy, and loved. Finn had, without a doubt, made the right decision to totally get away. While he was a top performing country music superstar in the US, that magnitude of celebrity did not quite reach the same level internationally. Therefore, he was able to be more himself during our time abroad—the self that only a few of us in his inner circle truly got to see and, even more so, the self that he used to be before the stardom. Whether it was drinking Guinness, singing, jigging, playing pool, exploring rock formations, shopping, or kissing the Blarney Stone, it was freedom, and it was love.

And not to be outdone or out-exhausted, when we flew back into New York on New Year's Day, we were able to go straight to our new, albeit sparsely decorated, home for the first time. Under the back deck, we found the packages Finn had requested Nola bring over for our first overnight—an air mattress, bed linens, and pillows. Plus, Nola included a few framed photos from our wedding and a loaf of bread, bottle of wine, and box of salt. I was confused. But Finn laughed, explaining that they were the same housewarming gifts given in *It's a Wonderful Life*. So, along with the drapery and two area rugs left from the previous owners, that was what we had in our home that first night. But it couldn't have been more beautiful.

Finn didn't miss a beat as he romantically carried his new bride across the threshold. We had Nola's wine and ate our first dinner in our new home—pizza delivery—literally on top of the kitchen's center island. And we made love in our master suite on the ever so comfortable air mattress.

\*\*\*

Reality rushed back soon enough, though. Cell phones were unmuted and my 5:35 wake-up alarm rang out the next day. While I had to return to work for two days before the weekend, Finn was in charge of all the deliveries of furniture we had ordered weeks before. It was fun to return home after work to discover something new each time. The dining room table.... The great room's soothing chairs, long comfy sofa, television, and multi-purpose wall unit.... The guest room's white bed and dresser.... Our sleek and stylish, king-sized master bed with black leather buttoned headboard. In addition, Finn immediately had a constant construction crew working on converting the lower level into his studio.

I decided to only wear my engagement ring at work and not my wedding band until the secret of our marriage was revealed to the public. When that happened, there would be a period of time when the press would be contacting us non-stop for details. And it was nice not to have to deal with that straight away.

What we *were* dealing with, though, was something that had bothered me before and now took a different spin since signing marriage certificates and joint agreements. I came home one day to tell Finn about a gorgeous, antique wardrobe with mirrored front that I had seen while shopping. He knew I had wanted one because it would give me more space to put some of my things and sit and get ready in the mornings. It wasn't a necessity, but it was beautiful, matched our décor, and we had the perfect spot for it.

"Why didn't you buy it?" Finn asked.

"Well, it's over six hundred dollars," I explained.

"Yeah? From what you described, it's perfect and a decent price."

"Yeah."

"Okaaaay…," he said in a leading, speculative way.

"Finn, I'm not going to spend that amount of money without asking you!" I exclaimed, wondering why he was confused.

"Lara…." He breathed out while shaking his head.

Walking over to my purse, which I had rested on the coffee table, he looked at me and then started to go in it. It didn't bother me at all. We had no omissions.

Finding what he was obviously looking for, he pulled out one of my credit cards and brought it up for my examination. "Is that your name on there?" he asked.

It was my turn to shake my head. I knew what he was doing…where he was going with his inquisition. "You know it is," I answered plainly.

"Oh, good. I was thinking maybe I was married to the wrong person. Because this is the credit card for my wife. So if it has my wife's name on it—your name—that means it's yours—your money."

"Finn…." But I didn't know how to proceed. I understood what he was saying. It just didn't seem true or right. And I didn't quite know how to explain that to him.

"Baby, it's money. It's fine. It's 600ish dollars. If it was 600,000 dollars I might want to know."

I understood he had more money—more money than I could possibly ever fathom. And when we got things, it was going to come from his earnings. I accepted that…pretty much. That was what got us the beautiful home we were living in. That was what got us all the furnishings and the studio below. But we had picked those things out together and, in essence, had agreed on the price. I couldn't just buy expensive things without talking with him. That's what was bothering me.

"Do you want me to tell you every time I spend more than fifty dollars?" He dipped his head down so that my slightly lower head would be looking at his.

"No. Of course not," I had to admit.

"Then it is fair. Why would *you* do that? Beauty," he

said trying to even my slightly elevated temperament. "I don't want to argue about money. Please," he pleaded. "Just like you not wanting anything on that damn prenup, there's a reason why I insisted on joint accounts. I want to make sure that what's mine is yours. I trust you. You know that. I trust you with my past, my truths, my love." He itemized them slowly for effect, and it worked. "So a plastic card or a bank account number is nothing. No matter how many zeros I have behind my name, it would mean nothing without you."

I took a moment to both soak in his words and try not to cry at their sentiment. Then I relied on my sarcasm. "What *do* you want to argue about then?"

His gorgeous smile appeared, and he went along with my banter. "Getting the laundry or cleaning the bathroom or eating potatoes for dinner."

I playfully smacked him on his red T-shirt. "You're doing all three."

"I'm putting my foot down on the potatoes."

"Then you'll be eating mashed potatoes." I laughed, pretty proud of myself for coming up with that answer so quickly.

His laugh told me he knew he had me back to the relaxed girl he loved. "Yes, Boss," he joked. "I'd even eat them burnt." He took my hand in his and twirled me dramatically around in a complete circle. "That's how much I love you, Lara Murphy." He then pulled me into his taut chest and swayed our bodies for a moment together. He was humming something, but I think it was just lovely, random bars. "We'll work on the money stuff, okay?"

Knowing that he truly did understand, I repeated those magical words back to him. "I love you too."

***

With our permission, Reese sent out a wedding press

release when Finn flew out at the end of January for the ACM announcements. That way, he figured, he could take the brunt of the press. When my cell phone belted out "Roxanne" in the middle of the day, I immediately grew concerned. Finn didn't normally call when I was at work.

I answered the phone while motioning to Vanessa, who was in my room during her prep. period, to give me a minute. "Hey," I tried to sound casual but then asked, "What's wrong?"

"Nothing," came my husband's alluring voice across the line. "You all right? Press or anybody bothering you?"

"Nah. All good. I never realized how many noises an empty house makes when you're not there, though."

"You've lived by yourself for years!" He half-laughed.

"Yeah, but this is a different house. I'll get used to it." I reassured him.

"I don't want you to. I'll be back soon."

"Yeah. Hey, li—" I started.

"I know, you can't talk. I just had to tell you something, though."

"What? Press is killing you, aren't they? Is it bad?"

"Lar?"

"Yeah?"

"I was nominated for Entertainer of the Year!"

"What?!" I screeched suddenly not caring that I was in my place of employment.

"I know. I was hoping for the Male Vocalist again, and I got that too, by the way, but—"

"Say it again." I interrupted him.

"Entertainer of the Year." It was his first nomination in that category.

"Oh! Oh! Oh! Aaaaa!" I yelled out putting my hand up for Vanessa to high-five me. As she did, I mouthed the words "Entertainer of the Year nom."

As I was literally dancing around the room, Finn's voice came through again. "It's just a nomination."

"Finn, that is awesome. Congratulations!"

"Thanks, Beauty. I'm kinda excited," he admitted.

"You should be. Call your parents. They're going to be stoked."

We exchanged "love yous" and hung up. Vanessa instantly began to pepper me with questions as she followed my lead, dancing halfway into the hall and high-fiving me again. I was so excited I didn't even care that students and teachers alike were glaring through their open classroom doors.

\*\*\*

On the days where our schedules meshed the right way, and it seemed Finn's star and demand on time increased even more since the nomination announcement, we canvased our home into a calming escape, especially since I had officially moved everything from my apartment. Instead of hiring some outsider, Finn and I spent snowy February weekends painting parts of the house. First up was the Yankees/boys adjoining bedrooms. Now our guest rooms, we painted those a color that reminded us of the sea glass embedded in my engagement ring. Next was the powder room—a quick coat of paint made it more earthy and attractive. And our master suite we painted in a sandy color to further enrich the black leather bed.

It was on one of those days that Finn was surely confused why he was getting a phone call from his own house while he was inside it. "Hello?" his perplexed voice emerged just before the fourth ring.

"Can you come up here?" I spoke into our landline.

"What? Yeah," he answered into his cell. "Where are you?"

"In the laundry room."

"Why are you whispering?"

"There's a spider. It's huge." Keeping my eyes planted on the creature, I ignored my husband's laughter and tried to defend my request. "I don't care about those little ones or the…Aaah…Aaah!" I cut myself off by screaming as the black furry thing decided to move ever so slightly in my direction.

Finn's laughter increased as he tried to give a calming directive of, "Step on it."

"It will crunch, and I don't have shoes on. It's so big. It will, ugh, crunch." The mere thought of that feel and sound under my foot nauseated me. "Can you just come up here?" I asked again, knowing he was in his downstairs studio.

"Isn't there a broom in there? Shoo it away." I got a double dose of my husband's voice as he opened the door to the laundry room.

But just as he did, the spider scurried under the bench where Finn's running shoes sat. Luckily, he saw the eight-legged demon and didn't think it was just my imagination. Hysterical housewife? Perhaps.

I hung up the landline and said, "See."

He acknowledged, "That really is big."

"I told you." I was still partially whispering as if the creature would attack based on the volume of my voice.

"And fast," Finn said, handing me his phone and bending down toward his running shoes.

"Uh-huh." I couldn't help but cringe and jump up onto the running washing machine.

The shakedown of the shoes proved pointless…no spider emerged. Finn grabbed the afore-mentioned broom and shoved it under the bench a few times, sweeping out toward us. Eventually, the predator emerged, letting Finn slam it with his shoe. I scrunched my nose as Finn picked up his shoe to inspect his handiwork.

"Is it dead? Just like that?" I asked.

"Looks like it." He put the broom and shoes back in their place. "Anything else you need me to do while I'm at your disposal?" he teased.

"Uh…." Suddenly, I felt foolish.

Finn mockingly shook his head. "How about a hug?"

Not waiting for an answer, he pulled me off the appliance and into his embrace. His voice now behind my ear, he asked, "What would you have done if I wasn't here?"

"I don't know. I would have had to do something. Run? Be really scared to come back in here?" As a thought crossed my mind, I pulled slightly away from my husband. "Do you think there's more? There have to be more. Where there's one, right?"

"Probably," he said honestly, if not exactly the answer I desired.

"I'll wear shoes next time," I said, causing him to laugh. "It's not funny. I got bitten badly once." I cited a time in college when my thumb actually bloomed to double its size.

"You think I don't remember that, Bed Bug?" he asked referencing the "don't let the bed bugs bite" quote he had said that night all those years ago.

I, ever so slightly, squinted my eyes at him. Of course he remembered. It was the infamous night of our first kiss. Being awakened by the bite, I had gone out to sit in the dorm lounge to monitor the situation when he and co-ed Decan had stumbled in drunk. One thing had led to another.

"The bite that started it all."

"For one of us." He raised one eyebrow, very well knowing that all those years ago I had blown him off thinking a) his kiss gesture was alcohol induced and b) I wasn't worthy of being loved. Unfortunately, it took more than seven years for me to realize that neither of those facts were true.

"Come here, Damsel." He smiled and scooped me up into his arms. "I'll protect you no matter what...."

# CHAPTER SIXTEEN

It could only work if everything went just according to plan. And it was completely possible even with having to coordinate schedules, times, and locations with not only Finn, but Nola, Will, and Kelsea. I was even looking forward to it.

Finn was performing and appearing on a late night television show. And since one of the other guests was a favorite actress of Nola's, he brought his sister along. Even though it would air later in the evening, it was recorded mid-day in Manhattan.

The plan was for me to get Kelsea from preschool after work and have a fun couple of hours with her at our house while Will was on an important work conference call at their home. He would then pick us up and drive the three of us into the city since I detested driving there myself. We would meet up with Finn and Nola at the penthouse and enjoy some downtime before all the grandparents flew in for Kelsea's mid-March birthday party the next day. The special location was because the Jamisons had purchased tickets for the little girl to see a Broadway show adaptation of her favorite animated television show.

That was the plan. It should have worked. It didn't. It

didn't by far.

Everything was fine until Will showed up. He was running a bit late. And while it didn't really matter since we had no specific time we needed to be somewhere, it made me anxious. That was just me. I liked things orderly. I liked things being timely and scheduled.

I took Kelsea out to Will's waiting car and was getting her in the back seat when I realized I forgot the wedding album I wanted to bring for Finn's parents to see. So Will took care of buckling Kelsea in, and I scurried back to the house. And then we were off.

Kelsea started telling her dad all about our afternoon while I texted Finn to let him know we were on our way. When the preschooler fell asleep almost as quickly as she had been rambling, I asked Will about his conference call and about when his parents were coming into the city. No longer distracted by Kelsea and texting, it was then that I realized something was off. Will wasn't saying much besides a couple muffled curse words at drivers who didn't really seem to be doing anything wrong. And his driving was a little fast especially when going around bends. I was trying not to think what my mind immediately went to. But then he totally blew off a stop sign.

Pulling at my seat belt to confirm its strength, I glanced at a sleeping Kelsea and tried a light-hearted approach with Will. "There was a stop sign there."

"Oh," he said. "Oh. Yeah, guess I didn't see it. Strange place for one. No need."

"Will," I started and scrunched my eyes. Visions of my childhood were screeching in my brain. I knew what was happening. I had been in a car one too many times with a person who had done the same exact things. But I didn't want to say or accuse Will of anything, especially when he had all of our lives in his hands at the moment. I had no idea what to do.

"What?" I noticed his voice was more gruff than normal too.

"Nothing." I backed down and looked at the speedometer and then out my side window. My stomach was churning, and it wasn't because of his driving. I needed to do or say something, but I couldn't.

"What's wrong?" he asked, and I wondered if I had made an outward sound of the one that was screaming in my head.

"Maybe we can stop and get a coffee," I managed to suggest.

"Uh, I don't know where there's some place convenient. Besides, we'll be there soon enough. You really need one?"

"No," I paused and then went for it. "But I think you might. You've been drinking, right? Will?"

"Oh, great—another wife. Geez, yeah…a couple cocktails. I'm fine."

I knew it. But hearing it confirmed made my stomach almost completely somersault. "Will…."

He shook his head in a semi-disgusted manner and continued to look directly ahead. I didn't know what to do. I couldn't think straight. And then the decision was made for me.

\*\*\*

"Roxanne" was blaring from my phone and Kelsea was yelling out for her dad. Will was being taken into the back seat of the police car. I had to make some decisions quick. Putting Will's car in gear, I followed the police car, keeping a safe distance, of course, in between, so I knew how to get to the station. Then I tried to soothe Kelsea the best I could with just my voice. I didn't dare turn and look at her. It felt like the police had a camera angled behind them just hoping I was another convict to haul into custody. They had already, after all, extensively questioned me about why I hadn't been the one driving and then lectured me about reckless endangerment. But, luckily, I think they believed my sincerity and also Kelsea's fright.

I was watching Will's head bobbing a little, and I wondered if he was talking with the officers or if he was just shaking it in wonderment of how we all were in the situation in the first place. That was when "Roxanne" belted out again, and I managed to hit the speaker button and answer. "Hey." I breathed out more than anything. My blood pressure was so high.

"Hey, Baby." His jovial voice was such a contrast. "How are you? I just tried calling, but—"

"Finn, you're on speaker and remember Kelsea is listening when I tell you something."

"Um, all right."

"Something happened. Is Nola with you? Is she…. Can she hear me?"

"Yeah." That was my sister-in-law's voice coming across the recognizable tinny sound of Finn's car phone speaker system. "What happened?"

"We were pulled over. Will…he…he was drinking. They—"

"Oh, God." Nola said at the same time as Finn yelled out a "What?"

"He's in the police car in front of me."

While Kelsea called out for her mom, Finn said, "Jesus. Are you guys all right? Are you all right?" The second question surged with more urgency.

"Yeah." I breathed out. "Yeah, I guess."

"What?" my husband asked, and I wasn't sure if he didn't hear me or if he just didn't like the "guess" part of my statement.

"Yeah, we're fine. You can meet us though, right?"

"God, freaking, yeah. I'm already turned around. I need to know where Lara. I need to know what station you're going to."

I said the name and offered little more. I *knew* little more. I was hoping between him, his sister, wi-fi, and GPS that they could figure it out. I needed to concentrate on

Kelsea and Will and my inner demons that were raging.

***

"Where's Finn?" I stood and asked my sister-in-law as she entered the police station and approached Kelsea and me at the hard plastic, blue seats.

"He's still in the car."

Her eyes were darting around the station looking from the active police officers at the desk, to the looming back hallway where I had last seen Will go, to her daughter who was innocently coloring in a small coloring book the nice receptionist had given us. It made me wonder how often children were subjected to the scene at hand. It made me sad.

"Mommy, can I show you something?"

"No, um, in a minute."

Kelsea, not waiting that minute, waved her picture at her mom. "I made this for you!"

She hadn't seemed to noticed her mother's distraught demeanor. I wondered what it was like to still have that innocence, especially after all she had already been through in her life. I wondered how long it would last.

Nola must have realized her abruptness with her daughter too, for she switched to a new gear and managed a, "That's beautiful, Kels. I love it. Make me another one just as nice."

"Okay!"

"He doesn't want to be seen?" I got back to my conversation with Nola.

I was referencing my husband's career and the precautions he had to take regarding what could get out to the press. Country music superstar in police station surely would be a PR mess. It didn't matter if he didn't have any part in the wrong-doing or not.

"He's talking with a lawyer—" Nola was just getting her reply out when Finn bustled through the door and beelined to me.

His look at me was so straight on, it was as if he was taking a picture so he could reassure himself that I was there in front of him. It almost brought a smile to my face had the situation not been so dire. The fact that he hadn't hesitated upon entering a public place—one that had cameras and dealt with reporters—reinforced his love for me. I had been brave up to that point, but knowing he was there and could take some of that armor away helped. I melted into his arms.

He pulled me away after just a few seconds, though. There were so many questions. "What's going on? Where is he? What exactly happened?"

"They're processing or something. I don't know what else is going to happen, but there's definitely a fine." I explained to both Finn and his sister. "I was going to offer to pay it—"

"Let his ass pay his own—"

"Finn!" Nola warned and glanced at Kelsea who seemed oblivious.

So did Finn to his sister's demand. "He was drinking. Damn it!" He looked from Nola to me, anger still bubbling through his pores. "Why did you get in the car with him?"

"I had no idea. I tried—"

"You son-of-a-bitch," Finn bellowed, and it took me a second to realize that he wasn't talking to me but Will who had approached from behind. Nola and I both took a precautionary half-step toward the men as Finn got closer to Will and continued. "What the hell were you thinking? That's my wife you had in your car. That's your little girl."

"I know, man. I know, okay? I know." The grumpy demeanor Will had portrayed in the car before being pulled over was gone. He just looked worn, deflated, and sorrowful.

"Daddy?" Kelsea's little voice made everyone swirl and chill for a moment.

"Hi, Curly Top." Will forced a smile. "You okay?"

"She's fine," Nola reassured in a fast-paced, weird kind of jovial manner. "Everyone is fine. It's all good. We'll just get you out of here and—"

"It's not fine, Nola," Will contradicted in a raised voice. "It's not. Christ, we're in a police station. I.... Everything is not fine. Quit pretending it is. It hasn't been. It hasn't been for so long now. You need to recognize that. You need to grieve. You need to let what happened happen, and let us be a family—the family we are now. We can't live like this."

I know my eyes grew wide. I could feel them. Finn was silent as well.

Poor Kelsea, she shouldn't have had to be witness to any of it—the car ride, the station, her parents arguing. I had been a Kelsea. I knew what that was like all too well.

"She"—I looked at my niece and spoke to the three other adults gathered around her—"she shouldn't be here."

"Can you take her, Lara?"

Finn was the one who asked. Will was still beaten down. Nola appeared to be in a state of shock from her husband's words.

"Yeah. We'll wait outside."

Finn dug into his pocket and handed his key fob to me. "Take her home...to our place," he clarified and seemed like he was a little less emotional and more in charge. "I don't know how long this is going to take."

I looked toward Nola and Will, who were still stoic. Then, looking back to my husband, I agreed. "Kels, your mom, dad, and Uncle Finn have to take care of some things. You and I are going back to my house. We'll have more fun there."

I tried to take her hand, but she went to Nola. "Mommy," she whined.

When Finn bent down to his little niece, I was so happy to see the interaction. Each time Finn saw Kelsea, he seemed to be gaining confidence about being with her. It was pretty much the way he used to be with her before Wyatt's accident. "C'mon, birthday girl. Aunt Lara might even let you open one of your gifts early."

That turned her around. "I like Aunt Lara."

"Yeah. I like her too." He smiled a quick, soft smile in my direction.

"I said it first." In that moment, she was pure preschool. But then some of that childish demeanor evaporated as she looked once again to her parents as if wondering if going with me really was the right thing to do.

And then it dawned on me that she might be remembering the last time I took her for an overnight and the three other adults had to deal with something. It was almost a year ago, but it was traumatic. It was the death of her brother.

"They're good, Kels. We are too. Everything…everyone is fine," I tried to reassure her.

She let Finn connect her hand with mine, and I was able to walk with her and her coloring book out of the station and to Finn's car. There wasn't a car seat, but we made do. I needed her and her little eyes away from the sirens, lights, uniforms, questionable figures, and, perhaps most of all, her sad parents.

\*\*\*

I hadn't been able to coax Kelsea into sleeping in our guest room. So, using my lap as her pillow and the sofa as her bed, she was softly gurgling in her sleep when Finn finally returned home. I held my index finger up to my lips in the universal quiet sign and pointed to the innocent child sprawled out on me. He, in turn, nodded and, without waking her, gathered her into his arms. I let him take her up the stairs while I breathed in a couple calming breaths. I needed those few minutes completely to myself to try to make sense of the chaos that had turned out to be that evening.

After Finn came back down, he silently sat on the sofa and opened his arms up to me. When I immediately found my natural fit in his strong, sturdy torso, he semi-sighed in a relaxing way and said, "This is the best feeling there could ever be."

"How are they?" I questioned without moving an inch. "Is everything okay?"

I had pretty much already found out via texting with Finn throughout the night that Will was being let go with a fine and had his license suspended for a while. He had also agreed to go to an AA meeting. I think a lot of it was because Finn was there to help.

"It's gonna work out. It's not gonna be easy. But right now, my concern is you. I know all of this…. God, Lara. I know this hit you in a way that—"

"I was scared," I admitted. "I was scared and weak."

"What?" He adjusted his body a little when he spoke so he could look at me.

But I remained snug. "I kinda…I froze. I couldn't do anything. It was like it was back all those years ago. My dad drunk and insisting he was all right to drive. I was too young then. But I'm not now. You're right, I should have done something. But I didn't know until we were already in the car and driving—"

"Lara," This time he forced me to sit up a little more erect. He wanted the direct contact of my eyes with his. "I shouldn't have said that to you at the station. I know you wouldn't have gotten in the car or put Kelsea in any kind of harm. Baby, I was so mad and worried when you called and told us. I couldn't release any of that until I saw you. And that's how it came out."

I nodded my head in a jittery way to accept his explanation, which I had kind of understood before he even told me. But it was still good to hear. "I'm mad at him, Finn. I know I shouldn't be—"

"Yes, you should be. And you should be mad at me too."

"You? What? Why?"

"You saw this happening with Will. You told me, and I didn't believe you. I blew it off. I think sometimes I'm around so much drinking in the business that I don't see it. But Will wasn't doing it for fun. He—"

"I know," I lamented.

"I know his pain. I get that. They have so much to work out. But I'm mad at him too. God, I could have torn him apart when I first saw him there in the station. The thought of you or Kelsea being hurt?" He exhaled at the same time I felt his muscles tighten. "But I need to work through that, because they were there for me. They were there when I did the same stupid stuff with…with drugs." It was always difficult for him to admit how hard he had fallen in the past—before his diagnosis and before me.

"You made it, and he's getting help. That's what matters. That's what will make it all right for all of us. I hate to say it, but it's almost like this had to happen… not only for him to see but for Nola too."

What Will had told me about Nola back at Thanksgiving and had alluded to at Christmas finally made sense. Nola's escape wasn't drugs or alcohol or building walls around her heart. Hers was to create a dreamy world of denial, and she was now being forced to wake up from it.

"Yeah." Finn's one word was so solemn.

"Thanks for taking care of all of us." I couldn't help but think of the stress he was under considering all the different needs of his loved ones and, at the same time, trying to keep his PTSD symptoms under control.

"Can we maybe stick with spiders next time?" He offered a closed but relaxed smile.

"I love you, Finn Murphy."

He patted his chest. And as I curled back into his body, he rested his lips on the top of my head for an extended moment. There was going to be a lot to deal with the next day and those to follow. But he was right— that embrace, that closeness of our bodies with our hearts beating against each other's was the best I-can-get-through-anything feeling in the world.

# CHAPTER SEVENTEEN

Spring seemed to go by at warp speed. Finn was really making an effort to stay in our New York home rather than be in Nashville as much. It worked out for the most part, but there were necessary trips there and elsewhere. Even though, of course, I missed him when he was away, I had been used to it and was now super busy with work and home ownership and neighborhood things. Besides, the rapture-filled reunions were almost worth him being away.

Finn did snag the Male Vocalist of the Year award at the ACMs that April. The awards took place on my birthday weekend. So he, unfortunately, had to fly out on my birthday. His apology for missing it, embarrassingly enough, was that I got a long distance happy birthday serenade via podium and television screen at the end of his acceptance speech. And, of course, it made every trending social media post possible. Finn did not win Entertainer of the Year. But I had a feeling it was a close vote. Everyone knew it was his to take in the near future.

My husband stuck to his word and backed up his brother-in-law in every way possible. While Finn wasn't Will's official sponsor, I knew there were a few phone calls or so between them that were the just-need-an-ear-to-listen-and-relate-to sort of thing. And because Nola was more accepting of how things were, they were slowly rebuilding.

Neither Finn nor I mentioned it, but we kind of entered a serene and careful phase during the end of April/beginning of May. Memories of the year before still lingered gravely in our minds. Our break-up back then had been sudden and terribly painful. And it was all because he didn't trust me to know something that he considered a fault, a chink in his armor—the PTSD/abandonment diagnosis.

Of course, now, a year later, we were in such a better place. And I loved him unconditionally. So, perhaps, it shouldn't have crossed our minds. But in a way, it was maybe best that it did. It reminded us to trust, love, and be there for one another no matter what.

Then, of course, the real day we both dreaded found its way into our lives. Finn had been moody for days. I could see the tension mount as he held his head and rubbed his eyes when he talked on the phone, finalizing plans for the summer tour beginning in just days.

It was the beginning of Memorial Day weekend and we were sitting in the airy great room. The sunlight was beaming brightly in through the expansive window wall. I was curled up in the swivel recliner reading a book. Finn was on the sofa with sheets of paper scattered around him and on the floor. They were all separate details that made the tour come together. The paper configuration made sense to him but not to me. His frustrated groan did though, as he hung up the phone. I set my book on the end table and walked over to him.

"Can I—" *Help* was what I was going to suggest when he interrupted me.

"Lara, c'mon, you almost stepped on that!"

"Sorry!" I tried to have it come out sincere, but it didn't have much of a chance. I challenged him to meet my eyes by staying still and quiet. When he did, I spoke a little more softly, "Can't we talk about it?"

"I just need some space. I told you before, you've gotta realize when to let me be. You've got to know when it's just too much."

"Oh, sorry I'm cramping your style." I hadn't put a filter on the sarcasm, and I should have.

"Lara…." The way he said my name was a mix between warning and sadness.

"I'm sorry. I don't want to fight…especially not today."

"Then why would you say that?"

"I don't—"

"Then damn it, let it be. Just…"—his voice crumpled a little as he stood up and said slower —"let…it…be."

"I want to be here for you and help."

His right fist quickly and violently found his other hand and then he put them up to his face in shame. "I've gotta get out of here for a while." He spoke much more softly and looked at me with those watery eyes.

I took a staggered breath. I didn't want him to leave. He was upset. And I knew why, but nothing was helping. *I* certainly wasn't.

"I'll give you space," I compromised. "Stay and work."

"No, I'm going for a run. I need the air." He looked at me for a second, gave me the quickest and slightly rough peck on the lips, and then proceeded to the laundry room for his running shoes.

\*\*\*

Finn had been gone a while—too long I was beginning to think. When he ran, he ran long and hard, but he should have been back. As I was trying not to worry, my phone rang announcing his call.

"Finn?" I answered, very well knowing.

"Hey." His voice sounded mellow. "Do you think you can pick me up?"

"Uh, sure. You all right?"

Pick him up? From running? Was he hurt? Did he get hit?

Before my manic mind could go any further, Finn answered my question. "I'm at the cemetery."

Oh. "You ran that far?"

"Yeah. Kinda don't think I want to run back."

I softly chuckled, glad that he was in a lighter mood than when he left. "No, I don't think so. Just let me grab my keys, and I'll be there."

"Thanks, Rox."

I smiled, hearing my favorite term of endearment of his, and then said one of my own, "Sure thing, Cowboy."

\*\*\*

I found him with his back propped up against the indoor mausoleum wall, legs outstretched, and his baseball cap next to him. The light came on when I opened the door to the room filled with the etched names of so many families' deceased loved ones. The light, triggered by motion, meant that Finn hadn't moved from that position in a while. Pre-opening the bottle of sports drink I brought, I sank down next to him, handed him the beverage, and leaned my head onto the shoulder of his sweat-soaked navy blue T-shirt. Finn silently tilted his head onto mine.

I looked at the wall in front of me. On some graves were photographs of the people who had passed. On others, there were mementos placed alongside flowers. Many of the grave markers were of couples. A few were single people. But there was only one so very young on that massive wall.

I hadn't been back to Wyatt's grave since right before I flew out for the wedding. I had gone by myself, somehow needing his blessing and/or wanting him to know that he was a part of our happiness. I never told Finn that I had. It wasn't a secret. I just knew he had a hard time seeing the concrete evidence of his nephew's death. He was better going to the beach where the memorial service had been. But he really didn't go there, either.

So seeing my love at this place, on this day, tore and melted my heart at the same time. I could only imagine the images flashing through Finn's mind. A year before, he and Wyatt had been singing in Manhattan, they had been riding a train, they had been walking on a sidewalk…and then a car was barreling right at them. There were also the images I didn't have to imagine—the devastating ones in the hospital I had been witness to… the ending of a life.

"Wy," Finn said out loud. "Aunt Lara's here. Too bad you never got to call her that. You would have thought you were the coolest kid in the school."

My hand in Finn's, I slowly stroked his index finger with my thumb. I had never thought about how Wyatt would have reacted to me being his new aunt and someone who worked in his school. I did think Finn's assessment was pretty accurate, though. "Just because I'm married to his cool uncle," I added, knowing how much Wyatt had idolized Finn.

"Well, there is that," he jested, and I looked up to witness an actual smile appear.

"There you are." I brushed my hand along the rough, emerging whiskers on his usually clean-shaven face.

"Lar, I think I'm ready."

"For?" I questioned although assuming he meant to go home.

He stayed seated though. "I know you think I've been moody because of, well because of today, and I have been, and I'm sorry." Before I could tell him he didn't need to apologize, Finn continued. "But the fact is, I've also been thinking a lot about…about having a baby. I think it took me sitting here somehow to realize how the love outweighs the pain. And it can overcome anything. I know we haven't talked about it in a while, but if it's something you want—"

Well, that wasn't what I was expecting. But, somehow, it made sense. I kissed him softly in the serene, peaceful setting.

"You. That's what I want. And it scares the crap out of me too," I said, because that was, essentially, what he was saying.

Did I want to be a parent? Yes. But could I be one? Did I deserve to be one after giving up a child?

"I know it does," he acknowledged, this time stroking *my* hand. "And, Lara, it shouldn't. You should be and would be the best parent a child could have," he said as if reading my mind.

"Together we could be."

"So? What do you think? Should we make it happen?"

I could see the excitement starting to enter his being. I could see the love already forming for this unknown child. I could see life returning after loss.

"Y'know, I just sliced open a watermelon while you were running." I touched my index finger to his nose.

"Did you now?" His grin was wide. "Don't think I need it, Baby, but if I'm—we're—planning on another workout, I might have the munchies afterward."

I leaned back into him. It was the first time in days that I felt like we were ourselves and, ironically, it was in the middle of a cemetery. We stared in silence at the wall in front of us for a few moments, lost in our own, yet, most likely, similar thoughts. I felt Finn's chest rise and fall as he took a gulp of the sports drink before standing both him and me up.

I took a couple steps forward and traced my hand along the hard, defined indentures of Wyatt's name on his grave marker. "Bye, Wy."

Finn placed his hand flat against the corner of the cold, rectangular surface. "See ya, Buddy."

Turning, he put his hand firmly in mine and opened the door. The bright sunlight contrasted the setting that we had just been entombed in, and it took a moment for our eyes to adjust. But the warmth felt good on our skin. Finn put his ball cap back on as I fished the car keys out of my clutch purse. I started to hand them over to him because he always took on the traditional, macho-man role of being the driver when we went somewhere together. And…it was in our vows.

"You mind driving?" he asked.

I looked at him query-eyed. "Uh, sure. No comments about my driving, though," I cautioned in a joking manner.

"Nope. I'll just enjoy the ride," he said with a touch of seduction. As I sat behind the steering wheel, Finn entered the passenger side and stated his reason for releasing the driving to me that afternoon. "I want to call Nol."

His eyes briefly acknowledged my soft smile before looking back down at his phone. I knew it was a big deal for him to call his sister on a day of such remembrance— the biggest of all. I knew some of that "what if" guilt found its way back to the surface of his brain where it had been buried a little deeper but had never fully gone away. And I knew my husband. If he didn't do it when he had the courage, he wouldn't do it.

"Tell Nola I'm thinking of them," I said in support for hitting the send button.

I listened to Finn's conversation with his sister on the ride back to our place. Being a captivate audience, I had no other choice. I think Finn wanted it that way. I was his security blanket.

The beginning of their conversation was generic with Finn hearing about the start of their long four-day weekend getaway. Nola, Kelsea, and Will were visiting Will's parents in Boston. They had chosen to get away and not be near all the remembrances of a year prior. Their relationship was still a work in progress, but things seemed to be definitely on the upside of the deep, dark hole it had been in.

I could tell Nola must have asked about me because Finn put his hand on my thigh. "Yeah, she's right here.

She's driving." After listening a moment, Finn replied to his sister with, "Well, we, uh, actually are coming home from the cemetery." Finn was looking out his side window and listening before responding to a litany of his sister's questions. "Yeah...Yeah, it's all okay....It was. I'm fine though. I'm calling to check on you...Of course. I just wish—"

I knew what he wished and his sister did too. But it didn't need to be verbalized. That would be too hard. And, the fact is, some wishes just can't come true.

So I cut him off with, "Tell her I said I'm thinking of them."

After a second, Finn turned to me. "She heard you and wants to know if we want to do dinner before the tour kicks off."

That, thank goodness, turned the conversation back. Everyone talked. It was acknowledged. Everyone knew that everyone loved and cared for one another. But sadness and regrets weren't going to help.

"If you can fit it in," I said to Finn, knowing that the tour was mere days away and those days were jam-packed and stressful.

We were pulling into the garage as Finn and his sister were hashing out the details of the dinner. I left him to finish his conversation and strip out of his sweaty clothes in the laundry room as I walked into the great room. The papers were still where he had left them. And I knew when he re-entered, reality would set back in. Although calmer, he would dive right back into the chaos of being Male Vocalist of the Year.

His hands surprised me from behind, wrapping ever so tightly against my waist. His chin dipped down to rest on my shoulder. Still from behind and still with his hands in place, he started walking us both through the center of the room. I resisted, knowing I was going near the papers.

When Finn urged me on, I recalled our earlier testy conversation. "I'm going to step on those."

Finn, now just in his boxer briefs, spun me around. "I'm sorry, Beauty. You didn't deserve to be treated the way I have been—"

"Finn, no," I interrupted. "It's all right."

"It's not." He put his hand up to my cheek. "I just forgot what was important."

"That's not true at all. You were remembering what was important, and sometimes that's painful and sad. I knew that."

"You are my rock, Lara...my lifeline. I love you more than I can say. Thank you for being my girl."

I loved how sensitive Finn could be. I knew I was deeply blessed in that area. It was just that I still, because of my upbringing, wasn't used to the raw, honest, outward emotion.

So I replied with, "I love you too," and then chose to go with my sassier, sarcastic side. "You want to be Entertainer of the Year? Why don't you start by entertaining me in the bedro—"

My sentence was broken up because Finn started tickling my sides. With him chasing me into the room's name that I couldn't finish, our playfulness turned to passion. We made love that day not to conceive a child but because of how much we needed, wanted, treasured, trusted, and, most of all, loved one another.

# CHAPTER EIGHTEEN

Finn left almost a week after that day. He flew to Nashville for the CMT awards and to finalize a few things. Then he was off for the first stop of his tour.

In contrast, during that time, I was busy with the final days of work before summer and getting things in order for both Finn and I to be away for a couple months. Because, yes, I was going on tour again. I don't think he would have toured otherwise. Although I'm sure all his managers, reps, etc. would have had quite a few choice words to say if he hadn't. It was a moot point, regardless, because I simply loved the freedom of the road and experiencing that side of his life almost as much as he did. And he beamed on stage. It was why he sang his songs— so that others could enjoy and find their escape too.

I met up with Finn and entourage a week after I was done with work. He was at his third tour stop—Cleveland. The crew and band welcomed me whole-heartedly. Although Carter was a little reserved…and with due reason. He had broken it off, via text nonetheless, with Vanessa. Not that they were hot and heavy and seeing each other on any sort of routine basis. But they did speak regularly and had spent part of the holidays together.

Vanessa had tried to play it off that she knew what the situation was from the start—casual, fun, no commitments. But like most of womankind, her feelings got involved and, consequently, were wounded. Sex is never just sex. My first time with Finn was proof of that.

Finn was sensitive to the awkwardness initially between Carter and me, but I didn't want him to be caught in the middle. So I stuck up for my "sista," giving Carter disapproving glares and nothing else for a day or so. But the day of the next concert stop, I walked straight up to him and slapped him across the face. I hadn't realized Finn was nearby. But I found out quickly enough when he tried to pull me away.

"Hold up, Cowboy," I directed my comment to my husband and planted my feet firmly.

"Lara, what are you doing?" *Astonished* pretty much summed up Finn's reaction.

Looking at Carter, who was simply staring at me and rubbing his cheek, I stuck out my hand for Finn's drummer to shake. "All square?" I asked.

"You're a cool chick, Lara." Carter took my hand as an offering. "And I deserved that. You know, I'm sure I'll regret ending it with Nessa. But I'm not your boy here. I'm not ready for happily ever after. So it's better now—"

"You better just hope that when you are, there's someone out there," I prophesized, now feeling a slight sting from the slap.

"C'mon, Slugger," Finn mocked. "Let's get some ice for the hand. You all right, Carter?"

"Yeah. There was no wind up. We're cool, right, Lara Li?"

"Until I beat you at poker tonight," I smiled teasingly.

"Oh, geez." Finn shook his head and started walking off with me. "Thanks," he said once we were out of earshot of Carter—an obvious reference to my unorthodox peacemaking efforts.

"I feel sorry for him. He's a good guy, you know? He's

gonna miss his chance."

"Glad it's not me."

"What? The sore cheek or the being single?"

"Both." Finn smiled.

"Me too."

"You need ice?"

"No. It wasn't that hard. It was more for effect. Maybe a little kiss would help?" I taunted.

"Uh-huh." Finn brought my hand up to his lips.

"And my lips, for some reason, sting too," I pouted.

"If you mention any other part of your body, right now, I might be late getting on stage. Not that I would have a problem with that." He laughed but kissed me softly on the lips as if he were actually healing me.

\*\*\*

It was at a different tour stop, mid-summer, when I almost slapped someone else. And this time, it wouldn't have just been for effect. It was the legitimate fighter in me.

It was the fifth of July—post-concert. Even though the sun had set hours before, the heat and humidity still clung in the dark, night air. I was in Finn's arms, gathered with the band and some crew. There were the traditional drinks and relaxed chatter as we sat in a haphazard circle just outside the area where the busses were parked. I was noting how spectacularly clear the night sky was when somebody from afar must have set off a random leftover firework from the night before. The sudden, out-of-the-blue sound caused me to jump, ruining the tranquility of the night and instantly putting my nerves a little on edge.

Finn soothingly ran his hand down the back of my hair a couple times before kissing the top of my head. "You're okay."

"I know," I replied. "I just wasn't expecting it." I could be backstage at his concert every night without headphones or watch an entire fireworks show and be fine, but any unexpected loud burst threw me every time. It was just like my dad had been when drinking—explosive without warning. "I don't like—" I started, only to be interrupted by another unforeseen disruption.

A blonde, probably in her early twenties, strolled right into our gathering, asking if anyone had a light. I didn't recognize her. But I knew, with the exaggerated make-up and hair piled crookedly on top her head in a bunch of curls, that she wasn't a member of Finn's team. The only thing I could figure was that she one of the crew's family members that I hadn't been introduced to and who had just joined us for the night.

But Finn didn't recognize her either. "And you are?" he asked.

"Poppy like the flower," she pronounced a bit slurred.

"Who are you with?" Finn asked sitting both of us up a little straighter. "Sorry, I don't seem to—"

"I'm with you Finny, all the way." She giggled, approaching my husband while playing with the sleeve of her leopard print dress.

I felt Finn's body tense at the same time mine did. Poppy wasn't a member of the team or invited by one. Finn grabbed my hand and stood both of us up. Most of the rest of the group, who also seemed now more on alert, mimicked him. A fan should not have gotten through to where we had all been gathered.

"Miss, you are not permitted to be here. You need to leave," Hawk interjected, taking a couple steps toward the three of us.

"I paid for a ticket," she proclaimed as if that justified the trespassing.

"And thanks for coming to the show." Gracious, Finn, I knew, was just trying to pacify the situation. "But it's time to go."

"Here, in fact," Hawk offered. "I will be your personal escort—"

"Finn?" She didn't even acknowledge Hawk. "Wanta have some fun? I can lick and suck you until you're numb. We can go all night."

I let go of Finn's hand then so I could turn away. It was bad enough watching all the screaming women in the stands yelling for my husband as if he were theirs. But to hear those words come from one of their mouths…. I just needed to breathe. It was a worse intrusion than the firework.

"That's right, bitch, move aside," came her voice from behind my back.

Instantly, I spun back around. "What did you say?"

I had had enough of her behavior. She was acting more childish than an actual child. While I accepted the sidebars that came along with being Finn's wife, I had an extremely hard time dealing with ignorant people in general. If they were drunk and obnoxious, forget it.

"I said," she spit out vehemently yet garbled. "I'm going to kill you."

"Hawk!" Finn belted out while simultaneously shielding his body in front of mine.

Hawk stepped up as I tried to get in front of Finn and toward the more-tramp-than-woman. She had no idea who she was dealing with. I had been through so much worse in my life.

"Lara," Hawk gently took my arm. "Come on, let's get you to the bus."

"But, what about Fi—" I started.

"He needs to know that you're safe."

When I looked to my husband, he pleaded. "Baby, please."

I hesitated and then took note of the loyal members of his band and crew. He was well covered. So I conceded that, at that moment, I was more of a distraction. Reluctantly, I let Hawk walk me and a couple of the other women in our group to the bus. Once secured, we could hear some arguing from outside and Hawk left to assist. I was worried, but I was also pissed. I was a rule follower, and it irritated me that someone like that girl would just blatantly abuse someone's right to privacy and take away what limited personal time he might have—what extremely limited time he had—to be with me.

The incident was over in the matter of minutes, but it changed the whole evening. When Finn entered the bus, it was just with Hawk. And it was obvious how angry he was.

"How the hell did she get through?" he bellowed. Despite being furious, he walked straight over to me, securing me in his muscular arms.

"I don't know, Chief," Hawk answered.

"Heads are going to roll," Finn's voice came from above my sheltered body.

"It's dealt with. Just...just calm down," Hawk attempted to pacify Finn.

I looked up at my husband. He was truly angry. I pulled my body tightly into his and started to stroke his back with my hands. I needed him to calm down too. He didn't need this to escalate. Everything was fine. I willed him to feel my touch and my calmness.

"She fucking threatened her," was what I heard from him instead.

"Finn, she was drunk and young. Don't get me wrong, it wasn't right what she did, but it's taken care of," Hawk countered, and I watched out of the corner of my eye as the rest of the group that had gathered in the bus left.

"It better be." Still pissed, Finn looked at me but spoke softer, "Are you all right?"

"I'm fine."

I felt more than heard his exhale. "I need some time with Lara," Finn stated while slowly rubbing circles on my T-shirt covered back.

Hawk stretched his hand out wide and clamped it down on Finn's shoulder the way men do. "You got it," he said before exiting the bus with the click of the door handle.

Now alone, Finn gently pulled away from me. "Thanks for going with Hawk," he said searching my eyes. "I know you didn't want to. But I promise you, you know I just wanted to make sure you were safe. I wasn't trying to dismiss you."

I claimed his hands with mine. I appreciated his sentiment. Finn knew I detested being regarded as an insignificant child, and he wanted to make a point of letting me know that was not his intention or purpose.

"I was worried about *you*." I emphasized the last word.

"I know you were." He rubbed his knuckle along my cheek. "But it wasn't me that she threatened."

"It wasn't me that she wanted," I rebutted. "Have you ever had anyone do that before?"

He dropped his hand. "Get into camp? No. But the comment? Yeah. I mean…sometimes. Not usually that, uh, suggestive…sexually straightforward. You know, it's usually innocent flirtation."

"That didn't seem innocent to me."

"Lara, seriously, it was nothing. I overreacted because of you. And like Hawk said, it's taken care of."

I knew it was. And I even knew that the girl was not a threat—just a combination of one too many and how the world celebritizes those in the entertainment industry. In a way though, I was glad Finn took it seriously and, at the same time, remained calm enough not to let his anger build up or explode.

"Lar?" he asked after a moment.

"Just so we're clear," Knowing I was calmer, myself, I decided to further pacify the situation with a serious statement underscored by lightheartedness. "If anyone is going to do those things to you, it's going to be me."

That got a genuine chuckle from my husband. "You were like a fierce lioness out there."

"I meant every word."

"I know you did." He smiled and opened up his arms. "Come here. Wrap those arms around me. Tell me that you love me."

"Every day, every moment," I declared and did exactly as he asked.

"That's my girl."

\*\*\*

Between me extending my stay on tour five days longer than the year before and Finn finishing up earlier because he started earlier, it was a little less than a month that we were apart at the tail end of the summer. Finn's tour wrapped a couple days before his September 11 birthday. And he took almost a month off just to unwind. Meaning, he was focused on writing music and setting up business opportunities via telephone rather than actually going out and attending functions or performing. And, as a reunited couple, that was a little piece of heaven on earth.

But in early October, Finn flew down to Nashville to record some new songs and be the guest co-host on a national weekly country countdown radio show. It was a short visit, but it also signified the end of his mini-break. The demand on his time was revamped with television appearances and photo shoots and meetings, particularly because the CMA Awards were a month away and Finn had been nominated for Entertainer of the Year for those awards too.

I thought I had his fast-paced schedule down and was okay with it...until I wasn't. Until that last straw. Until I broke.

First Finn had moved his departure date for the CMAs up five days—making the time before I would join him now nearly ten days. And then on the first Saturday in November—the last night that we were supposed to be together before he left—he had to back out of an engagement party for my friend Dinah. He was, unexpectedly, going to have to spend the night holed up in his downstairs studio.

Disappointed, I, regardless, told him it was all right and went to the party alone, not really knowing anyone besides the bride-to-be. I tried to mix and mingle, but I wasn't in my social Lara mood. It was even to the point that the food didn't even seem appetizing. I hung in there for Dinah's sake, though—the solo act at a couple's party.

When I got home around 11:30, Finn was, as suspected, still cocooned in the studio. He smiled from behind the glass and motioned with his finger that he would be done in a minute. Exceptionally tired from the evening's festivities, I retreated back up the stairs, and, before I knew it, fell instantly asleep in our master bedroom.

\*\*\*

Standing at the foot of our bed, Finn had a towel wrapped around his waist and his hair was still wet from the shower when I awoke the next morning. "Hey, Sleepyhead," he joshed. "How often is it that I'm awake before you?"

I glanced over at the bedside clock. It was much later than I usually slept in. "Yeah. Guess I was tired. When did you come to bed?" I swung my feet out from under the covers and toward the floor.

"Right after you. You were zonked, though." He made his way to me, planting a few soft, feathery kisses on my lips. "Morning." He smiled.

"Mor—" I started and then retracted both my word and my body.

"What's wrong?" he asked, alarmed while sitting next to me on the bed.

"What are you wearing? Do you have on some type of cologne?" It wasn't a bad smell. I just couldn't handle any strong scent.

"Of course not." He actually sniffed his own arm. "What are you talking about? You know I won't wear anything because of your allergies."

I leaned over to his damp hair and drew in some air through my nose. "It's your shampoo."

"Lara, it's the same shampoo I use all the time. It's not even a new bottle."

"It's too strong," I whined and got up to go into the adjoining bathroom.

It was definitely the shampoo. The scent from the shower still lingered, actually making me a little nauseous. I started to brush my teeth hoping the minty taste and scent would erase my sudden mini-allergy attack.

"Do you want me to rinse my hair again?" Finn was beside me now.

"No," I denied while walking back into the bedroom in search of my Yoga attire. "It's fine. The smell will fade."

"That's so weird." He strung his legs through a pair of boxer briefs and then changed the subject. "How was the party?"

"It was okay."

"Yeah?" He sat back on the unmade bed, casually watching me getting dressed.

"Yeah."

"That's it? It was okay?"

Between the shampoo and the fact that he was leaving again, I really couldn't handle any more questions or comments about the miserable night before. Now with leggings and a T-shirt adorning my body, I turned to him. "I just thought that getting married meant I didn't have to do things—go to things—by myself." I hadn't said it in a harsh tone, but the statement was enough.

He answered in a similar tone but opposing view. "I thought getting married was about being in love with only one person forever."

"Finn…," I started, but realized he was right. I should have never defined marriage that way. It was a false representation of the point I was trying to make. "I know you work hard to make all of this happen—your career and being here. I know you have made a lot of sacrifices. I do. I get it. And last night, it shouldn't have been a big deal, but, I…you know—"

He had started getting off the bed mid-way through my dialogue and was now in front of me. "You know what I'm dealing with right now. The media surrounding the Entertainer of the Year nominees is insane, even if it is a long shot. An engagement party? It's not a priority."

"I guess I'm not either." Maybe I shouldn't have said it, but I, unfortunately, meant it.

"Don't." His eyes pierced mine momentarily letting me know I had crossed the line. "You know that's not true. And you told me you were fine last night. You said—"

"Well, I guess I wasn't." Damn it! I was near tears, and I didn't want to be. "I've gotta go."

"What? Where?" The man who had hundreds of lyrics memorized in his head and never forgot an important moment in our lives was truly perplexed.

And it pissed me off. So sarcasm escaped immediately. "Thanks for remembering. Piloxing class and then lunch with Vanessa."

If he felt bad about not remembering my mundane suburban schedule, he didn't let it be known. "And that's a priority?"

"That's a commitment." I punctuated each word, knowing that the truth stung.

Finn took a breath. "Look, Lar, I would have rather been there last night than here dealing with all this crap."

I appreciated that he said it, but, in reality, I knew he would probably have preferred anything with music over attending something with people who weren't used to being in the company of a celebrity. "No you wouldn't have," I said a little more softly.

"Well, I would rather have been with you."

That I couldn't argue. I knew in my heart that he would have wanted to be with me. But the fact was, he hadn't been. And I also knew I should have been used to doing things on my own. In all actuality, before Finn, I had been quite used to it—it had been the only option as a single woman. I had gone to the movies by myself and attended parties by myself before. But something was bothering me—whether it was him changing his mind at the last minute, his amped up schedule, or just me being needy. I knew I was both a little right and a little wrong. But I had to let it go, at least in the moment, because he was leaving, and I couldn't let that happen without wishing him well. It was almost a superstition of mine.

"Have a safe trip." By the time I got home from a late lunch, Finn would be on his way to the city for a press conference and then was spending the night at the penthouse before taking off for Nashville early the next morning.

His eyes bounced all over mine as if they were searching me for the right words...knowing that we had stopped mid-disagreement. Finally, he rested on the forgone conclusion. "I'll see you in a couple days."

"A lot more than a couple," I clarified in the same tone that the rest of our conversation had taken, because ten days was nowhere near a couple.

"I'll see you in a 'little more than' a couple days." He offered a middle ground and leaned in to kiss me. But it was short and not so sweet on either of our parts.

\*\*\*

I had a lot of energy to burn up in Piloxing class. Every side kick or air speed bag had Finn's or the music industry's name on it. Every bead of sweat took the place of a tear. Until it didn't. About two-thirds of the way in, I tired out. I wasn't running as fast or following the moves as well. And the juice and protein bar I had gobbled for breakfast were even threatening to come up. I had exhausted every emotion except for a tiny bit of regret. But, again, I made it through.

When Vanessa noticed at lunch that something was off, I didn't even try to deny it. "Finn and I had words."

"What are you—a proper English grandmother? You 'had words'?" She laughed with robust.

She was laughing so hard, I couldn't help but join her which, admittedly, helped my demeanor. Wiping a laughter tear from my cheek, I clarified. "We argued. Is that better?"

"Wording is better. The fact that you now ruined my fairy tale view of the two of you is not."

"Oh, please!" I threw my napkin at her.

"It was bad?" she asked more seriously.

"No. I was pissy," I admitted to both Vanessa and myself. Exercise, a good friend, and a little nourishment had helped bring that clarification to my brain. "And he didn't give in. But the worst part is, he's leaving today to go to Nashville for a couple weeks."

"Then you better find a different word—a better word—than whatever words you did have"—she smiled—"before he leaves."

I thanked her and left some cash for the restaurant bill before taking off to my car. When I looked at my phone, I noticed how late it was and calculated in my head where Finn would be. He would most definitely be on his way into the city by then. Even though our conversation would not be in person, I had to at least call him. I was still upset, and I'm sure he was too. It had not been a good way to leave things, especially since we wouldn't see one another for a while.

When he picked up, the slight vibration sound of the car's speaker confirmed that he was, indeed, driving. "Yeah?" As suspected, his greeting was abrupt.

"Thanks for answering."

"Yeah. What do you need, Lara?" He was definitely setting the tone—no soft sounding words, a direct question, using my proper name not a shortened version or nickname….

And knowing I deserved it, I answered honestly. "I need us to be okay."

He paused only slightly before questioning. "Where are you?"

"I'm getting ready to leave New Italian Diner."

His response was something between a sigh and a calming exhale. "I can't backtrack that far. Hold on." After a moment, "Do you think you can meet me?" he asked, giving me directions to a rest stop off the highway.

"Yeah," I agreed. I hadn't expected to see him in person but was glad that he suggested it. I knew we couldn't end things the way we had. We had to make things better before he left. Absence making the heart grow fonder wasn't always true, especially because his absence the night before was what had ignited the furious flame in the first place.

# CHAPTER NINETEEN

Conveniently apart from most of the other vehicles, I found Finn's car parked at the side of the rest stop's building. I pulled the Jeep into the empty spot next to his and turned off the engine. Finn, who was texting something, looked over at me, laid his phone on the dash and reached over to open the passenger door. I acknowledged his invitation by exiting my car and sliding into the passenger side of his.

As soon as I closed the door, he said, "First of all, I love you."

It was my turn to sigh. "I don't need to hear that, Finn. I know that." *But it never hurt*, I silently made the postscript to myself.

"Well, I need to say it. And you know, maybe *I* need to hear it."

"I love you," I said without hesitation. "I will say it as many times as you need me to. But I'm not going to say I'm sorry."

"Well, Lara," he said matter-of-factly. "I'm not either. You know what my life is like. And you told me...you told me," he reiterated as if I didn't remember what I had said. "it was okay not to go last night."

"I know I did. That was a mistake. But I'm not apologizing. I'm not apologizing for saying what I did…wanting you to be with me."

He wrung his hands through his hair in an obvious show of frustration for our word merry-go-round. "So? So, what then? What do we do?"

I didn't answer. I didn't have an answer. I didn't even know why I was reacting the way I was. Everything he said was true. I had never, ever been the needy type or dependent on someone else. Yes, I loved him and would always like him to be around, but this emotion was different. Where was it coming from?

It was Finn's phone that broke the standoff between us. He looked from it to me and said, "Lara, I need to go. I'm going to be late for that press conference."

"Now? Now you're concerned about being late?" I queried to the man who was, at best, laisse faire about promptness.

Tears started to threaten to release. Damn it! Why couldn't I keep anything together? His hand started ever so slightly to go toward me in an act of comfort. But he resisted, surely thinking of my unkind, if accurate, words.

"Look,"—his voice seemed to be restrained—"do you want me to postpone or cancel it so we can hash this out? If you think we absolutely need to do that and that we can—"

"No," was my monosyllabic answer.

"No? You don't think we can resolve this? No? You're not willing to—"

Before he got more upset, I clarified. "No. Go to the press conference. It means a lot that you offered." It did.

"Lara," I could see in his still non-superstar gray eyes and hear it in his best friend voice, how concerned and torn he was. "You're still upset…we're upset. This day just did not start out right." When I didn't deny it, he devised Plan B. "Can you come with me? I'll do the press conference and then meet you at the penthouse. I'll make sure to tell them I am not to be bothered. We can spend the night…have the time to just—"

"But I have work tomorrow."

Finn's white-knuckled hands grasped the steering wheel. "I'm trying to meet you ha—"

It was more than halfway, and I knew it. "All right. I'll call off sick tomorrow and have Vanessa put anything that needs to be out on my desk."

"Okay." He exhaled.

"I hate driving into the city."

"Leave the Jeep here. I'll have a driver drop you off tomorrow. It'll be fine. There's always tons of cars at a rest stop day and night."

"Let me just get my purse."

I did just that and secured the Jeep with a sounding, locking beep before stepping back into Finn's car. Before I even had my seat belt fully snapped, he had the car whipped into reverse and was tearing out of the parking lot. Part of it, sure, was because he was late. But I knew him. He also needed the speed of the automobile to release some of the tension that still hung awkwardly between us. To his credit, he first got on his phone and made the call he promised and then turned on the radio. I could hear a commercial and then a D.J.'s voice filling the otherwise silent car. Discreetly drying my tears, I got lost in my own thoughts, replaying what did, indeed, go wrong that day.

My introspective ended with Finn saying, "Shit!"

"What?" I turned my head toward him obviously concerned.

He didn't answer directly. He just turned up the radio. Broadcasting in all its old school glory was "Roxanne."

"Well, that's random," I offered.

He twitched a smile in my direction and held out his right hand. When I took it with my left, he grasped on securely. I confirmed our unity with an extra squeeze before our entwined hands found a resting place on his leg.

But that moment didn't last. It was only a matter of minutes before we were in the hubbub of the noisy, bustling city, which required Finn's absolute, devout driving concentration. And then he literally dropped me off at the front entrance of the building that was home to the penthouse and sped off to his destination.

\*\*\*

When Finn eventually arrived back at the penthouse, he found me looking out the balcony doors to the stretching Manhattan skyline and Central Park. Thanks to a shower, change of clothes, and talking with Vanessa, I was refreshed and renewed. In contrast, he looked a little worn from the day. Ceremoniously, he turned off his phone, placed it in his small carry-on bag, and stuck it on a dining room chair.

"All right, Lara, let's get into it. Yell. Tell me I'm neglecting you. Whatever. But let's get through this."

I felt like a cartoon character. In slow motion, my mouth fell open and my eyes sadly widened. I thought we *were* through it. Spontaneous "Roxanne" on the radio had done it for me. He had gone to the press conference with things still festering, while I had welcomed the warm spray of a pulsating shower and thought how grateful I was that he had arranged the night.

I plowed into his body, taking him by surprise. As he slowly encircled his arms around my lower back, I said, "I'm sorry." And then I tugged him in even tighter.

After a moment, he pulled me away to arm's length. Looking directly into my eyes, he asked, "You sure?"

"Yeah."

"You're all right with everything?"

"Yeah," I answered. "Do *you* need to yell at *me*?"

"No." He kindly touched my face with the back of his soft hand, reassuring me that I wouldn't have to face one of my fears. "But, Baby, I don't want to have to worry about you seemingly changing your mind about things like this," he said in a serious tone. "The weird thing is, I think I'm usually pretty good at reading you, and I really thought you were okay with me not going last night."

"I was. Really. I don't know why, but it got to me at that party. I'm sorry I got so emotional about it."

"Don't be. It's all right. But I don't want you to ever doubt that you are my topmost priority. I know sometimes it may not seem that way, but you are. Tell me. Tell me if you fe—"

"Can I tell you something now?" I interrupted.

Apprehensively, he agreed. "Yeah."

"I love you."

"God, Lara," With the descent of his tight shoulders, I could see him relax instantaneously. "I love you too…forever."

I sank my body back into his. I felt his strength, love, and commitment by the way he immediately and securely held me in return. I was so thankful for those words, that night, and especially that classic rock song.

\*\*\*

It was my third year in a row attending the CMA Awards. Every year seemed to bring a new chapter of my life. The first year was when Finn and I had made love for the first time. The following year, we had just gotten engaged. And, now, in year three, we were married. And the excitement I felt eclipsed any of our firsts that came before.

Finn had told me that he should be at his Nashville home when I arrived. So we would have a little time alone together before getting ready and heading out to the pre-party and awards ceremony that night. But when I got to the ranch and called out his name, there was no reply in return. I immediately hit his speed dial.

His voice on the other end sounded genuine if not a bit

tired. "Hey there, Beauty. Flight get in okay?"

"Yeah…finally." I growled my exasperation over the flight. "I'm at your place."

"Our place." Finn emphasized the first word.

"Whatever." I sighed. It was still weird to think of Nashville as partly mine, especially because the only part I wanted was the part that wasn't there. "Where are you?"

His hesitation was accompanied by an explanation that neither of us wanted. "Well, there's kind of been a change of plans. I'm stuck at rehearsals. There were a lot of last minute changes."

"Oh," I said, starting up the stairs toward the master suite. "All right." I could at least shower before he got home.

"I'm not going to make it back before the pre-party." His words made me stop mid-track in the master suite's sitting room.

"What?"

"No. I'm sorry. I need you to meet me here. I'll send a car." He paused as if anticipating my wrath. "All right?" When I didn't reply, he added, "There's nothing I can do." I heard the sincerity in his voice.

I knew he was sorry. I knew especially after our mini fallout before he left New York that he would have made every effort not to be in that situation. And I knew it was the night—the biggest night. I wasn't going to jeopardize any of it by being sad. I would just have to wait a little bit longer to see him. "You need me to bring you anything?" I conceded, looking down and finding a good inner-calm.

"Uh, yeah. Do you mind grabbing my clothes? There's a bag hanging—" he started.

But I had moved into the master bedroom. "…on the back of the door," I interrupted, spotting his all black ensemble that most definitely confirmed he had planned on being at the ranch before going out for the evening. "Yeah, I see it. I'll bring it."

Finn responded with, "You in the bedroom?"

"Yeah."

"Wish I was there with you."

"Tell me about it." I smiled, hearing his seductive tone.

"I *am* sorry, Lar."

"Finn, it's okay. It's just…I wanted some alone time with you before all of…everything." I was thinking of how fast paced and accompanied the entire night would be from the moment I stepped out of the car and into the chaos of CMA night.

"I know, Baby. I'll make it up to you. I promise."

"I have no doubts." I hugged his pillow against my torso.

"I love you," he said before telling me the details of everything I needed regarding the house, when to expect the car, and where to meet him.

\*\*\*

The day hadn't started how I planned and early evening followed suit. When I arrived at the center, there were people bustling around like they were bees having a contest to see who could make honey the fastest. The immediate rush of the scene literally made me want to hold my ears and sit down. I had to ease myself into this. Everything seemed to be happening so fast, and it was a bit overwhelming. At least I kind of knew what to expect. It was just that Finn had always been with me in the past. I knew once I found him, though, and he was at my side, things would settle down, and I would be beyond ready to start what was sure to be an amazing evening.

Looking sexy in simple jeans and his label's black T-shirt, Finn greeted me the moment I entered the area where he and his band were gathered for a quick rehearsal. "Hi." He pulled me into a welcomed embrace and lengthy smooch. The teasing whistles from a couple of his comrades made the action stop and him turn, smile, and say to them, "Aw, knock it off! Go. Go. Catch ya in a few."

I heard a few "Right, Chiefs" and "Hey, Laras" before everyone quickly tore out of the room. They also had dates and families to see before the star-filled night really kicked off. And I'm sure they were almost as anxious to be with them as I was to see Finn.

"You look amazing." Finn acknowledged, scanning my black halter dress crisscrossed with a silver ribbon pattern. "That dress…it complements you…how you light up a room." He started playing with my loose, long strawberry blonde hair. "I've missed you."

I was suddenly so much more relaxed in his arms in that vacant room. "I've been so looking forward to coming down here."

"Really?"

"Yeah, of course," I replied curious as to why he would question such an obvious statement.

"Good. It's just our last few phone conversations…I don't know…you seemed quiet or short or something. Everything all right?" He touched my face—he truly was concerned.

"Yeah. Yeah. Everything's great, Baby. Sorry. Guess I was just trying to get everything at work and the house ready to come down here."

"You sure?"

Before I could confirm or refute his question, we were interrupted by one of Finn's assistants. I forgot her name for a moment because I was upset that we had only been alone for what was it…five point two seconds?

"Finn, can I see you a sec?" she asked before smiling at me. "Hi, Lara."

"Hi, Shelly."

Yep, Shelly. That was her name. It came to me just as I opened my mouth. She was an older, skinny brunette with a wide smile and a bad case of adult ADHD.

"Uh, yeah," Finn replied.

"Just a sec," she promised, echoing her previous

statement.

"Yeah." Finn reassuringly stroked my hand, knowing, with regret, that at events like these, his attention on me had to be limited. He stepped aside with Shelly as I fished my cell phone out of my purse and put it on vibrate. The way he tentatively touched my arm alerted me to the fact that the interruption was going to be about something I wasn't going to like. "Lar?"

"Yeah?" I looked from my husband to his assistant.

"Audrey's here." His words came out cautiously.

"Aud—Uh, um…." Well, in all of the scenarios that had quickly played in my mind—and there had, remarkably, been a lot of them—that was not even remotely one. "Audrey?" I questioned, detesting the sound of Finn's ex-fiancée's name coming out of my mouth.

"Yeah."

"What is she do—?" I started.

"I guess she works for one of the radio stations somewhere in California that was nominated. She wants to see me." He was searching my eyes. "What are you thinking?" When I didn't answer—because I wasn't thinking much of anything besides shock—he tried again, "Lara?"

I attempted to sound calm, cool, and collected, but it did come out a little cruel. "What? I'm not going to tell you what to do. That's your decision."

I tried to continue to meet his eyes, but my armor was not very strong. I hadn't realized I was going to need to wear it under an evening gown. Once my eyes dipped, the blinking was a little more rapid. Any amateur psychiatrist could tell that I was hurt and didn't even know why there was a decision to be made at all. I didn't want him to ever see Audrey again but especially on such an important night.

Finn touched his hand with mine and turned to his assistant. "Tell her I'm sorry. I can't see her."

"Should I tell her—" Shelly started, and I wondered

what she had thought Finn's answer was going to be in the first place.

"Just what I said." He was abrupt, feeling me pull my hand away from his.

"K. Taken care of." Shelly smiled her obnoxiously white veneers at both of us. "Need anything else?"

"No. Thanks." He was polite but brief.

"Got it." And she exited as quickly as she entered.

When I started to follow, Finn quickly grabbed my hand causing me to look at him. "What?"

"Audrey's not in the hall is she?" I asked, feeling my blood pressure start to simmer. Who I was upset with at the moment confused me, though.

"No. No. She's in the front lobby or something." Finn looked perplexed, probably thinking how quickly the feeling in the room had changed...and not for the better.

"I've gotta get out of here. Is there somewhere more private we can go?"

"They set up a dressing room." He gave the answer I predicted, seeing as an aide had immediately taken Finn's garment bag from me upon my arrival.

We made our way through the halls which, amazingly, were even busier than when I had arrived just moments before. Wanting to make a connection between the two of us, Finn tried to put his hand on my lower back. But I shrugged him off. Although, I did keep to his side, knowing that neither one of us wanted the many onlookers to note any kind of friction.

Once we entered his small room and Finn shut the door, which only muted but not completely silenced the noise from the hall, he immediately questioned my behavior. "What? I said I couldn't see her."

I turned from the mirrored wall, not wanting to see my own sad expression. Facing Finn, I finally realized what had upset me beyond just *her* presence in the building. "You told Shelly you were sorry. You have nothing to be sorry about, Finn. Why do you feel anything?"

"What is it with Audrey? You're not like this with anyone else. I have female friends. I have female co-workers. And it's not like I have even seen Audrey since she le—"

I interrupted, not wanting to hear any re-hash of the Finn and Audrey saga. "For one thing, it's because of that…because she hurt you."

More than she even knew, I thought. Audrey's leaving was a big part of what caused Finn's breakdown years before. It had life-altering effects on such a kind, warm, generous, loving man.

"And the other?" He moved on, knowing that what I said was true.

I paused, calming myself so that I had an honest, rational answer for him. "I don't know. I guess because I knew her, and I saw you with her. It's more real for me. She had all of you. And, no, I'm not talking about just sex."

Wow! Sometimes, my mouth answers before my brain processes. And it's pretty darn accurate.

"What then? What did she have?" Surely not needing any more stress that day, he sounded not exactly mad …but edgy. When I turned away so that I was now facing the piano and green sofa, Finn continued honing in on what I had been referring to. "Are you talking about a piece of jewelry? Because that's all that was. That was years ago. I was a twenty-two-year-old kid not knowing what real life was all about. A twenty-two-year-old kid thinking that's what you're supposed to do at that point in your life. That diamond? I walked into the store and picked out something I could afford in less than fifteen minutes. She didn't have me. Good old-fashioned American standards did and…the mall jewelry store."

I tried not to laugh, because somehow we were in a disagreement. And how did that happen? I couldn't help but glance at my engagement ring and think about how much thought and love my man had put into its creation.

Sensing his opening, Finn gently took my arm to turn me once again completely toward him. "Lara, it would have never worked out. Never. It was always gonna be you. I might not have known it at times, but it was always you. No one…no one has ever come even remotely close, and they never will." Seeing my silent tears fall at his sentiment, Finn softened even more. "Geez, Baby, you know that. I know you do. What's this all about?" His thumb pads came up to my tear-stricken cheeks. "You have been all over the place before I came down here and—"

I hugged him fiercely and murmured into his chest. "Hormones."

"Yeah?" I heard the skepticism in his voice knowing I was not a typical PMSy girl—tired and hungry perhaps but not moody.

I broke from our embrace but kept within arm's length. "I was going to tell you at home before we drove over here."

"Did you just call Nashville home?" he teased with a now little more relaxed smile.

"So not the point, Murphy." I shook my head. "But when you couldn't make it, I knew when I saw you, I wouldn't be able not to tell you. So…" I opened my purse and pulled out a small box. Holding it steady but extending it toward him, I said, "Go ahead. Open it."

His pre-show, soft, gray eyes widened and brightened in an absolutely extraordinary way. "What? What! Whoa! Really? Lar? Lara?" He looked at me for confirmation. But knowing what a sign on a white stick meant, he hardly gave me time to nod my head up and down before taking me in his arms and swinging me around mid-air. "Oops, maybe I shouldn't." He slowly and carefully placed my feet back on the brown-carpeted floor.

"No." I smiled, suddenly forgetting anything else that happened that day besides the joy in my husband's soul. "You definitely should." When he followed up with an energetic kiss, I added, "And definitely lots of that too."

"I love you so much." He hadn't let go of my hands or let his eyes drift from mine.

"Not too scared?" I questioned nonetheless smiling.

"Yeah," he admitted. "Petrified. But good petrified. When did you find out?" He was so full of life, he was acting like he had downed three espressos in succession.

"About a week ago. But you were already here. And I wanted to tell you—show you—in person."

"Wow. Oh, man. Wow! Really?" He didn't wait for an answer. "Wow! Did you tell anyone?"

"No. No. Of course not. I guess that's why I may have sounded a little short to you on the phone. I didn't want to give anything away. And it's why I've been so moody. And the allergies—your shampoo—I remember them intensifying with…" I stumbled a bit, but, after all, it was the truth and he knew all about it. "…my first pregnancy. Anyway, I started putting the pieces together and took the test."

"I love you so much, Beauty." He was so focused on me, it was downright mesmerizing.

"You said that." I laughed.

"Sorry that Au—"

I cut him off not wanting *her* name to ruin any more of our evening. "No. I'm sorry. I know what we have." And I placed my hand over his cotton-covered heart.

Finn trumped me by putting his hand on my stomach while kissing me so damn sweetly. "I don't know how I'm going to make it through this evening."

"Finn," I cautioned. "We can't tell anyone yet. It's too early. It's really early."

"Just the three of us." He beamed, rubbing my stomach.

I smiled back. "Aren't we going to be late?"

"Who cares? Here sit with me. I want to hold you." He led me to that sofa where, despite me being in an elegant evening gown and him in jeans and a T, we fit each other perfectly. "This is a moment I don't want to ever forget."

# CHAPTER TWENTY

For as scrambled and unpredictable as CMA day began, it ended on two unbelievable high notes. Of course, there was Finn's and my shared happiness about our little bun in the oven. And then, there was Entertainer of the Year.

Finn was not seated next to me when they announced the nominees. He was backstage because he and his band had just finished performing. The monitors showed him backstage clowning around, crossing his fingers for luck. I know he didn't expect to win. This was a first time nomination at a highly esteemed awards ceremony. He was just having fun getting off his high of performing and, of course, his secret, personal news.

But when they called his name as the winner, all joking went aside. The camera was on him and his eyes grew wide in shock. Carter knocked him on the shoulder and Finn's hands went to his knees. Then I slowly started to see him go onto the stage. He was wiping tears from his eyes as if his hands were windshield wipers. And, as if I were up there and experiencing it with him, tears started falling from my eyes too. The world seemed to go mute around the two of us—a major fete in a room full of hundreds of cheering people. Danny Roth's wife, who was sitting next to me, handed me a tissue. I dabbed slightly and stood with everyone else while watching my husband hug the presenter and accept his trophy. I knew his emotions were on overload. God, yeah, he might have had a tear in his eye if he had won Entertainer of the Year any other night. But this night, it wasn't a tear, it was a waterfall. And I appreciated it more than anyone else.

After a second or two to collect himself, Finn finally stepped up to the microphone. He moved his head so that he could zone right in on me. I hoped that my smile beamed through even though my hands were folded in front of my chin. The microphone announced everything to the auditorium. The television cameras announced everything to the viewers. But his words were just for me.

"I know I have a million people to thank but…" He looked right into my eyes. "Baby," Then he paused, looked a little lower and said what everyone besides me thought was a reiteration, "Baby, this is for you."

And the show ended. I had a terrible time trying to practically claw my way back to find Finn. Everyone seemed to be dispersing in different directions, and they were doing it in an unorganized mob-like fashion. Colleagues of Finn's who I had gotten to know over the years congratulated me on Finn's success—some asking questions on the way, some just rubbing my back or giving me a cheek kiss.

When I felt my phone vibrate inside my clutch purse, I pulled it out and read the text message from Finn. *I love U*

I texted back, *Ditto, Cowboy. Where R U?*

Before Finn could respond, Hawk tapped me from behind. "Hubby sent me," he smirked. "C'mon, I'll get you to him."

I texted back quickly. *Never mind…w/Hawk. C U in a few.*

To say that it was a scene from a bad war movie where the lovers were reunited after trials, tribulations, near death experiences, and years of longing, might be an exaggeration. But it did seem like that because as soon as Hawk and I entered the press room, there was a parting of the seas. Finn stopped talking, walked across the room, pulled me tight against him, and kissed me. Flashbulbs were of course swirling and going off. This from the man who for so much of our relationship was adamant about privacy and no PDA.

"I'm so proud of you." I placed my hands on his cheeks and tried to ignore the others around us.

"It's unreal." His face was up against mine.

"But it's not. All of it...all of it is real." I smiled.

"Finn, picture of you and your wife?" one of the reporters questioned.

Finn winked at me and said, "If she's okay with it."

I turned my body so that we were side-to-side and arm-in-arm. We took a few shots straight on. Then Finn kissed the top of my head for more photos. Surprisingly, I was more than okay with it. I was happier than I had ever been in my life and, for once, I didn't mind the world seeing the true me.

When one reporter dared to ask me a first question, though, Finn immediately put an end to it. He was still steadfast about me not having to put up with his professional life. He pulled me out of the room and into the VIP hallway for a little privacy. "Go with Hawk. I'll meet you in a few to go to the after party." He paused and then said, "If you feel up to it."

"Of course I feel up to it." I laughed. "And Finn, I don't need Hawk. You're not going to be like this the whole time, are you?" I semi-teased.

"It's only been a couple hours. Geez, give me a break. And, yes, you know me, I probably will be." He smiled.

"Oh, boy." I tsked.

"Or girl," he whispered in my ear and then called Hawk over who had remained a few steps away to give us the moment to ourselves. "Stay with her."

"You got it."

"I love you, Roxanne. You're my real trophy tonight," he said and kissed me.

"And we haven't even gotten home yet." I seductively winked.

***

Most people probably thought Finn was drunk at the after party. But if they had been paying attention, they would have noticed he only drank slightly more than me. And, of course, I wasn't drinking at all. Finn was buzzed on life, and it was contagious. Everyone wanted to be around him and follow his lead. He, of course, kept me glued securely to his side and made every excuse to leave early. But it wasn't easy because he was now the king kahuna of country music.

However, in our Tennessee home, he was the softest teddy bear ever. Finn, even as a college co-ed, was sensitive and considerate. But finding out I was pregnant with his child put him on a whole new level. He carried me into the house like we were on our honeymoon and then proceeded up the stairs to the master bedroom. I kept protesting that I wasn't an invalid, and he kept insisting that he wanted to take care of and pamper me.

And, oh my God, did he ever. The way his hands softly caressed and treasured the outside of my body made me melt with every delicate touch. The way he said my name with a catch in his voice and a tear in his eye made me appreciate on a deeper level how true our love was. And then there was the way his body gently, rhythmically rocked mine as if I were the newborn and not the little peanut lying in wait.

***

Along with congratulatory pats about his big award, Finn was receiving other celebratory hugs from his family a few weeks later. And, of course, so was I. We had decided Thanksgiving was the perfect time to tell everyone in our immediate clan that I was expecting. The rest of the world had to wait.

"Looks like she's already scheming up a new set of pajamas," Will cocked his head toward our mutual mother-in-law.

I looked over to Mrs. Murphy who was beaming brighter than a candelabra. She had her son in an embrace and was smiling at me from across the Jamison living room. Will's prediction, I thought, probably wasn't too far from the truth.

I laughed. "It's once a year, and she enjoys it."

"I'm really happy for you both," Will said more seriously that time.

"Thanks, Will."

"Kelsea will be over the moon. Someone in her class has an obnoxious number of cousins, and she keeps whining about why she doesn't have any."

"Well, I'm glad we can help that situation out." I silently acknowledged the fact that Will was an only child. "That's really the whole reason, of course," I joked.

"I figured," He softly chuckled. "Lara, thanks for sticking by me and my family. You had every reason to never speak to me again."

His sudden sensitivity after a humorous start to the conversation threw me, so I resorted to a little sarcasm. "Will, c'mon, us Murphy outsiders have to stick together."

"I mean it. I was dealing with too much right after...right after that day in the car, and I never got a chance to really apologize. I know I've seen you since then. And I know I've said it, but everything is really, truly clearer now, and I want to say it up right."

"Accepted. Thanks." I nodded. "I'm glad you got the help. I'm glad both of you—all of you—are doing better."

Not a drop...not one drop of alcohol since that day in March. And, even better than that, his relationship with

Kelsea and Nola seemed more solid than ever. As if to prove my fact, Nola approached us then and gave her husband's hand a kind squeeze. The smile between them warmed my heart.

"Looks like the cookie monster has another one in her hand." Will shook his head as he looked at his daughter. "I'm gonna go con her into sharing them so we all don't get the after effects of a four-year old sugar rush."

As he took off toward Kelsea, Nola grabbed both of my hands and started telling me how pregnancy was the most wonderful, unique privilege any woman could possibly have and about some of the experiences along the way. Of course, I knew all of this firsthand, but it wasn't something that I wanted to reveal. No one knew about my teenage past except for Finn and my mom, and I was still determined to keep it that way.

Finn came to stand next to me as Nola said, "Wait until you experience that first kick."

"Oh, I know, I—" I started and caught myself.

"You couldn't know that yet, you're too early," she stated.

"Right. I just was going to say, I know," I tried not to verbally stumble. "I'm looking forward to it."

"Leave her be," Finn said a little too abruptly in my defense.

"Okay, Munch. Geez."

My husband walked off toward the foyer, prompting his sister to ask, "What's up with him?"

"Y'know, just being over protective." I tried to laugh it off, but I knew there was more to it—his thoughts had most likely been where mine were.

"Oh, boy." Nola laughed, accepting the answer at face value. "You've got a long nine months."

"Hey, I'd rather him care than not." I knew firsthand how fortunate I was in that department. Watching Finn exit out the front door, I continued, "I'm going to go check on him."

When I stepped out to the front of the house, that over protectiveness rang true when, despite it being in the high forty-degree temperature range, Finn asked, "Coat?"

"I'm fine." I slid into his side. "You all right?" I asked looking up at him.

"Yeah," he answered and then, after a moment, said, "It's just…I just wish this was your first pregnancy." On that admission, he slowly looked down at me with something close to guilt in his kind eyes. "Sorry. Was that insensitive?"

"It was honest." I rubbed the cottony fabric over his washboard abs to let him know I appreciated the truth. "And, Finn, don't believe I'm not thinking that too. I don't want to take anything away from that boy who is hopefully out there somewhere safe and happy. He may have been my first pregnancy but *this*," I placed my hand on my stomach, "is my first child."

Resting his hand gently on top of mine, my husband and his smile warmed whatever chill may have been in the air. He peppered me with a series of gentle pecks on my lips. Nestled on that suburban New York porch, a sense of serenity washed over me, knowing both the unconditional love of a man and our babe-to-be.

\*\*\*

It was that Sunday after Thanksgiving, when we had just gotten back from seeing Finn's folks off as they made their way back home to Kentucky, when Finn told me something I had not been expecting. He waited until we were home and alone until he let me know why he had been on the phone practically non-stop for the past so many days. He waited until everything was finalized, because he knew I would probably protest. And I did.

"No. No," I said. "I didn't ask you to do that."

"Lara, it's done."

"No. Undo it. You don't have to do this."

He looked worn to me. I had assumed that it was because of all the additional interviews and appearances that were being asked of him since winning Entertainer of the Year. I did not expect that it was because he was making such an important decision. I did not expect that he was cancelling his tour for the following summer.

"Finn!"

"Lara, Beauty, it's done. Let it be. I always told you that you come first. And I mean it."

"But I know what touring is for you. I know how important it is for your career. And I know how much you love it."

"Not as much as I love you and Little Munch in there."

I couldn't help but do a half chuckle at the name Finn just proclaimed on our unborn child—a mini-version of his childhood nickname. "Little Munch, huh?"

"Lara, it's okay. Really. I needed a break, anyway."

"But you're on top right now. Now is when you want to roll with it."

"Not without you. And besides, I'm doing pretty good. That means my fans will carry me through. I'm not struggling to be out there and gather fans at different venues."

"Pretty good." I shook my head at his modesty.

"Beauty, listen, I'll do some local shows if they come up and some promos in the city, but I am going to be here for the birth of our baby. I am not going to be half way across the country and get the call that you are in labor and however many inches."

"Centimeters! Geez!" I laughed.

"Whatever." He smiled. "And I am going to be there afterward for him or her and you." When I stared at him in awe and admiration, he pulled me to him. "That's it then. Not another word about it."

"That was very dad-like," I teased.

"Hmmm. Maybe I should look into smoking a pipe too."

"Oh, brother." I pulled away. "But I do have a question."

"What?"

"I guess everyone knows then…your peeps? They know I'm pregnant?"

"No." He lightly chuckled at the word I gave the masterminds around his career.

"No?" I was shocked. Didn't we just have the everyone-is-working-to-cancel-the-tour conversation?

"You told me it was too early."

"It is. Then why do they think you're doing this?"

"I told them it was personal. They're probably gossiping right now about how we're getting divorced."

"Oh, God. Finn!"

"Don't worry about it." Before I could interject, he continued. "They're my staff. They are certainly not going to put it out there. They'll know soon enough."

"Baby?" I looked him in the eyes. "You are absolutely sure about this? We can work it out if you want to change your mind."

"As long as you love me, I'm absolutely sure."

"Finn, not only do I love you now, but I will love you until the day I die."

"Then, it's all good." He smiled and kissed me just as sweet.

# CHAPTER TWENTY-ONE

"Clover?" The expression on Finn's face was priceless.

"What? That's Irish, right?" I rebutted.

"I don't know! Listen, I told you I would do anything for you, but I might have to draw the line there."

"She could be our lucky charm. Besides, do you know how hard it is to pick a name when you're in a building full of kids?"

"If you haven't heard of a Clover before, there's a reason." He shook his head. "But I agree with the lucky thing."

It was a little early, but previous blood work and an ultrasound that morning—exactly twelve weeks into my pregnancy—indicated that we were having a girl, and a new giddiness between Finn and I had settled in. Somehow, knowing the sex of the baby made everything seem more real. And if Finn had treated me with kid gloves before, he was even more protective of his now two girls. It was a rare December evening where we had nothing to do. So we were spending it cuddled on the sofa, drinking hot cocoa, getting excited about décor and clothes and, of course, names.

"So how can we make it work?" I asked, trying to think

of a name that encompassed our thoughts but didn't sound like we were living in an ashram.

"How about Shamrock?" he jested.

"Finn!" I hit his shoulder.

"You know I love those shakes." His smile was wide and irresistible. "I don't know how it's different than Clo—"

I interrupted. "Chloe? What about Chloe?"

"Chloe," he repeated, paused, and then said a little more seriously, "Chloe Murphy. Yeah. I think I like that. Yeah?" He looked to me for final approval.

"Yeah." I warmed even more to the name hearing it come from my husband's mouth.

"What about the middle name?"

"Oh, man, let's just quit while we're ahead for now."

I felt truly fortunate that Finn was able to experience so much of my pregnancy with me. Not only did he make sure he was at the doctor appointment where we heard the heartbeat and found out she was going to be a she, but he was with me during those times when morning sickness would creep in. It was so much different than my first pregnancy. I had rolled through the mandatory obligations back then without feeling much besides shame and remorse. But now, everything was new and bright and wanted and, most of all, loved.

"You know," I stretched my legs out and brought my body more forward. "I think I'm gonna go to sleep. I'm getting tired all of a sudden."

Finn rubbed my shoulders. "You all right? It's pretty early."

"Yeah." I squinted. "I'm just starting to get a headache."

"Lara, you don't have to pull the 'I have a headache' bit," he joked.

"Ha!" I laughed, but the pain increased. "It really just started. And don't make me laugh, it hurts worse when I do that."

"Sorry." He acknowledged my distress. "I know you won't take anything. Hold you?"

"No," I replied. "It's one of those touch sensitive things." Although not a regular occurrence, a headache wasn't anything unusual for me, and with the pregnancy, I didn't want to take any type of medication that wasn't specifically prescribed. When I turned to face him, it forced him to drop his massaging hands. "I'm just overly tired." It had been a busy day and week for that matter. "I'll be better in the morning. Stay. Watch some sports thing without me talking through it for a change."

He shook his head, but he didn't deny the validity of my statement. "What?" he mocked. "Never."

"I love you," I said as a tear strictly from the headache formed in the corner of my eye.

"Me too. Night, Lar." He kissed me ever so gently on my lips and then my stomach. "Night, Chloe."

"G'night." I tried a half-hearted smile, stood up, and hoped that dreamland would take the sudden pain away.

\*\*\*

Fortunately, as predicted, my headache was MIA the next morning when I woke and got ready for work. Finn was flying to Memphis for a couple days. His first engagement that night was at St. Jude's. Along with the military, it had always been one of the charities Finn helped out with. From Nola's kids to the charity concert at my work to our little one in the womb, it was evident that Finn had a special place in his heart for kids. The following day he was going to be part of a tribute concert that was being recorded in memory of B.B. King. There were artists from across all genres, and it was quite a privilege for Finn to be included in the ensemble.

It was on that final, second night of Finn's trip, around 11 p.m. New York time, when I knew I couldn't wait any longer. I was hoping his part of the B.B. King gig was complete. Regardless, I had to hit that speed dial number. The sound in the background when he picked up the phone told me that he was, at the very least, still at the event. But he did pick up. So I knew he wasn't performing at that moment.

"Hey, Beauty. I just got off stage. How'd you know?"

"Oh, good. Good." I took a deep breath. I really hadn't wanted to ruin that for him—he had seemed so psyched. "Finn?"

"Lara? It's pretty loud. I'm going to try, but can you maybe call—"

"Finn? Can you come home?"

"I am."

"Right now?" I clarified.

"Well, yeah, you know, tomorrow." I heard the dumbfounded inflection in his voice.

"No. Now? Can you come back now?" My voice broke despite trying so hard to stay brave and levelheaded.

Finn heard it immediately, and I heard his voice change just as quickly too. "Lara? What's wrong? What's going on?"

"I need you," I pleaded sounding more desperate than I remember being in such a long time.

But it couldn't be helped. I knew I couldn't do this alone. This wasn't about going to a party by myself. This was…this was…so much more real.

The background noise was no longer as loud. It was obvious Finn had moved to a slightly more secluded area. He knew by my tone and request that something serious was going on.

"Lara? God, Beauty, what's wrong?"

"Please, Finn, if you can, please come home tonight." I didn't want him to worry, and I didn't want him to change plans, but I knew there was no way around it—he needed to be home.

"Lara! Tell me! What's going on?" He was practically bellowing, and I wanted to cry just knowing how panicked he was. Before I could answer, I heard him call out to someone on the Memphis end, "I need a flight out—now! I don't care how you get it, whatever, get me a flight back to New York. Get me home, now!" And then he returned to talk to me. "Lara?"

"Thank you." I breathed in a huge exhale knowing that he was going to be on his way home.

Once he was back, it would all be better. Finn would make it that way. I knew it.

"I'm scared to death. What's going on? Are you all right?" His series of questions fired off like a machine gun.

"I'm…I'm okay." I managed.

And then he went to the next logical conclusion. "Is it the baby?"

"Finn…," I started but, due to my emotions, exhaustion, and relief that he was coming home, his name was all I could get out.

"It's…." He sounded heartbroken.

"Sort of." I gained some of the composure back that I had before starting the phone call—before hearing my love's voice across the line. "There was just an incident. That's it. And I just…well, I need you. I need you to be here, okay? I need to see you. You're done, right?" I had waited for him to have his moment, but now I needed mine.

"Yeah. Yeah," he answered to me before yelling at someone else. "God! Damn it, do we have a plan?"

"Finn," I tried to calm him over the phone. "It's all right. It's okay. Just let me know—"

"I'll be home soon. If I have to, I'll drive the whole way."

Oh, God! That was the last thing I needed. I didn't want him in a panicked state driving an insane amount of hours.

"No, Finn. No! Promise me." It was my turn to yell.

"It won't come to that. As soon as I get details, I'll call you. I'm gonna see what's going on. I'll call you right back."

"Yeah."

"I love you, Lar. I'm coming, Baby. I'll be there."

"I love you too."

"I'm gonna call you in a little bit. As soon as I make the arrangements."

"All right."

We were repeating everything. Neither one of us wanted to hang up. But we had to.

***

When Finn called back, he already had a driver taking him to the airport and someone getting his stuff at the hotel. "The earliest the commercial liners could get me back was after 11 a.m. I told them that was unacceptable."

"Finn, that's fine. It's okay."

"No. It's shouldn't take twelve fucking hours to get from Memphis to New York. It *would* probably be easier to drive."

"No!"

"Don't worry. Quince has a private plane. He's having his pilot take me and come back."

"What?"

Quince? Quince? It was late. I was upset. Oh, Quince Dall. The number one recording blues artist born and raised in Memphis.

"Yeah. He offered s—"

"Finn, you don't need to do that." All this changing of plans was making me nervous, and that was the last thing I needed to be.

"You need me, right?"

"I do." I broke. I've never needed him more.

"All right, then. Lara, listen," His voice revealed that he was trying to soothe me while attempting to stay in emotional control himself. "By the time the pilot gets there, everything is checked, the flight, everything…I'll be at the house no later than seven. Okay?"

"Finn?" I had to tell him.

As if reading my mind, "Lara, tell me. I need to know."

"Don't come to the house. I'm at the hospital."

"Oh, God. What? What happened? You told me you were all right."

"I am."

"You're not. You're not." He was crying. There was no disguising it, although I could tell he was trying. "You're in the hospital."

"It's precautionary. But, yes, I'm in General."

"General." The sudden plummet of his voice told me he had rapidly flashbacked to Wyatt's last moments at that hospital and the hell that had surrounded all of us.

"I'm sorry." I was wiping the tears away from my eyes, hoping my nasally nose didn't give me away.

"You don't...Is anybody with you?"

"No. There was, but it's late now, and I just...I just want you."

"Was Nola—"

"No. She doesn't know. She doesn't need to be here." I didn't want her to have to be in the place where her son died, not unless she really needed to be. I knew it was going to be hard enough on Finn, but he would run on adrenaline.

"Hey, we're pulling into the airport now."

"Already?"

"Yeah. It wasn't much of a drive. I'm gonna have to take care of a lot of things."

"Fine. Do that. I need to get some sleep. I'm pretty sure the doctors wouldn't approve of me being up right now."

"Lara, you tell me...you tell me straight out. You're okay?"

"Yes. The doctor will explain things in the morning. I'll be able to go home. I need you to get some sleep on that plane. Be safe." He was my priority at that moment.

"We'll be safe. You get some sleep too."

"Call me when you land?"

"Of course." He knew our routine. And then he remembered something else. "Lara?"

"Yeah?" I thought he was going to tell me that he loved me, but what he said instead had almost more meaning.

"Sleep tight. Don't let the bed bugs bite."

"I love you more than life, Finn," I cried more than said.

"You are my life, Lara. Nobody…nothing else matters. I'm on my way."

\*\*\*

I was in a private room. It hadn't started out that way. When I had first been admitted, I was in a room with another woman. But shortly after, they moved me to another room—a private one at the end of the hall. I'm almost positive it was preferential treatment, because as soon as I moved rooms, the attendants started asking if I had contacted my husband yet and if he was coming. They never said Finn's name, but the implication was definitely there. How they found out about my relationship to a celebrity, I wasn't quite sure. I certainly hadn't broadcast it. I figured it was most likely Vanessa who had played pseudo ambulance driver and brought me to the hospital from work in the first place. She was the type who would promote it in an innocent, trying to do the best for me, kind of way.

I do have to say, having that personal privacy when Finn arrived did help. When he called to tell me that they had landed, it was still very early in the morning. I pulled my hands through my hair to smooth it, pinched my cheeks to get a natural blush, and bit my lips to wet them. I wanted to look the best I could sans makeup so that there could be some pretense of everything being all right. It didn't work, though.

He shed the disguise of his ball cap, scarf, and glasses the moment he crossed the threshold of my room. Approaching my bedside, he put his hand to my face. "My God, I just saw you. What happened?"

Wanting to alleviate some of the fear, I tried the sarcastic approach. "I didn't tell you? Sick of food shopping. Needed a place for free meals."

But he was distraught. It showed on every part of his being. And he did not want to joke around. "That's not funny, Lara."

"Sorry," I repented, taking his hand in mine as he eased into the bedside chair. "Finn, you didn't sleep."

His eyes were neither their gorgeous sparkling gray nor their fake starlit contacts green. They were bloodshot red. They were tired. They were wary. They were scared.

"How could I?"

"Here." I took our hands joined together and placed them on my hospital gown covered abdomen. Seeing me and feeling our baby I thought had to help.

"There's still…there's still a baby?" His eyes moved from my stomach to my face but his hand did not move.

"Yeah. Oh. Yeah." I hadn't realized he thought that…I hadn't said that. "Little Munch,"—I forged a smile using the nickname Finn had given our daughter—"seems to maybe even be hungry today."

"What's going on, Lar?" Some of the worry had dissipated, but he was still downright worn. "What happened? Why are you here?"

"There was a little episode."

"Lara, what does that mean?" He was frustrated with the twenty questions, and I was prolonging telling him because I knew what his reaction was going to be.

Nevertheless, "I collapsed yesterday during work."

"What? At work?" His hand left mine. "But you only called me…Lara…" The warning version of my name.

"I'm sorry you had to come back here like you

did…earlier than you planned. I probably should have just waited until you came back tonight."

"No. You should have called right away. Right…away."

"I didn't want you to worry. I just…I needed somebody. I needed you."

"My wife—my pregnant wife— is hooked up to an IV. There are monitors making strange sounds around you. Of course you needed me. And, of course, I would be worried." Before I could respond, he changed directions. "What do you mean you collapsed?"

"I suddenly wasn't feeling well. I had a horrific headache and the room felt warm. I felt like I needed air. But I couldn't open the windows. It was freezing outside. I was sweating and couldn't get rid of any clothing. I went to sit down on the floor and I…I guess I fainted."

"Lara!"

"Not sure how long I was out. Couldn't have been too long. I woke up to hear Vanessa asking me if I was dead. I probably looked that way sprawled out on the floor." I tried to joke, putting my hands in a haphazard way above my head.

Finn did not laugh. He instead asked, "What did you hit?"

"My head but not bad. I felt it coming."

"Oh, God. Your head? Hard?"

"No. No. I was already on the floor when I just toppled. I needed an ice pack. That's it." I took his hand in mine again to reassure him. "Vanessa ran and got the nurse. I was tired…so tired."

"I don't understand. What happened? Why did you pass out?"

"The doctor's coming. I told him when you were going to be here. He'll explain it best." When Finn started to shake his head slightly, I continued. "I'm glad you're here. It'll help to have both of us listen."

"You should have called me." He reiterated his previous thought.

"Baby, please. I did. You're here now. That's what matters. I—"

"Okay. Okay." He scooted his chair as close as he possibly could to my bed, reclaimed my hands, brought them to his lips, and held them there locking his wary but loving eyes with mine.

It was the doctor's entrance then that brought an end to our alone time. Finn got up to shake his hand as I slightly shifted in the bed. Even though I had, obviously, lived through it and had heard the medical explanation the day before, I listened closely as the doctor detailed the prognosis to both of us. Because it wasn't my first time hearing it, I could process the information more clearly. Finn, however, exhausted and emotional, seemed to be swirling.

Dr. Weinstein believed I was experiencing vasovagal syncope. He explained that when a woman is pregnant, there are a lot of intense changes in the cardiovascular system. Heart rates increase, etc. Most of the time a woman's body adjusts to the change but sometimes, depending on circumstances, it reacts adversely. There had been warning signs—the lightheadedness when standing up too quickly and the nausea that I thought was just morning sickness. And because of the nausea, I wasn't eating or drinking enough and was most likely dehydrated. They could all be signs and triggers along with anxiety, which probably prompted the headaches.

Finn eyeballed me on that comment. "Were you stressed about something?"

"No," I said but didn't meet his eyes straight on.

"The plane. Me being away." They weren't questions.

"Finn, c'mon…. No, I don't like it when you fly or are away, but I deal with it. I don't pass out because you're gone." We'll leave that to the front row ticket holders, I wanted to say, but bit my tongue, knowing the mood in the room did not warrant sarcasm.

"Pregnancy can cause all kinds of hormonal

changes…intensify feelings and anxiety without you even realizing it," the doctor interjected, landing more on Finn's side of the debate.

"What about the baby?" Finn forged on while filling his hand with mine. "Did this affect her? Will it happen again?"

"The baby is fine. Your wife wasn't passed out very long, and she didn't have a hard fall. Now, we need to monitor the situation." Dr. Weinstein turned a tad more serious. "While I believe that by just following some simple guidelines, you should have a smooth pregnancy, we want to make sure it's nothing more and that it doesn't happen again. You were lucky you could tell it was going to happen." He looked directly at me and then said, "So no driving for at least a month, maybe more, while we get things regulated and make sure there isn't a recurrence or there aren't any other factors."

"No driving?" I asked because he hadn't told me that tidbit before.

"No. We don't want you behind the wheel in case—"

I stopped the doctor with my words. "I got it." I squeezed Finn's hand extra hard. Or was it the other way around? "Absolutely. No driving."

Wyatt. Wyatt. There couldn't be another Wyatt. That driver had a stroke, but it was the same action…the same consequence. I turned my head and looked at my husband. His bloodshot eyes were now misty. I nodded slowly and reassuringly.

"Don't worry, Beauty." Finn affectionately called me. "Meet your personal chauffer. You're not going to have to worry about planes. I'm not going anywhere. You're going to be attached to my hip and the passenger seat."

I smiled softly. "Oh, I'm sure you will just love both of those."

The doctor then gave me a list of dos and don'ts, like eating many small meals and healthy snacks in lieu of three large ones. Drinking eight to ten glasses of water each day.

Getting up slowly. Not taking too hot of a bath or shower and avoiding standing for long periods. That final one was, perhaps, the most troublesome. I had to guarantee Dr. Weinstein and even more so, Finn Murphy, that I would try to sit more at work. But I knew that was nearly impossible.

"If you have to stand, you should keep your feet moving as much as you can. It will help circulation," Dr. Weinstein said.

"Can you do that?" Finn asked me.

"Finn, it's not like I am standing behind a podium delivering a Power Point presentation. God, yeah, I move all the time. It would be like you just standing there at the mic and not dancing or shaking or whatever you call that on stage." I smiled a huge grin, knowing that a lot of the tension had been released.

"Okay, Rox," he relented and jokingly covering my face with his full hand. "That's completely choreographed by the way."

"Uh-huh." I laughed.

Looking at his beeper, Dr. Weinstein said, "Excuse me for one second" and left the room.

"I save all my good moves for you," Finn whispered in my ear and followed up with a kiss on my forehead.

"You okay?" I asked.

"Me?"

"I'm fine, Finn. We're"—I held onto my abdomen—"fine."

"That's all that matters, then." He squeezed my hand again. "But I meant it when I said you're not leaving my sight."

"I thought it was your hip," I said seductively.

"Then *I* might be the one passing out from heart palpitations." He winked and then kissed me in a way that I knew, despite his ease in words, he was still very concerned.

\*\*\*

Finn wrapped his arms extra securely around my body after turning out our bedroom light later that night. He was in his protective state. But part of that tight lock was also the tension still residing in his body—the tension from getting that phone call miles away and feeling helpless.

"I'm glad you're home." I rubbed his hands with mine.

"It should have been sooner," he said with a parental tone, obviously still upset that I hadn't called him straight after passing out.

Knowing what was done was done, I chose to ignore his statement and concentrate on the present goodness in the room. "I feel so safe in your arms."

"You are. I told you, I won't let anything happen to you," he recited the words he told me right before our wedding. But now, rubbing my belly, he added, "Or this little one in here."

"Promise?" I asked, needing his vocal reassurance as much as the one his physical embrace provided.

"You know it…with every ounce of my being." I felt him nuzzle his face into my shoulder and neck, drawing us as close as could be.

Gently turning to face my husband, I let my lips softly collide with his, wanting him to know with that touch how much I believed in his words and in his love. "Get some sleep," I coaxed.

"Mmm-hmm," was as much as an admission to sleep deprivation as I was going to get.

"You're gonna need it. Driving Miss Daisy starts tomorrow," I jested.

"Driving Me Crazy is more like it," he joshed back, but nonetheless kissed me sweetly before settling back into our cocoon to finally get some much needed rest.

# CHAPTER TWENTY-TWO

I thought I was going to have to convince the principal, Xenia, to hire hovering Finn on as an assistant the way he not only drove me to work but took me on the elevator and catered to my every need until I kicked him out. Then he showed up around noon with a lunch in hand and physically put my feet up to make sure I was following doctor's orders. Admittedly, he did good by bringing treats from my favorite coffee shop, Java Mug. And it was kind of romantic if you could block out the computers and piles of work as a backdrop. But it was definitely protectiveness overboard.

"Finn?" I said that night, curled up with a brown blanket on the oversized rocker.

"Yeah?" He looked up from his lyrics journal that he had been scribbling away at on the sofa. "You need something?"

I left the blanket behind and walked over to sit next to him. As I curled into his side, I said, "I love you."

"I love you too," he answered sincerely yet puzzled considering my seemingly out of the blue declaration.

"You know what I need right now?"

"What?"

"Just that. Only that. Just your love. I want you to trust what you told me…that everything is going to be all right. It was an isolated incident. I don't need you to do everything. Drive me back and forth to work, but do your thing too. Sing, record, meet, whatever. I can always get someone to drive me home if need be. Right now, what I need is for you to be you. Just love me." I said rubbing my belly. "Forget about the rest. Then everything will be all right."

He kissed me then deeply and with understanding. "I want to make love to you."

"I want that too…so much."

"And it's okay?"

"Being loved by my husband? I think that's more than okay."

"You know what I mean." He was so concerned about everything.

"Have I done everything the doctor said?"

"Yes," he admitted.

"And am I going to be on my feet, Cowboy?"

"Not tonight, Roxy." He smiled a wicked grin. "In fact, let's get you prone, right—" He literally swept me off my feet to take me into the adjoining master suite.

"Finn!" I bellowed but laughed all the same.

***

We were both more relaxed after making love. It helped us unwind and refocus. As I traced my finger randomly on Finn's torso, he couldn't help but ask, "You all right? No headaches?"

"No. Ready enough for round two if you wanted," I teased.

"Geez!" He laughed and kissed me on the forehead. After a few moments snuggled in each other's arms, Finn spoke again. "You mind if I play you something?"

"Sure. Yeah. What?"

My curiosity was piqued. While Finn would deal with the business or writing aspects of his career at home, he wouldn't often sing. I'm not sure exactly why. Maybe it's like how I never wanted to help friends set up their blog page or hook up their new computer. I did it for a living and needed the break or differentiation. Finn would sing for others or hum some random song, but he wasn't apt to just sitting down and singing around the fireplace.

"It's something I've been working on." He put his legs into his boxer briefs. "I just gotta get my guitar and notes." He pecked me on the lips before exiting.

While waiting for Finn, I put on a pair of floral shorts and a powder blue, spaghetti-strapped cami and started talking to our daughter. "Hey, Daddy's coming right back. You are so lucky, Chloe. You have such a caring dad. I ne—"

Finn's re-entrance stopped my soliloquy at the perfect time before I could dwell on my lack of a positive father figure. Guitar in hand, he climbed back into bed and frogged out his legs so that I could sit in the opening facing him. Leaning over, he kissed me sweetly on the lips and again on my stomach before saying, "It still needs some work. Just in the poem stages, but tell me what you think." After a few chords, that beautiful voice began crooning the words…

*"The first time that I shaved and didn't have a nick,*
*Or when I snuck the beer and got don't-tell-Momma sick*
*Graduation meant that I was finally going to be free.*
*I set out in the world to be the man I was meant to be.*

*I thought I had become a man so many times in my life*
*But it only began when I met the girl who'd become my wife."*

Finn looked from his guitar to me then. When I sucked in my lips and smiled warmly back, knowing the special words were meant for me, he continued…

*"Not too long ago, I thought I had it all.*
*I must be a man cause I was standing proud and oh so tall.*
*People gave me some awards and tons of accolades*
*My hometown even had me as master of their parade.*

*I thought I had become a man so many times in my life*
*But it only began when that beauty became my wife*

*There were things before her when I thought I was complete*
*But ratings and fame could never ever compete*
*With the day that I saw that positive stick of white.*
*I knew then that everything was all together right.*

*I thought I had become a man so many times in my life*
*But it only began when that beauty, my amazing wife,…*

*She told me that we were now parents soon to be*
*I knew it didn't matter if it was a he or a she*
*The babe already had a special place in our hearts*
*A love that set everything else miles and worlds apart.*

*I didn't know I could love something as much as I do…*
*I thought I had become a man so many times in my life.*
*A white stick, a plus sign, and Beauty especially you….*
*I thought I had become a man so many times in my life.*
*Today, I think that dream is finally coming true."*

Although briefly looking up at me a couple times during the song, Finn had for the most part concentrated on the guitar strings and the lyrics in front of him. I leaned forward and took the guitar from his arms, gently placing it on my side of the bed. With this motion, he ventured to look me in the eyes.

"Oh, my God," I said because no other words would form. I was not the word master in the family. I slid my hand softly down his cheek and kissed him the same way.

"When did you write that?" I asked as I leaned back and he took his hands in mine.

"I've been kinda playing with it, but everything came together in Memphis. Do you like it?" My husband was always sensitive and equally confident, but this was the rare, vulnerable Finn.

"Were you really in a parade?" I teased, because otherwise my emotions were on overdrive and the tears were going to pour.

"Only you, Lara." He shook his head.

"I love it, Finn. It's absolutely amazing." I felt his thumbs rhythmically circle my palms. "I might have to put little headphones up to my belly and play her the track when you're out of town or maybe even during labor."

He smiled. "The album will have to wait. I'll play with it and record the song just for the two of you if you'd want it."

I shook my head at his modesty. "Of course. And, Baby, you became a man when you listened to the story of my past that late September night a couple years ago and didn't run away. You are the best man there ever was."

\*\*\*

Unfortunately, because of my hospital stint, there was a leak about my pregnancy, or at least rumors thereof in the media. It really could have been anyone. We knew people talked, including my co-workers, hospital guests, etc.. So Reese put out a formal announcement, playing down any trouble that I may have had. But it would have been around that time that we should have been telling people, anyway. So it was fine. We were fine. It was all good.

But the following day, Finn had to face something that was quite the opposite. He and Nola had received a call that the end was imminent for their Grammy Murphy, who was in hospice care in Florida. It created quite a dilemma for my husband as he was torn about going to see her. He, of course, wanted to say goodbye to the woman he always said was one of his biggest, most encouraging fans from the start. But, then again, he was incredibly fearful of leaving me. I convinced him to go, saying I would be more stressed thinking I was responsible for him missing the opportunity.

And as it turned out, Finn being away and flying didn't stress me out, at least not to the point of collapsing. I knew in my heart that hadn't been the case when he was in Memphis. It was simply a pregnancy/hormonal imbalance that needed monitoring and directives—no stress, water, off feet, and so on. And, if for no other reason, I was glad that Finn had to make that sad trip to see his grandmother if just to prove to him that his leaving hadn't been the issue.

I was reading a book aloud, wanting our unborn child to hear the rhythm of my voice too, when the security system announced that Finn had returned home. He walked through the front door after a long couple of days of sadness and traveling. He looked weathered. But his first concern, as always, was me.

Placing his leather duffel down, he reached his arms out to my shoulders. "All good?"

"Yeah. We're fine." I said using the plural tense and reaching my hand up to his face which looked even more worn due to the whiskers piercing through. "Baby, I'm so sorry," I said and brought him into my body.

Grammy Murphy passed away just a couple hours after Finn and Nola had arrived. Which, as sad as her passing was, thankfully, Finn's father and the sibling grandchildren got there in time. The funeral was going to be simple and local. There wasn't much family as all of Grammy's siblings had proceeded her in death, and so it would just be her long-time husband, children, and grandchildren in attendance. Both Nola and Finn were not going to be a part of it, though. They decided to fly immediately back home to New York upon her passing. Everyone understood as they knew about my little hospital stint, and it was also just a few days or so before Christmas. They agreed that the important part was that the siblings had been there for their grandmother at the end.

"I want to go first," came my husband's muffled voice as he was still in my arms.

"What?" It wasn't that I didn't hear him. I didn't understand.

"It was only a few hours and he already looked so lost."

"What?" Again. "Who?"

"It wasn't like he didn't know what was going on. It was who was going to complete his life and heart...who was living the same story he was." Finn broke our embrace and looked me in the eyes. Those eyes were as watery as mine, for it was then that I realized he was speaking of his grandfather...and of himself. "I want to go first," he reiterated. "I don't think I could bear living without you on this Earth."

*\*\**

While Finn and I were alike in many ways, good and bad, it was also the differences that made us so compatible. There was one thing, though, in which we were polar opposites and clashed on every single time. Finn seemed to have no regard for time. I, on the other hand, arrived at any destination early—even if it meant sitting in the car for twenty minutes waiting for doors to open. Being ten minutes early is late for me. In contrast, Finn feels free to waltz into a location whenever. He doesn't do it on purpose and doesn't do it all the time. And he certainly doesn't mean it to be rude. He is just laissez-faire about the whole thing. I believe it's most likely because, with his career, he knows that everyone or everything will wait for him. I can't be late for work. Finn's late and the crowd is even more energized and happy that he has graced them with his presence.

Our differing views on promptness conflicted that next day—the day of Kelsea's preschool's winter holiday show. Because of Finn being out of town, my hospital drama, and his grandmother's passing, that event and getting ready for Christmas snuck up on us. So, having taken the day off of work, we were bustling around that morning getting some last minute gifts, including a custom made doll that was the spitting image of Kelsea herself—blonde bouncy curls, light brown eyes, and, of course, sparkly purple shoes nearly identical to the ones she wore at our wedding. But Finn also had a local jeweler make Kelsea a personalized necklace. That was our last stop before heading back home to get ready for the preschool play.

On any other day, we would have had plenty of time. The jeweler was on the other side of town but not too far away. It wasn't like we lived in a metropolis. Early winter snow was just starting to fall on our ride over. The forecasters weren't calling for much...just a coating. So it was just enough to make the world pretty and magical— the perfect setting for Kelsea's day. The necklace was just as magical. Her name was engraved in the center piece with stars around it. And dangling from that were three aquamarines—her birthstone. We knew she was just going to love it.

"I think you have completely spoiled her this year," I noted to Finn as he started the car to make our way back home.

"Nah."

"Whatever." I laughed.

"How about I'm just practicing for our little princess?"

"That I partially believe." I smiled, taking Finn's free driving hand and placing it on my stomach. "But I think that niece of yours has a pretty special place in your...Oh, crap." I stopped my own train of thought seeing all the brake lights ahead of us.

"What do you suppose that's about?"

"I don't know," I said, realizing it had to have just

happened because it wasn't that way on our drive in on the same road. "But it's not good."

Finn looked to the rearview mirror. Similar to what was ahead of us, traffic was backing up as far as the eye could see. "Well, it doesn't look like we're going anywhere fast."

"Great," I pouted, thinking how quickly things had gone from almost splendor to disaster.

Finn put the car in park since we weren't even inching forward at that point. "How do you suppose we should pass the time?" He smiled and winked at me, more, I am sure, to try to get me back in a good mood than to actually contemplate sex with all of the vehicles around us.

Neither reaction transpired. "How about calling your sister and telling her we're going to be late?" I offered instead.

"We're not going to be late. There's plenty of time. Besides, Nola said Kelsea's group is at the end." I must have grumped or sighed or something because Finn added, "Baby, there's nothing we can do about it."

I exhaled and leaned my head back against the headrest. Shortly afterward, we saw a police car drive along the curb lane to move ahead of us, followed a few minutes later by a tow truck. Then, about twenty to twenty-five minutes after that, I felt Finn shift the car back into drive. We began to move ever so slowly. It took a while but we finally cleared the accident site and, the worst part was, it really didn't seem like anything at all—a basic four car fender bender. Granted, debris was scattered on the road and front ends were pushed in and sides of cars were scratched or dented, but there were no ambulances and everyone seemed to be moving around.

When we finally got home, I raced to the bathroom. I was pretty sure my bladder wasn't going to make another mile. Stripping out of my loose white T-shirt and pants, I hurried just as quickly into the shower. I hadn't showered prior to leaving. I had just thrown my hair into a messy bun and put limited make-up on so that we could make it to the shops and back quickly. Ha! I laughed to myself. Best laid plans, I thought, as I let the warmth of the shower attempt to calm me. I turned it on extra hot in an attempt to forget the cold end-of-December weather that had caused just enough havoc for a four car pileup.

When I got out of the shower, I noted the time on our nightstand clock. We only had thirty-five minutes to get there, which would be just about right if we left right then. But that wasn't possible. My mind raced through the litany of items that still needed to be done as I threw on my underwear ensemble and then did the same with my turquoise dress lying innocently on the bedroom chair. I had to dry and fix my hair, put make-up on, find shoes to wear....

"Finn?" I called out. When he didn't answer, I called out again, "Finn!"

"What? Yeah?" He appeared in the bedroom doorway.

I caught sight of him in the same attire we had spent our lovely ride in. "God, you're not even ready. I thought you would be dressed."

"I'll get there. I'm probably just gonna change my shirt."

"Fine." I was trying not to be mad at him, but it was slightly infuriating the casual way he was moving around when there was obviously so much to do in so little time.

"Lara, you need to relax. Listen, you haven't eaten or had anything to drink. That's what I was doing. I was cutting up a pear for you and there's some pretzels—"

The hot, loud rush of air from the hairdryer silenced his voice as I sat on the bed and started the extensive process of drying my hair due to the thickness and length of my mane. Flipping my head upside down to get underneath, I saw Finn's feet turn and exit as I ran the brush through my hair while still allowing the hot air to caress it. I did this for a couple minutes before deciding it was fine being partially dry. When I started to unplug the cord, I felt Finn sit next to me on the bed.

"Hey," he said in a firm, yet compassionate, voice. "You need to eat." In his hands was a small plate of food and a glass of water.

"Okay." I slowed down for a second, recognizing his kindness…his love. "Thanks." I swallowed a good gulp of water, not realizing how thirsty I was. As I bit into one of the pear slices, I stood. "I'm gonna take these with me while I go upstairs to find a pair of shoes." Admittedly, I was pure girl that way. I had so many shoes, they had their own separate closet upstairs in the spare bedroom.

"Let me go get them for you. Sit. Eat."

I couldn't help but laugh. "First of all, I am not a dog, and second of all, like you would know the best shoes for this outfit. I need to get out of this room, anyway. Between the hot shower and the blow dryer, it's like a coffin in here. I'll be back."

\*\*\*

*My mind obsesses about those final words. I cry and ache every time I think of her having that stifling feeling. Were they also her last thoughts?*

*It's as if my brain is on an endless, pointless cycle, searching and searching for a rewind button—a mechanism that would empower me to go after her. She was overheated. She was stressed. She had hardly eaten a thing. What was I thinking? Why didn't I insist on her sitting down and me getting those damn shoes?*

*My body rebels against anything that comes remotely close to it. I don't want food. I don't want anything to drink. I don't want a bed and sleep. I don't want meds. I don't want a hug or to be comforted. All I want is Lara.*

*Shortly after, they made me look at those papers. Those damn papers. I had to sign them. I had to let go. I had to accept that she left me.*

# SNEAK PEEK AT *TAKE ME HOME*

## CHAPTER ONE

Her voice . . . it was haunting. She seemed so far away and, worse yet, in pain. But it was more than pain. She was sad. It was sadness in her voice. And, I knew that voice. I knew that voice well, and I wanted to be there to comfort her. But that wasn't possible, was it?

Her voice became clearer then, and I concentrated on her words wanting to know what was causing her such distress. "You have to," she pleaded. "You have to take your meds. Everyone loves you. We need you. Please, Finn."

*I love you. I need you. Yes, the same applies.*

Even though I wanted to say those words, I couldn't. I started to, but something was stopping me. Was it my heart? No. It was emotional, but it was something more. I put up my hands.

"Lara!"


Pressure. There was pressure all around. Next to me. Around me. In my head. In my brain. I needed to escape it. I wanted it to go away. I wanted to be free. I wanted to be me again. But how?

It felt like there was pressure on my chest, too. God, near my heart. My eyes were heavy. Regardless, I managed to open them. There was a reason for that pressure. A guardian angel lay haphazardly across my body protecting and watching over me. I was tired. I was so tired. But I wanted to stay awake and just watch. I wanted to soak in the peacefulness before it all came crashing back in. Because, I feared it inevitably would.

# ABOUT THE AUTHOR

There really wasn't any other path. Grea Warner knew from a young age that she wanted to write. She was born to write. First it was in diaries with little metal keys and in written tales that she slipped to friends in study hall. School newspapers, a college television drama, and internships in the soap opera world were next. After producing and writing a local show, she decided to delve into the world of the novelist. When her fingers aren't tapping out her latest book filled with angst and romance, Grea can be found hiking the trails or jamming to her favorite country artists on the radio.

Website: http://www.greawarner.com
Facebook: https://www.facebook.com/grea.warner.7
Twitter:@grea_warner